MORGAN COUNTY PUBLIC LIBRARY
110 SOUTH JEFFERSON ST
MARTINSVILLE, IN 46151

P9-ELQ-648

FIC
CLA

Clawson, David.

My fairy godmother is
a drag queen.

My Fairy Godmother is a Drag Queen

My Fairy Godmother is a Drag Queen

DAVID CLAWSON

Sky Pony Press
New York

Copyright © 2017 by David Clawson

All rights reserved. No part of this book may be reproduced in any manner without the express written consent of the publisher, except in the case of brief excerpts in critical reviews or articles. All inquiries should be addressed to Sky Pony Press, 307 West 36th Street, 11th Floor, New York, NY 10018.

First Edition

This is a work of fiction. Names, characters, places, and incidents are from the author's imagination, and used fictitiously.

Sky Pony Press books may be purchased in bulk at special discounts for sales promotion, corporate gifts, fund-raising, or educational purposes. Special editions can also be created to specifications. For details, contact the Special Sales Department, Sky Pony Press, 307 West 36th Street, 11th Floor, New York, NY 10018 or info@skyhorsepublishing.com.

Sky Pony® is a registered trademark of Skyhorse Publishing, Inc.®, a Delaware corporation. Books, authors, and more at skyponypressblog.com

Visit our website at www.skyponypress.com.

10 9 8 7 6 5 4 3 2 1

Library of Congress Cataloging-in-Publication Data is available on file.

Cover design by Sammy Yuen

Print ISBN: 978-1-5107-1411-3
Ebook ISBN: 978-1-5107-1412-0

Printed in the United States of America

Interior design by Joshua L. Barnaby

To Wendy West -
because once upon a time
she was my fairy godmother
when I really needed one

My Fairy Godmother is a Drag Queen

Hello

It's really weird to see yourself on the cover of a tabloid. I mean, you go into the convenience store at the corner to get an energy drink because you need something to help you stay awake so that you can study for your Calculus exam the next day, and there's your entire family on the cover:

* Your stepmom trying to look like she's had to deal with the paparazzi every day of her life since she was born, not just for, like, a few weeks.
* Your stepbrother, who you'd think was really hot if you didn't know what an idiot he was.
* Your stepsister, who thinks she's living the American blonde version of Kate Middleton's life.
* Her boyfriend, with whom you're in love—more on that later—and . . .
* YOU, half-hidden in shadow because you were trying your best to get out of the shot, but when all of those guys with cameras were coming from so many directions . . . well, you know that's you. Plus, you realize how badly you really need a new winter coat. The one in the picture just doesn't flatter you the way it did when you got it, when you were thirteen, eight inches shorter, and fifty pounds skinnier.

Is it weird that I keep referring to myself as "you"? Because all of this really happened to me. *Me.* I still can't believe it.

I suppose it would be logical to think you wouldn't have picked up my story if you didn't already know who I was, but just in case, I'm Christopher Bellows. Although, for all of my seventeen years up until then, everyone just called me Chris. I'm not really sure why the press always identified me as Christopher. Yes, it's *the* name on my birth certificate, but if they'd ever just asked that question, I would have told them. But they were interested only in other details—not that they got those right—and never really interested about me. I admit, I bear my share of the responsibility for their getting it all wrong, so I guess I'm just going to tell this story as if you knew nothing, because, in reality, even if you read every single article published up to the moment of the big announcement, about the truth you *do* know nothing.

So, yeah, the first thing I'd like to make clear is that I was never their maid, their captive, or their slave. (I'm rolling my eyes here, just like you probably would if you ever read or heard that about yourself. And this time I really mean *you*, not me.) I'm not saying I can't see how someone could interpret our lives that way if they wanted to, especially since I think it might have been Coco who got that whole rumor started, but since being a drama queen often goes hand-in-hand with being a drag queen, consider the source. Actually, the night I met Coco was the same night we all met J.J. So it's basically the night that separates the before from the after in this story. I should probably start there. Even if you have read all of those inaccurate news accounts that began the next morning, these were the last few hours of relative calm before the proverbial storm.

Chapter 1

A Vision Appeared

"Chris! I need you!" came loudly from three different rooms—my stepmother, Iris, from her bedroom suite; Kimberly, my stepsister, from her bathroom; and my stepbrother, Buck, no doubt from his usual place sprawled on the couch in front of the TV. Since he was downstairs, and the rest of us were upstairs—I'm speculating—I called down to him that he would have to wait. He growled loudly in response.

My hands were already filled with a curling iron (which was what Kimberly was most likely calling for), the steamer I'd forgotten to put down after using it to remove wrinkles from her new Vera Wang dress that had arrived minutes before, and a bottle of white wine plus a corkscrew (which was almost certainly what my stepmother was yelling about).

"Chris!" Kimberly bellowed again, just as I rounded the corner into her bathroom, and jerked my shoulder to draw her attention to the arm which was precariously clutching her curling iron to my side. She took it resentfully as she said, "You'd better not have been using this as a dildo."

"You're disgusting," I responded with a wince.

So, Kimberly. The stepsister: nineteen, blonde, perfect body, hours away from entering the bubble of fantasy that leads to being named one of PEOPLE Magazine's "Most Beautiful People," and someone with whom I have always had, and perhaps always will have, a complicated relationship. More on that later, too.

After quickly plugging the curling iron in and turning it too high, she put her free hand on her flowered-silk-robe-covered hip, and looked at me accusingly. "I'm serious. When and why did you remove one of my possessions from this verboten territory? You know you're not allowed in here without my permission."

"Do you really want to interrogate me while Iris waits for this?" I asked, holding up the bottle of wine to avoid explaining I'd been using Kimberly's iron to curl construction paper for a diorama of the French Revolution for AP History.

Kimberly blanched, saying, "Dear God, run," but then, stopping me with a hand on my upper arm, whispered, "Get her to drink as much of that as you can before we leave. I don't know how I'll make it through this night if she's not good and mellowed by her 'medicine.'" The look of miserable anxiety that came over her face was almost enough to make me feel sorry for her. But, seeing as how I was the only member of the family not going to the night's big event, I was still sulking in my quiet little way and chose to ignore any feelings of sympathy for the spoiled little bitch. So there. I left the room without comment and headed toward Iris's rooms.

Now if you're flipping back to what I wrote before about not being a maid, captive, or slave, I can understand your confusion. Maybe I can explain. First, remember that for most of the time before my dad married Iris—the first ten years of my life, really—he and I had been dirt poor. Since my mom had died of pneumonia when I was still an infant, I learned to take care of myself at a very young age. Although my dad tried his very best to do as much for me as he could, probably by the age of five I was doing more to take care of him than he was doing for himself. But the American Dream being what it is, my dad worked as hard as was humanly possible. With a healthy dose of good timing and even better luck, when I was eleven he hit it big. Suddenly we were rich. Like, stinking rich. At least on paper.

We didn't really change the way we lived right away, though. I was just glad that I got to spend more time with my dad, and that finally being able to work only one job (managing his new assets) gave my father time to sleep enough to get rid of the dark, under-eye circles that I had always thought were just the way he looked. It turned out I didn't have to worry about inheriting the genetics of a raccoon after all.

But eventually Dad met Iris Fontaine, of the Upper East Side Fontaines, at some business-slash-charity event, and suddenly our grungy little apartment in Queens didn't really make sense for a guy now worth over fifty million dollars (on paper, at least). And within a year, we'd moved twice. First to our own large apartment in the upper 80s, and then later into the historic and storied Fontaine brownstone in which Iris's family had lived for over a hundred years.

In just a few short years, I went from collecting plastic bottles off the street to help add to the household budget to living in a house where Rockefellers and Vanderbilts had once dined. Plus, I had a new stepsister and stepbrother and another new school. It was all too much and too fast, but when I saw the way that my father looked at Iris, I couldn't resent him for it. Somehow I knew that the love in his eyes was what he'd also felt for my mother, and although he'd never, ever made me feel like he needed anyone other than me, I finally understood how lonely he'd been.

But, oddly, after our family had grown by three, I felt alone in a way I never had before. Plus, we had maids and drivers and assistants and a cook—people to do things that had been my responsibility. (Not to mention the decorators and architects and construction men who flooded into the house. While the place still looked terribly fancy compared to our small apartment in Queens, I was told that the house was a shadow of its former glory, and now that was all going to change.) While I know a kid is supposed to jump for joy when all of his chores and responsibilities are suddenly lifted off of his shoulders, I felt useless instead. I never complained, and I tried to always be pleasant to everyone, but I spent a lot of time alone in my room reading. A lot. Which I guess is pretty much what I'd always done when it was just Dad and me, but back then it had never felt like I was hiding out or missing anything. It was just the way it was. But now it definitely made me feel removed from all that was going on around me, and other than meals and "required" family events, I guess avoided dealing with my new reality by ignoring it as much as possible.

Sometimes, late at night, I would sneak into the kitchen and cook something, just so I could feel useful. But then I was so afraid of getting in trouble with the cook or making her feel bad because she might think I didn't like her cooking, I would slip out of the house and leave whatever I'd made at a little park where I'd once seen a homeless person

6

sleeping. The next day on the way to school, I'd check to see if the food was still there, and it was always gone. For all I know some city maintenance worker might have tossed it, but it at least made me feel like *maybe* I was doing something good for someone who needed help.

I guess I would have adjusted to this new lifestyle eventually—maybe—but I never really had the chance. Because when the stock market crashed in 2008, I learned that the danger of being rich on paper is that paper tears very easily. At least the kind of paper of which my dad's wealth had been made. Since we've just met, I'll save the grim details for later, but suffice it to say that I was technically an orphan, and it left me shell-shocked and overwhelmed.

All I do know is that although I was pretty new to her family, Iris didn't throw me out. As flawed as they may be, they're all I have. So, if I have done more for them than some people think is right, well, those people weren't in our house and don't really know what they're talking about. I'm always amazed by how readily people judge the right and wrong of things they know only from the outside. Honestly, it kind of pisses me off.

"Chris!" Iris called again, in more of a desperate whine than a yell.

"I'm coming!" I said, trying to uncork the bottle as I ran along the hall that separated Kimberly's end of the house from Iris's. As I passed Buck's open door I noticed that his tuxedo had slipped off his bed and onto the floor. I stopped short, bent down to leave the clothes steamer I was also carrying just inside the door, and muttered to myself not to forget where I'd put it, while adding "de-wrinkle suit" to the mental To-Do list running through my head. Which reminded me of all the homework I had due on Monday.

Now that my hands were freer, the cork came out of the bottle easily just as I entered Iris's dressing room. She heard the *pop!* and practically melted onto her faded, chintz chaise lounge.

"Thank God you're *finally* here," she said, extending a limp arm in the direction of the wine glass I was filling with a modestly priced Chardonnay. Although she was only in her early 40s, and had been considered the great beauty of her debutante year, Iris Fontaine-Bellows had a haggard puffiness that belied her best attempts to make the world believe that everything in her life was just as perfect as she had always been brought up to believe it would be.

"Are your nails dry?" I asked, holding the glass just out of reach. Partially I was toying with her, I'll admit, but also I was the one who'd spent much of the last hour giving her a mani-pedi—high on my list of *NOT* My Favorite Things— so there was some self-preservation involved.

"My nails are drier than Prohibition. Give me the glass!" She even went so far as to partially sit up, and I couldn't help thinking of the ceiling of the Sistine Chapel as her fingers reached out for her own spark of creation. The possibility of getting that into my AP Art History paper flew through my mind before I handed her the glass, which she half-emptied with her first "sip."

I waved the bottle in the air as I asked, "Shall I leave this?"

She answered with only a dark look, then pointed at the TV. "Turn up the volume."

"The remote is right beside you," I said, gesturing with my chin to where it lay on the side table.

She squinted her eyes as the corners of her mouth hinted at the pleasure she took from using my words back on me. "But my nails. You wouldn't want me to chip them, now, would you?"

Momentarily bested, I reached over for the remote and turned up the volume. Since I'd gotten home from a Calculus study group a little after lunch, every TV in the house had been turned to NY1 for any and all updates on the night's big social event at The Plaza, The Autumnal Ball. This was both the reason the house was filled with so much anxious activity as well as the reason I was sulking. Obviously, I could understand that thousand-dollar-apiece tickets were prohibitively expensive, but if the money could be found for everyone else to go, then why not me, too? I sighed.

"Would you stop that!" Iris said. "Do you think I like that we can't afford for all of us to go? Do you think I *like* having to live this way?" Entirely free of irony, she gestured around her large dressing room. To be fair, it was faded, threadbare, and out of style, but in a weird way it was comments like this that reminded me more than anything how different I was from my stepfamily. While it was always frustrating, it also made me forgive them a little. To put it simply, they just didn't know any better. They had always lived a certain way and had never learned to adapt. It all sounded so Henry James or Edith Wharton, and yet a hundred or so years later, for some people, very little had changed.

As the news anchor on the TV announced that they would be going live to the remote reporter at The Plaza, Buck called for me from downstairs. "*Chris!*"

"You'd better go check on him," Iris said. "And tell him that if he's not showered, shaved, and perfect by seven-thirty, I will kill him and his Xbox."

"You want Buck to be 'perfect' by seven-thirty?" I asked.

"You know what I mean," she said, wrenching out of my hand the wine bottle. "And check on Kimberly. How's her dress? Did you steam it? She has to look perfect. She has to *be* perfect. We all have to. God, this is all too stressful. I think I'm going to vomit." And then she filled her glass to just below the rim and downed it like a shot. "I'll need you back in here soon to help me get dressed. Well, what are you waiting for? Go!"

As I walked down the stairs to the ground floor, I could hear the news reporter from the living room TV. ". . . But what really has tongues wagging about tonight's Autumnal Ball is the expected attendance of the man being called "The Most Eligible Bachelor in America," none other than J.J. Kennerly."

I entered the living room to see video footage from some other red carpet event of the ridiculously handsome, brown-haired, brown-eyed, square-jawed, cleft-chinned J.J. Kennerly, the only child of the closest thing America has to royalty.

"I don't really get why everyone thinks he's all that," my stepbrother Buck said from the couch. He was stretched out over the length of it in sweat pants and a t-shirt that barely contained his pecs and biceps. The tennis shoes he'd kicked off lay sloppily on the floor. "I mean, seriously, would you want him humping your buns?"

"You're not funny, Buck." Over the last few months, he and Kimberly had both taken to making rude comments like this to me incessantly.

He acted as if he were thinking about what I said, then responded, "Yeah, I am."

I sighed deeply. "What did you need me for?"

"Do we have any Fritos?"

"I don't know. Did you get off your lazy ass and go look?"

Buck sat up, leaving his legs outstretched. "First off, I don't want you thinking about my ass. That's disgusting. We're semi-related. And B, you're the one who is anal-retentive about the kitchen—among other things—so I didn't want to disrespect your purview." He lay back, proudly crossing his arms over this chest, as if he'd just won the Academic Decathlon.

Here's the thing about Buck. He's annoying, obnoxious, a total jock, Xbox-worshipping meathead, but then he'll throw in an SAT word like "purview." And even use it correctly. I have a theory that he's not actually as stupid as he likes to act, because often he'll play the stupidity card in a really smart way. He's especially good at using it to give Iris and Kimberly shit, but getting away with it by acting like he has no idea what they're talking about when they get upset with him for whatever he just said. It's either really good luck or a little bit of genius. I can never quite decide.

"Do you need anything other than Fritos?" I asked. "Because I'm not making two trips. I have too much to do getting them ready for this thing tonight, and Iris said if you aren't ready by seven-thirty, she's taking away your Xbox. And, by the way, you didn't hang up your tux like I told you to, and it fell on the floor, so now it's wrinkled. I left the steamer in your room, because I don't have time to do that along with everything else." I hadn't planned on asking him to steam the wrinkles out, but I figured it was worth a try.

His brow momentarily darkened. "Why can't I just put the tux in the bathroom while I'm showering and let it get steam that way?"

See what I mean? Lazy . . . or stupid-smart? Very dangerous.

"That's worth a try," I said as I started out of the room. "Decided on if you want a soda or not?"

"Nah, too many empty calories." As if the Fritos wouldn't be.

Soon after my father's death and the reality of our financial situation became clear, not only did the restoration and redecorating of the house stop, but all of the help was quickly let go. Since I was the only one of us with much experience taking care of a house or cooking, it fell onto my fourteen-year-old shoulders to take the lead. It gave me a purpose, and a way to avoid sitting in my room all day thinking about my dad, so I was more than willing to assume the responsibility. It never occurred to me that the role might be forever, but even that probably wouldn't have stopped me, because at that time I was mostly just terrified of being sent to an orphanage or somewhere equally Dickensian. Iris still got some money from a trust fund at the beginning of each financial quarter, and I quickly learned to get money for groceries and household incidentals the first day the check arrived. She had never learned to adjust the spending habits she'd developed in her youth, and the money was always gone long before the next disbursement. So, typical Buck, he used my stewardship of domestic affairs to get himself some corn chips without ever having to get up from the couch.

No sooner had I placed the snack into Buck's hands than another cry of, "*Chris!*" came from upstairs. Kimberly again. Buck looked at me with something close to sympathy, although I wasn't sure if it was for me or for her once he said, "Mom has her totally freaked out."

"Well, we can't afford for our wine bill to double, so I guess I'd better get up there and see if I can calm her down." As I walked up the stairs, my cell phone buzzed, but it was only a text from Vibol, one of the study group kids, with a question. It's not like anything in my history would warrant my expecting an invitation from a schoolmate to go out and be social on a Saturday night, but the human heart has a bad habit of being hopeful.

The next two hours flew by in a frenzy of silk organza, hair products, and for Iris, another bottle of Chardonnay. But by seven-thirty, all three members of my stepfamily were standing by the fireplace in the formal sitting room, having their picture of perfection taken by me with Iris's iPhone. As she checked to see if the photo met with her approval, Iris asked, "Do you think it would seem desperate to email this to all of the society section editors?"

"Yes!" Kimberly, Buck, and I all said in unison.

She looked up at us like she wanted to say something, but a hiccup distracted her. "Maybe I should have one last drink before we go. But first, I need to use the powder room."

Once she'd walked out of the room with impressive grace, save for a little stumble going from the well-trod antique Oriental rug to the chipped marble of the entry hall, Kimberly looked at Buck and me with disarming fear and vulnerability. "Do I really look okay?"

"I'd do ya," Buck said in his version of high praise. "I mean, if you weren't my sister and all."

Kimberly smiled at him appreciatively. "Thanks, Buck." Then concern returned to her face as she looked directly at me. "Well?" she asked.

Remember how I mentioned that Kimberly and I always had a complicated relationship? Well, this was one of those times where I definitely had the upper hand and a golden opportunity to really screw with her psyche. It was just too tempting!

But if there's one thing that I've simply never been good at—and trust me there are thousands—at the top of the list is lying. So I told her the truth. "You look like a princess in a fairy tale."

Kimberly blushed, softly whispering, "Thank you."

"She should, as much as that dress cost," Buck said. I suppose he was making an attempt to lighten the moment.

"Shut up, Buck!" Kimberly said, swinging her dainty arm with impressive force at his shoulder.

"Ow!" Buck rubbed where the blow had landed.

Iris stomped back into the sitting room, still lifting the billowing skirt of her gown as she readjusted her undergarments. "Would you two stop it! Damn it, now I'm not going to be able to relax over a last drink. Chris, go get us a cab. Please."

I slipped out of the room as she began to lecture them on what an important night this was for the family's future. I couldn't help but think how fitting that I was missing a speech that started that way, and for maybe the, oh, ten thousandth time I felt that pang of loneliness orphans must feel anytime they see a family doing the sorts of things that families do together—weddings, funerals, Autumnal Balls at The Plaza—and I couldn't stop myself from thinking for the ten millionth time about my father, and what this night might have been like if he were still alive.

I was kept from losing too much time down that rabbit hole by the convenient appearance of a cab in the distance. I dashed down the stairs, waving an arm, and within a couple minutes, it drove off with Iris still lecturing Buck and Kimberly. I might have heard something about a scheme to make it look like they were getting out of somebody else's limousine, but I couldn't swear to that, because, honestly, the cab hadn't been as big of a distraction as I'd hoped. Its taillights hadn't even faded out of view before I was sitting on the front stairs with my head in my hands, indulging in one of my I-don't-think-unreasonable funks. Homework could wait a little while longer; I had self-pity to bathe in first.

I'm not sure how long I was lost in those unhappy thoughts before a voice said, "Child, if that frown gets any lower, you're gonna trip someone."

And then I looked up to see standing before me . . . Diana Ross?

Chapter 2

Saying it is Different

Okay, it couldn't actually be Diana Ross. I knew that because she's like a grandmother or something now, and this was a very young Diana Ross, wearing a shiny, long, tight, flapper-fringed gold gown like something out of The Supremes' high-glamour period. If you don't know who I'm talking about, think Rihanna without the piercings and tattoos. Or Beyonce in *Dreamgirls*, because I'm pretty sure she was really supposed to be playing Diana Ross, but for legal reasons they called her Deena Jones. Even Buck figured that one out. Lawyers.

"Um, so you're supposed to be Diana Ross, right?" I said with a lack of certainty.

"Well, darlin', who the hell else ever looked this fabulous?" she said, waving one glove-covered arm over herself like she was a part of a "Showcase Showdown" on *The Price Is Right*.

Now that I was paying more attention, I realized that "she" had a rather deep voice. But I didn't want to jump to any conclusions and say something wrong, because some women just have deep voices, just like some men have high ones, and both sets must get really tired of the wrong, "Yes, ma'am," or "No, sir," from telemarketers and the like. And she was really, really beautiful, with smooth brown skin dusted over with some sort of shimmering makeup.

After a longer pause than was natural, I finally blurted out a confused, "Where did you come from?"

"You mean like Harlem, or what the hell am I doing on your street?"

"Um, the second one, I guess? But without the 'hell.' You're perfectly welcome on any street, including this one. I've just never seen you before. Or anyone like you."

"Mm, ain't you a flatterer." She held out a gloved hand for me to shake, which I did. "Please allow me to introduce myself. I am Ms. Coco Chanel Jones. And don't you forget it."

"I don't think forgetting is an option."

"More flattery. I like that. Anywhoo, you asked how I came to be here. Well, it's a sad tale, but you look like you're trafficking in sad these days, so let's just say that cab driver did not take kindly when I realized I left my purse at home. So he dumped this fine piece of African goddess down the street there, and then carted off your fancy-dressed friends. You don't happen to have a spare Metrocard, do you?"

"Oh!" I said, feeling badly that I'd flagged down the cab that had just dumped her. (Him? Her? I still wasn't sure.) Then, wanting to make her (him?) feel better, I said, "They're not my friends. They're my . . . family."

"MM-hm, I heard that," Coco said, pursing her lips. "Let me guess. You're all sad because they're going somewhere that you want to go. Am I right?"

I nodded reluctantly.

"Where?"

"It's stupid," I said.

"Don't try Coco," Coco said, wagging a gloved finger with a huge sparkling costume diamond ring on it at me. "You're cute, but I get bored easily."

It's always a nice surprise being described as cute, but since I still couldn't figure out which sex was calling me this, I shifted uncomfortably on the cement step. "Really, don't worry yourself. It sounds like you have enough troubles on your plate." But before she'd even had chance to say anything else, I found myself continuing with more than I'd meant to say. "It'd just be nice to feel included for once."

Coco tapped the toe of one of her gold five-inch stilettos on the sidewalk a few times before crossing her arms over her chest, saying, "Don't make me get blood on my new shoes kicking in your head because you won't just say where it is you want to go. Do I really look like someone who has a tolerance for the repressed and soft-spoken?"

The look of good-humored intolerance somehow got me to actually blurt out to this complete stranger what it was I wanted. "The Autumnal Ball! Okay? There, are you happy? They went to the Autumnal Ball at The Plaza, and I wanted to go, too."

And then Coco let out the most unexpectedly cruel cackle I'd ever heard, and I immediately regretted sharing such a personal pain.

But it turned out her laugh had not been cruel. That was just the way I heard it at first, because she followed the laugh with a huge smile, saying, "Child, fortune just gave you a big, wet, tongue kiss!"

"Huh?" I said. For many reasons.

She began to struggle up the steps in her tight dress and five-inch heels, putting a hand on one of my shoulders for balance. "Baby, we've got to get you cleaned up and pretty. I'm going to be your fairy godmother, ya hear?" she practically shouted in my face. "And when Coco says fairy, honey, she means fairy! Hey, now!"

I struggled to stand while trying not to make her lose her balance, all while attempting to figure out what the heck was going on.

"I'm confused," I said.

Now standing one step below me, but with those five-inch heels, Coco was pretty much eye-to-eye with me. She put her hands on my shoulders, looked deep into my eyes, and said the most unbelievable words that I never thought I'd hear. "Child, I am taking you to The Autumnal Ball."

"The . . . but . . . but . . . I don't have a ticket."

"Don't worry about it."

"But how—"

"Don't worry about it."

"But I don't have a thousand dollars for—"

"I *said*, don't worry about it."

"But how can I not worry about it? Worrying is what I do! About everything!"

With an unexpectedly calm smile, Coco put I finger to my lips. "And *that's* why you need a fairy godmother. For the rest of the night you're not allowed to worry about anything. You have one, and only one, responsibility. To have a dream come true and have the sweetass time of your sweetass life. Do you understand me?"

I didn't really feel like I had much of a choice other than to nod in agreement. Besides, homework could always wait until tomorrow.

Coco ooh'd and ah'd as we walked up to the third floor where my room was. I'd started out apologizing for the deteriorated state of the house, just like I always heard Iris doing on the rare occasion she had to let someone inside. But after Coco interrupted me to say that she lived with her single mother and four siblings in a two-bedroom walkup in Harlem, I decided to keep my mouth shut.

That didn't mean she was very impressed with my bedroom. It was admittedly minimalist, but that was at least partially my fault. When my dad and I had first moved in, I'd asked to be put on the floor above the others, because I didn't want to displace anyone, or give them any extra reasons to resent my entering their lives. It also gave me the chance to remove myself a bit from a situation I wasn't entirely ready to embrace. And since the third floor had been where servants were housed back in the day, the decor was definitely utilitarian. But I had a bed (old, but surprisingly firm), a chipped antique dresser that must have been a piece of pride in its heyday, and a simple desk and chair. Luckily the desk was pretty large, because I generally had lots of books stacked on it, and the chair was comfortable, which was all I really needed to focus on my schoolwork.

The best part of the room was that I had my own little balcony. Since it was at the back of the house, it looked out onto the small garden alcove of one of our neighbors, the NYC version of a backyard. When the weather was nice, I often spent many hours there reading, enjoying the fresh air and the slightly muffled sounds of the city. Kimberly's much larger room was beneath mine, and her much longer balcony stretched out below me. There had once been a time when I'd first moved in that I thought she and I might somehow bond over this shared experience, her escaping to read on her balcony, me escaping to read on mine, and our eyes would meet and we'd realize that we weren't so alone after all. But that never happened. Kimberly wasn't much of a reader.

To be fair, since it had just been my dad and me up until then, I'm not sure I really knew how to be part of another type of family. I'd never had a mother I knew, and I'd never had siblings, so my expectations were based on what I'd seen in movies and on TV. Iris and her children were definitely not like that.

"You're kidding me, right?" Coco said as she looked through the clothes hanging in my closet. "That little cuntella was wearing this year's Vera Wang, and their cheap asses can't even buy you a suit?"

"How do you know what designer she was wearing?" I asked.

Coco raised a worldly eyebrow at me. "I'm your first drag queen, ain't I?"

"Oh. So you are a he."

Coco's other eyebrow raised to meet its partner. "We prefer 'she' when we have put this much time and money into our appearance, thank you very much."

"I can do that," I said.

I guess I looked a little spooked, because she shook her head with a soft chuckle and said, "Shit, next you're going to tell me you don't even know you're gay."

And then I guess I looked more than a little spooked, because for the first time I saw a glimpse of whomever Coco was when she wasn't in drag. Everything about her went sort of soft and quiet. "Oh, precious, I'm sorry. I didn't mean to say that. You don't have to be anything you don't want to be until you're ready. When am I ever going to learn to keep my big mouth shut?" She looked down at the floor, biting her lower lip.

So here it was, the moment I'd been dreading. And hoping for. When someone would say those words, "you're gay," and I wouldn't feel the knee-jerk need to deny it.

Because the fact is that . . . well . . . I am gay. The idea of it had taken a few years to solidify in my mind, and in the last year or so I would even experiment with saying the words out loud—always when I was in the house alone—just to see if anything cataclysmic would happen in the world, mine or at large. "I'm gay. I am gay. I like guys." Little one syllable words that changed everything. But no lightning, no thunder, no turning into ash and dissolving into the ground. Nothing really, except for the feeling that somehow I'd done something wrong.

I don't know if you're gay or straight, or even if you are gay, if you've ever felt this way, but for me, I always felt like the words, "I'm gay," needed to be followed by, "I'm sorry." *Dad, I'm sorry if I've disappointed you by being something other than the man you thought you'd been raising all of these years. Straight girl with a crush on me, I'm sorry if you were having visions of a long romance and eventual marriage to the only guy you've ever known who would also rather watch episode after episode of Gilmore Girls reruns than football or a Transformers marathon. Straight person, I'm sorry if the differences in our sexual and emotional wiring make you uncomfortable.* Because that's something that seems to get forgotten in all of this talk of sexual "preferences." Being homosexual isn't just about sex. It's about who we have emotional romantic connections with, whose arms we actually feel at peace in, who completes the—dare I say it—fairy tale of what romantic and domestic bliss is for that individual.

And then, after all of that hypothetical apologizing, I'd get kind of annoyed. You know what, yes, I'm sorry I'm gay and if that creates issues for you, but I'm having to deal with it, and so must you. Because it's not changing, it's not going away, it's always been there, whether we're talking about my history or the history of the world, so we're all just going to have to deal with it. Case closed.

So many words like that had run through my mind for years, but saying them aloud, to an actual person, was very, very scary.

"No, it's okay," I said. "I'm . . . I am . . . it's just that knowing it and saying it are . . . different. You know?"

When I looked up into Coco's eyes, I saw them beginning to tear up, and evidently that was not okay with her because she shoved me towards the bed as she reached into one of her arm-length gloves and pulled out a cell phone. "You just sit there while I make a few phone calls. We've got to get you a suit jacket, and I ain't walking through a field of cow shit with someone in Payless shoes. Those cheap motherfuckers. She gets Vera Wang and you're wearing Payless freaking shoes!"

After I gave up trying to argue that there was nothing wrong with nondesigner shoes and clothes, Coco sent me to go take a shower.

Since Coco didn't have her purse, I paid for us to take the 6 Train. One of the great things about living in New York City is that you can get on a subway on the relatively conservative Upper East Side with an uber-glamorous drag queen, and other than a few happily scandalized tourists, no one bats an eye. One elderly Russian lady asked how Coco managed to walk in such high heels, but her husband said, "If your legs had ever looked like that, you would have found a way."

For a second I thought she was going to hit him, but then she just blew out her cheeks and said he was probably right.

When a seat opened up, a rather handsome Dominican man motioned to it with a, "Ladies first," and Coco flirted with him so hard I finally understood what it meant for people to eye-fuck. Luckily he got off at the next stop, or I'm not sure she would have said a word to me.

"Whew," Coco said, after her eyes had followed him down the platform as far as she could. "I was afraid he was going to give me a hard-on while I'm tucked."

"What's tucked?" I asked.

Coco looked at me with slight exasperation before saying, "Child, did they have you locked up in that attic? Because no kid that grows up in New York City is that damn innocent. What do you *think* tucked means?"

My eyes briefly went to the crotch of her dress.

"That's right, baby. Men do not appreciate what a beautiful woman goes through."

I figured this wasn't the time to ask why, exactly, she felt the need to put in all of that effort to look like the sex other than the one she had been born. Being gay had certainly never made me want to dress or look like a woman. But to each his or her own, right?

Instead, I said, "So you still haven't told me how we're supposed to get into this high security event."

"I told you not to worry about that. What I want to know is why everyone else in your family gets to go, but you don't." She bent over to pointedly look down at my inexpensive shoes, as a way of pointing out that she was following my request to drop that topic.

I explained all about Iris being my stepmom, and dad's death, and so on and so forth, but when I finished, Coco just said, "Okay, so money is tight. I certainly understand that, trust. But why spend the money for them to go? Let alone the money that Vera Wang gown set y'all back. Lordy!"

"Okay, well, first, Iris had to sell one of her last pieces of serious jewelry to pay for that dress, and don't think she doesn't remind Kimberly of it every time she can, even though Kimberly kept saying she could get something cheaper. But Iris said 'there was no way she was having those other bitches at the ball talk trash about her daughter because she didn't have as good a dress as anyone else there.'"

"I'm starting to respect this Iris," Coco said with an emphatic nod.

"So, anyway, Iris has it in her head that since Kimberly is so beautiful—"

"I was far away when they got in the cab. Is she really that pretty?"

"She's gorgeous," I said. "I'm not saying that makes her a good person or anything, but she is sort of stunning. On the outside, at least."

"Go on," Coco said tapping me on the forearm.

"Anyway, now that Kimberly is starting NYU, and J.J. Kennerly is a sophomore at Columbia . . ."

I stopped because a faraway look had come over Coco's face, and I could tell she wasn't listening anymore. "What's wrong?"

Coco snapped back to attention. "Oh, nothing, you said the name J.J. Kennerly. That man is so beautiful, I just had to take a moment and picture him. Although, probably not a good idea while I'm tucked, if you know what I mean."

"Yeah, I think I've figured it out, thanks."

"So, what, Iris thinks if J.J. Kennerly sees Kimberly all dressed up in some Vera Wang maybe she can get a date or something?"

"Oh, no. Iris wants them to get married."

"Married? Is she cray-cray?"

"Well, Fontaine is a pretty big name in the Social Registry and that sort of thing, so it's not that crazy of an idea, and Iris will do just about anything to get back to her former glory."

"Ooh, it's all so Jane Austen, isn't it?"

"You read Jane Austen, too?" I asked. It would be nice to know that we had something in common besides being gay.

"No," Coco said. "But I've seen a couple of the movies."

Then she grabbed my arm and jumped up. "This is our stop." A gang-banger type stupidly tried to step in front of her to get to the door first, so quick as a whip she stomped the heel of her stiletto into the toe of his shoe. "Oops. So sorry. Pardon me." She smiled at him in a way that was both polite and a threat, and he let us both pass. I have to say if I ever get caught in a fight between a group of gang-bangers and a group of drag queens, I might want to be on the side of the drag queens.

Especially once I saw the first of Coco's friends. Special Kaye Ballard was a six-and-a-half-foot tall, red-wigged Amazon, dressed to compliment Coco—one of the backup Supremes to Coco's Diana Ross. As we emerged from the subway, she was standing at the top of the stairs holding a suit jacket and a pair of men's black shoes.

"You're the best," Coco said as they air kissed. "Mama loves you."

"We'd better hurry," Special Kaye said. "Aphra Behn is getting antsy."

"That bitch always goes Norma Desmond before a performance," Coco said, taking the jacket from Special Kaye and helping me into it. I felt slightly uncomfortable about the way this new drag queen was looking me up and down, but when she said, "Mm-mm-mm, what a cutie," I couldn't really pretend I hadn't heard it, so even though I blushed, I said, "Thank you."

Special Kaye started fanning herself. "You know that blush would go perfectly with my red hair."

"Hands off, you wretched old queen," Coco said. "This little innocent has already had enough shocks for one evening."

"But the night is so young."

"And so is he." Coco stopped adjusting the jacket on me and looked Special Kaye dead in the eyes. "I'm serious."

Special Kaye held up her hands, with a shoe in each. "Okay, okay, I get it. No chicken for dinner."

"Good. And make sure Aphra Behn knows it, too."

Special Kaye turned to me and said, "You won't have to worry about her. She prefers buzzards, all wrinkled and stringy."

I was a little confused, but before I could give it too much thought, Coco was kneeling down and telling me to lift my foot. Within seconds the shoes I'd worn had been carelessly tossed aside, and I was standing in a fancy pair of black leather shoes that looked and felt very expensive. There was just one problem.

"Um, these are way too big," I said.

Coco and Special Kaye both looked at me like I'd just farted in front of the Queen of England. Then they looked at each other, as if to confirm that their ears had not deceived them, and finally back to me.

"Baby," Coco said, "those are Ferragamo. If you don't think your feet are big enough to fill what you have so graciously been given, then I will gladly stop a cab driver and ask him to drive over said feet until they swell up enough, understand?"

"Um . . . they're perfect?" I said.

"That's better. Now let me see you walk in them."

I took a step, and the shoe immediately slipped off.

"Taxi!" Coco said.

"Wait!" I said. "Wait, just give me a chance to figure it out." Thus began an awkward couple of minutes while two impatient drag queens crossed their arms over their busts and watched me learn out how to walk in shoes that were way too large for my feet. Finally I thought I had the hang of it, but when I turned around to proudly walk back in their direction, somehow I kicked off one of the shoes, and it barely missed hitting Coco.

Slow as dial-up, she bent down to retrieve the shoe, then held it out to me. "If I can make walking in five-inch heels look easy, the least you can do is keep these damn things on your feet."

"We should go," I said. "I'm ready. Really. Besides, you still haven't told me how we're supposed to get into this thing, so why should I worry about—"

"Little one," Special Kaye said, throwing her arms above her head in a show-stopping gesture, "we're the entertainment!"

Confused, I turned to Coco. "Wait, what? You mean you're *invited* to this thing?"

"Invited?" Coco said. "Honey, we get *paid* to be here." She and Special Kaye cackled as they high-fived. "Let's go."

We started on our way, but then I remembered, "My shoes!"

Coco rolled her eyes, and then told me to wait right where I was. She walked back to where my old shoes had been abandoned, picked them up, and headed towards us. But then, as she passed a trash bin, she tossed them in, wiping her hands dramatically as she looked me directly in the eye.

I had a couple blocks to practice walking in the new shoes, and I thought I was getting the hang of it, even if I was dragging behind a little bit. By the time we rounded the corner to The Plaza's service entrance, I was feeling pretty proud of myself since I hadn't thrown a shoe in over a block.

Waiting with a hand on her hip and a perturbed look on her face was a much shorter and chubbier version of Special Kaye, also with a matching red wig. "Finally!" Aphra Behn said. "You're later than my first period!"

Chapter 3

Five-Inch Heels and Other Shoes

Jeremy, the earpiece-wearing, clipboard-holding, maybe five-foot-six assistant entertainment coordinator looked like he was about two hyperventilated breaths away from an anxiety attack when Coco informed him I was part of their entourage. "But he doesn't have security clearance!" I could almost see the vein on the left side of his forehead expand as his blood pressure rose. "You can't do this to me!"

"Honey, relax," Coco said, putting a hand on Jeremy's shoulder. "He ain't going to hurt anybody, but I don't think he'll sue if you want to have someone frisk him."

Special Kaye Ballard's arm shot up to volunteer, but Coco turned a droll eye on her. "You've already been warned once."

Jeremy wiped a hand over his moistening brow. "Well, I'll at least need a driver's license or something so that they can run a check."

Coco looked at me. "Do you drive?"

I shook my head. "Living in Manhattan? I only have my school ID."

I started to take it out, which Jeremy was in the process of telling me not to bother doing, when he stopped as he saw it.

"You go to McVities?"

I nodded as I handed it over. He looked down at his clipboard. "Are you sure you're not on the guest list already?"

"I'm pretty sure," I said. Jeremy pursed his lips in annoyance, then turned to walk over to a muscular man in a black suit, who I assumed was part of the security force.

I turned to Coco to find her looking at me with a raised eyebrow. "Vera Wang and McVities Prep, just how much jewelry is Iris selling?"

"I'm there on scholarship."

"McVities has scholarships?"

"Under special circumstances . . ." I said. Or at least in my one special circumstance. The combination of Iris's family name, my test scores, and my dad's new wealth had managed to get me into McVities for my freshman year. Buck and Kimberly, of course, were already students there, although Buck had almost had to transfer to Choate when he flunked his sophomore year. My first year had been paid for by the time of my father's death. While there was never any question of her biological children continuing to attend the expected academy of their ilk as long as Iris had things to sell off, I had worried that I might have been fighting along with everyone else to get into Eleanor Roosevelt or Hunter once that first year ended. However, since I was number one in my class and had the highest test scores, Principal Baskin found it in his statistics-loving heart to find a way for me to stay at the school. As long as my scholastic performance didn't slip, of course. (Now you see why I went to so many study groups?) Since Kimberly and Buck had both just graduated in May (thanks to his having to repeat that sophomore year), and I was now in my senior year, I had only about eight more months of 24/7 stress. Well, assuming I could figure out what I wanted to do with my life once I graduated. I was applying to colleges, of course, but in a rather nebulous, what-else-was-I-supposed-to-do way. I don't think I was the only high school senior who ever felt like that

Special Kaye cleared her throat. "Um, if you're still in high school, exactly how old are you?"

"Seventeen," I said.

She held up her hands and took several steps away from me.

"But I'll be eighteen soon," I said, not really thinking through how she might interpret the information. I was just excited by the idea of actually qualifying as an adult, at least from a chronologically legal standpoint.

"Oh, really," she said. She stepped closer. Much closer.

Coco slipped a gloved hand between me and Special Kaye, looking up into her much taller friend's heavily made up face. "Bitch, you are one pair of scissors away from going drag queen to post-op, understand?"

"What makes you so sure he doesn't want a bowl of Special Kaye for breakfast on his birthday, huh? Maybe he doesn't care for Coco Puffs."

Coco slowly closed her eyes, as if asking for patience, as she licked her lips. "I'm pretty sure this one is looking for a man who doesn't have dresses in his closet. Or fake Jimmy Choos."

"I told you, those were not fake."

"Jimmy Choo does not make a woman's shoe big enough for a man's size 13 foot!"

"Ladies!" This time it was Aphra Behn putting a hand between Special Kaye and Coco. "Mr. Hypertension is on his way back."

We all turned to find Jeremy waving us towards the entrance. "Well, he doesn't have a police record, but if *anything* goes wrong tonight, you will never work in this town again. I'm not joking. Because I will kill you." He handed me back my ID with a gracious smile. "Have a lovely evening." Then he dropped the smile. "But I seriously will kill you if you do anything wrong in there. You understand that, right?"

I nodded as I was pushed through a metal detector.

Now if you're thinking we then entered a gorgeous ballroom decorated with glittery lights and the orange, red, and yellow tones which the night's theme called for, well, then you've never been through a service entrance. It was a long, wide hallway of painted gray cinderblock. Service people of every imaginable stripe scurried about through an obstacle course of stacked chairs, racks of glasses, trays of food, cases of liquor and wine, and flatbeds loaded with just about every imaginable party item of which an event coordinator could think.

Eventually we were shown into a dressing "room," which consisted of four "walls" made of metal racks with curtains hanging from them, a lighted makeup mirror and table, and one chair. "One chair for the three of us?" Coco said to Jeremy.

Jeremy waved for Coco to be quiet as he listened with a panicked expression to someone through his earpiece. "Uh-huh, yeah, sure, no problem!" Jeremy said into his sleeve. Then he turned to us, yelled, "*Crap!*" and ran off at Olympic-caliber speed.

The four of us who remained all looked down at the one chair.

"We don't go on for almost an hour," Special Kaye said.

"I had to walk a lot more in these heels than I'd planned on," Coco said.

"Well, I was on time, so I've already been here for an hour," Aphra Behn said.

"Um," I said, "we passed several stacks of chairs on our way here. Do you think we could use a few of those?"

They looked at me like I was Einstein suggesting the Theory of Relativity.

"I love you even more now," Special Kaye said.

Coco put a hand on my shoulder. "I'll cut off her dick by the time you get back, I promise."

"Are you sure it'll be okay? I don't want Jeremy murdering me because I borrowed a few chairs."

Coco pointed at her feet. "Five. Inch. Heels."

I actually didn't have to go very far to find the closest chairs, but while running the errand I learned two interesting things. First, I discovered that I hadn't adapted to my new shoes as well as I'd thought, because while I was okay keeping them on when walking was the only thing I had to think about, the second I picked up three stackchairs and tried not to bump into anyone or anything, the right shoe somehow slipped off and shot through an open doorway.

I froze, waiting for loud repercussions, but none came.

I placed the chairs down and tentatively eased my head into the open doorway. Several security guards were looking at a wall of black and white monitors that showed every conceivable angle of the Autumnal Ball—the ballroom, the bars, backstage, the kitchen, the red carpet, you name it. As

I bent down low and stretched my arm to retrieve the shoe, which had stopped just shy of the console, one of the guards barked, "Don't even!"

My heart stopped. Luckily my bladder control did not.

I looked up slowly to find . . . that they hadn't even noticed me. The guard was pointing at the one of the screens showing the red-carpet arrivals. "Damn, that Kennerly woman is a MILF!"

I grabbed the shoe, extracted myself back into the hallway, slipped off the other shoe, and placed them both on top of the chairs, which I scuttled back to the safety of my new friends.

Oh, so if you're wondering what the second thing I learned was, it was that the Kennerlys had arrived at the Autumnal Ball. Which meant that Iris's plans for Kimberly, and the family, were on their way to possibly coming true.

"Her tits are as fake as mine," Special Kaye said as she peeked between the curtains screening the stage from the mingling socialites in The Grand Ballroom. Aphra Behn shouldered her aside to get a look for herself. "Well, hers are real. And she's got the warm knees to prove it."

I chuckled, but then turned to see Coco shaking her head. "Are they always so mean?" I asked.

"It's the oldest story in the book—the bullied become the bullies."

Special Kaye twirled away from the curtains. "I'm not mean. I'm just honest." Then she began to sashay towards the back of the stage. "And I'm so nervous I honestly think I'm about to vomit."

Turning to face us, Aphra Behn sighed jealously as she tapped her long fake nails against her distended belly. "If only I could vomit. For years I've dreamed of being bulimic, but I can only get the binge part right. It turns out I just have *no* gag reflex."

Special Kaye harrumphed. "I wonder how *that* happened."

Aphra Behn smiled proudly. "You're just jealous."

Special Kaye slid her hands along her flat belly. "Am I?"

Aphra Behn's smile turned into a sulky frown. "Bitch."

"Ladies, no fighting!" Coco said as she clapped. Then she held out a hand to each of them. "It's time for prayer circle."

"Prayer circle?" I asked, not expecting to hear anything about prayer from these three.

"It's what we do before every performance. Haven't you ever seen a Gaga concert video?" Coco said, as they joined hands. "Why don't you go find yourself a good spot to watch the show from while we get ourselves ready? Just meet us backstage afterwards, okay?"

I nodded, then walked off as quietly as I could as an unexpectedly serious mood overtook the trio. It occurred to me that for all of their frivolity and joking, this meant a lot and was very important to them. I guess acceptance and approval always are.

Once I left the backstage area and entered the ballroom, I had the strangest reaction. All I wanted to do was hide. I didn't know any of these people, and while my family was there, I had this weird feeling like I would get in trouble if they found out I'd made it in. Maybe just the idea of explaining it seemed too complicated. I'd have to justify hanging around a bunch of drag queens. After feeling sorry for myself for not getting to attend the ball with my family, now that I was there with them, I wanted to keep it a secret.

So I found my way to the corner of one of the side alcoves that bordered the ballroom so I could look out at the rich and powerful people. I tried to figure out which conversations were between old friends, and which were between people scheming to appear like old friends. There was definitely a sense of seeing and being seen, but it took me by surprise that no one looked like they were having much fun. It all seemed like so much work. Somehow I'd always imagined the kind of expensive event that I couldn't afford to get into as being lots and lots of fun. There was plenty of glamour, sure, but even the laughter had an oddly showy quality.

And then the first of the evening's many unexpected things happened.

I guess because I was trying to unobtrusively observe by slipping myself into the shadowed corner, unless you knew I was there, I was easy to miss. Because before I realized who was talking, I heard a young man's voice trying to be jovial while still complaining. "I wish I hadn't let you drag me to this thing. They're like piranhas."

And then a woman's voice said, "Some people would find the attention flattering."

And then an older man's voice said, "Just make sure you get a pre-nup."

And then the woman's voice mixed good humor with a tinge of exasperation, "Jonas, you're not helping."

Jonas?

I turned my head to see less than two feet away from me none other than Jonas Kennerly—American royalty, ex-presidential candidate, richer-than-God Jonas Kennerly. And beside him was the object of the security guard's MILF fantasy, Jonas's wife, the legendary beauty, Jennifer Kennerly. And they were both talking to the man I'd seen earlier on

TV and thought was probably the handsomest man alive, J.J. Kennerly, who turned out to be even better looking in person.

I'm not quite sure how long I managed to go without taking a breath. I'm not even sure if I blinked, I was so afraid of doing anything that might draw attention to the fact that their private conversation was being overheard.

"J.J., I just want you to meet Missy Easton's daughter. She's at Yale *and* was on the cover of *Harper's Bazaar* last month."

"Mom, you know it's tough out there for a pimp," J.J. said as he looked to his father for sympathy.

Jonas, however, put his hand on J.J.'s shoulder and asked, "Do I need to give you the St. Crispin's Day speech? *'The fewer men, the greater share of honour.'*"

"Thanks Dad," J.J. said, "but I'm thinking more about shuffling 'off this mortal coil.'"

His dad laughed, and I, if I'm being totally honest, might have swooned. How many guys can top a quote from Shakespeare with another quote from Shakespeare? Especially hot guys?

All I could think about was how lucky Kimberly was. I mean, sure, she hadn't even met him yet, but if anyone had a legitimate shot at it, it was Kimberly. Then my stomach soured a little, because even though she was my stepsister, honestly, she was kind of a bitch a lot of the time, and it wasn't fair for someone like her to end up with someone like him.

I almost ached as I watched the Kennerlys reenter the melee. Sigh. *Straight girls have all the luck*, I couldn't help but think.

And then the second—but not the last—totally unexpected thing of the night happened.

I was still trying to keep my eyes on J.J. Kennerly as he and his parents made their way across the room, when I heard a very familiar voice say, "I know I just saw him over here. I'm sure of it!"

"Mom, it's not well-lit, and you're probably seeing double by now anyway, so would you quit jerking me around the room with every supposed Kennerly sighting?"

"Kimberly, I'm *telling* you, it was him! If you had come with me the second I told you—

"I was in the middle of a conversation!"

"—we would have made it here in time. Damn it, that waiter with the wine is walking in the other direction!"

No sooner had they shown up than Iris and Kimberly were off in pursuit of one kind of refreshment or another.

If I hadn't breathed or blinked while the Kennerlys were standing so close, I'm not sure if my heart even beat while my own family was there. Maybe I was afraid that it would burst the bubble of my unexpected adventure.

And then, after that, it occurred to me that I'd also passed up the opportunity to warn them to tone down the pursuit. I'd just heard J.J. saying he felt like he was being attacked by little flesh-eating fish, and Iris's level of subtlety was somewhere between a barracuda's and a great white shark's. Later I would think about this a lot, questioning my own motives in a lot of what eventually transpired.

The ballroom lights dimmed as spotlights hit the stage curtains, and I had to abandon my safe little corner to get a better view. But that only meant finding a pillar a few feet away. Little steps are generally the way I like to take life's changes, especially when wearing shoes that are way too big.

Now I don't want to sound ungrateful, but I admit that when I had found out Coco and company were performing a drag routine to songs by The Supremes at the biggest society event of the season, I had my doubts. I just didn't see how all of those elements went together. But once they started performing, I finally realized the cleverness in choosing them to open the entertainment portion of the festivities. The old-school music had the more staid attendees bopping their heads, and having it performed by drag queens made it edgy enough to win over the more adventurous. Also, having only seen them bicker and kvetch for the last hour, I had no way of knowing how crisp their unison would be, nor had I been prepared for the fearless charisma that Coco exuded in front of a crowd.

After their third song, I added my own enthusiasm as they took their bow (actually, curtsies), then slipped through a door so that I'd be waiting for them in the hallway behind the backstage area. From the sounds of the applause, I think they took another curtain call, and then it sounded like the comedian who was emceeing might have engaged them in a little patter before he moved onto his regular shtick. I don't know exactly what they were up to after that, but I was left waiting for longer than I'd expected, and feeling rather antsy, I fell into my usual habit of pacing. Of course, I also started obsessing about all of the homework I should be doing instead of standing around waiting for three drag queens who were evidently not going to show up. It wasn't a terribly long hallway, and as I began to feel increasingly anxious when Coco and the girls failed to appear, I got distracted as to whether I was supposed to have met them somewhere else, and I wasn't really paying attention to the whole walking thing, because, you know, most of us don't have to by the age of seventeen, which meant I wasn't really paying attention to keeping on the too-big-for-my-feet shoes, and the left one slipped off, and I guess I was trying to slip my foot back in at the same time I was turning, and, well, I sent the shoe flying into the air like a David Beckham field goal. Right at the face of the guy who had just rounded the corner.

Who just happened to be—yeah, this is the BIG totally unexpected thing of the evening—J.J. KENNERLY!

Yes, that's right, I had just inadvertently kicked a shoe right at the face of The Most Eligible Bachelor In America, The Most Handsome Man I Had Ever Seen In My Life, and The Man Who Was Supposed To Save My Family.

Just the two of us. Me and him. Him and me.

And, of course, the shoe that I had just accidentally torpedoed at his no-doubt-ridiculously-expensive dental work.

And then, as if that weren't embarrassing enough, I GASPED. Yes, an honest-to-god, did-it-out-loud in a really big, fat, gay way, gasp.

Luckily all of those pictures in magazines and on-line of J.J. Kennerly playing sports aren't just photo opportunities, because just as quickly as I emitted my never-to-be-lived-down-at-least-in-my-own-head gasp, his hands flew up and caught the shoe.

Then, casually holding it out to me with a charming smile and a sparkly glint in his dark brown eyes that you'd swear was a movie special effect, except that this wasn't a movie, it was real life, and my miserable real life at that— have I mentioned that when I first met J.J. Kennerly at the Autumnal Ball, that I FREAKING GASPED?—he said, "Did you lose something?"

I think I stared at the shoe in his hand for an extremely long time. (Really nice hands by the way, doesn't chew his nails.) Or maybe it just felt that way. Maybe it was just a split second. But it felt to me like forever. Regardless, when I finally managed to lift my eyes away from the prof-fered Ferragamo, an inferno of embarrassment exponentially increasing my body temperature and breaking a sweat onto my brow, I looked up into J.J. Kennerly's eyes, and . . . .

I swear I'm not making this up just to make myself feel better, or to make it sound like I'm in denial about how queeny I must have sounded when I let out "The Gasp," but when J.J. Kennerly's eyes met mine, I heard just the slightest, softest, wouldn't-have-even-heard-it-if-everything-and-every-other-sound-in-the-world-had-not-just-stopped, intake of breath come from J.J. Kennerly.

We both stood perfectly still—him holding out the shoe to me, me unable to move a single muscle—and stared into each other's eyes. It was probably only for five or ten seconds, but it felt both instantaneous and infinite.

So, yeah, THIS turned out to be the most unexpected thing of the night.

But it wasn't the last one. Because there was one more. And it came just at the end of those five or ten seconds that J.J. Kennerly and I had been staring into each other's eyes.

"J.J.?" a female voice said.

J.J. and I both flinched, and then I realized I knew the voice.

"Kimberly," I whispered.

J.J. swallowed in what was really more of a gulp. "Is that your girlfriend?" he asked softly.

"My sister. And she doesn't know I'm here."

Suddenly I was moving very quickly, and it was in the direction opposite Kimberly's voice. Without even really being aware of it, I was running, in just the one shoe, which somehow stayed on fine. Through doors, and hallways, and out into the unexpected night.

CHAPTER 4

THE MORNING AFTER

I don't remember anything about the subway ride home. My mind was totally occupied by reliving that eye-to-eye moment I'd just had with J.J. Kennerly. I had looked openly at him, and he—I was quite sure of it—had looked openly at me. I wouldn't be able to explain it in any concrete way, but there was just something that let me know with one hundred percent certainty that we had shared one of life's rare and special moments—the moment of the indescribable wow. Love at first sight, the whole shebang. Me. And J.J. Kennerly. No matter how I tried to figure out other ways to interpret what had happened, none of them mattered, because it was just so obvious.

Okay, so maybe I can't say that I *really* believe in the concept of love at first sight, but I *do* believe in the moment when you see someone and know that you easily *could* fall in love with them. Even a cynic should be able to accept the possibility of this moment, because there's no denying that most of the people we see on any given day we know, even with a brief glance, that we could *never* fall in love with them. So, if the negative extreme inarguably exists, then why can't the positive extreme? It's only logical, right?

The first thing I did when I got home was hang up the designer suit jacket Special Kaye had brought for me, and that was when I let out my second gasp of the night. (Don't judge. I'm being honest about these things, so the least you can do is not judge. I'm already punishing myself enough as I recall all of this, believe me.) I had run out of there so speedily, with only the thought of getting back to the safety of my own room, that I had totally forgotten to say thank you and goodbye to Coco and the girls, and I had, arguably, stolen a very expensive jacket and one very expensive shoe. I could only hope that maybe Coco had run into J.J. Kennerly, seen the other shoe, recognized it, and somehow gotten it back.

Although then it occurred to me that if J.J. had high-tailed it out of that hallway as quickly as I had—well, almost as quickly, since I'd fled before he'd even reacted to Kimberly's approaching—then he was probably gone by the time Coco arrived. And *then* it occurred to me that if he *hadn't* gotten away before Kimberly arrived, and if he and I really had shared the moment that I knew we had, well, then Iris's plan for Kimberly to save the family's future by marrying into the Kennerly fortune had hit a major obstacle. Then I started to wonder if I'd been judging Iris's dependency on white wine too much all of these years. Because, although the one time I'd taken a sip and hadn't really understood the appeal, I was tempted to revisit something which I had perhaps previously discounted too quickly.

Instead, realizing how dirty my un-shoed foot had probably gotten even though I'd had a sock on, I decided to take a shower to see if it would help me relax. After I was cleaned up and in my pajamas, I went downstairs to wait for the report from the rest of the family's perspective on what had happened at the ball. I sat on the couch, and then laid down, and evidently I fell asleep, because the next thing I knew I heard the sound of laughter, and I opened my eyes to see Iris, Kimberly, and Buck all leaning over the sofa and smiling down at me.

"Oh Chris!" Kimberly said.

"We're so happy for you," Iris said, throwing her arms around me in perhaps the first genuine hug she'd ever given me.

Buck playfully punched my arm in more of a tap. "We're proud of you, guy."

I wanted to ask, *who are you people and what have you done with my family?* But instead, as I sat up, I said, "What's going on?"

"It's J.J. Kennerly!" Kimberly sat down right beside me, our legs touching, as she threw an arm around my shoulder. "He's in love with you! All he could talk about during the entire ball was Chris, Chris, Chris!"

As I swallowed my stomach out of my throat, I managed to get out, "But—"

Iris smiled understandingly as she sat down on my other side, kindly patting my thigh. "It's okay, Chris, we know you're gay, and it's okay. We just want you to be happy."

"That's right," Buck said. "And now that there aren't any secrets between us anymore, let's start acting like a real family."

It was all so surreal. My head was swimming, but they went on.

"That's a great idea," Iris said. "In fact, in the morning, I'll make breakfast, and Buck, you'll take out the trash." Buck nodded.

"What about me, Mother?" Kimberly asked, her flawless brow showing a slight wrinkle of concern. "What do I get to do to help?"

Iris thought about it for a second. "I know! You can take Chris shopping to get some new things for his first date with J.J.!"

Kimberly let out a squeak of excitement.

Although, alas, as it turned out, that squeak wasn't Kimberly. It was the front door. Because it *had* all been sur-real; it had all been a dream. A dream that it almost hurt to wake up from. They say that it's always darkest before the dawn, but sometimes it's really darkest the moment you realize a dream was just a dream.

But as I sat up and turned to face them as they entered the room, I had one of those confusing, groggy moments when you wake up, and the events in real life are too much like what was just happening during your slumber, so you aren't sure if you really are awake, or if it's one of those *Inception* dream-within-a-dream things. Because they all *were* beaming huge smiles, and Kimberly actually somehow looked even fresher and more beautiful than she had at the beginning of the night. There was a never-before-seen effer-vescence to everything about her and, perhaps even more disorienting, to Iris, too.

"What's going on?" I asked finally.

Iris tossed her clutch to the couch, just barely missing me with it. "Your stepsister was the belle of the ball! All of those other little jealous bitches were just drooling with envy! It was fantastic!"

Although it was still odd to see Iris looking so happy, this definitely sounded more like her.

"Now, Mom," Kimberly said with less than convincing modesty, "it was just one night of dancing. We don't *know* that it means anything."

"Yeah," Buck said. "I mean, he had to dance with somebody, right? Maybe he figured it was easier to keep riding the same horse."

Kimberly turned on him. "Just because you couldn't even get laid by a hunchbacked hooker if you tried!"

Buck languidly lowered himself onto the couch, putting his feet up on the coffee table. "Ha! Shows what you know. I nailed one of the waitresses." Noticing the eyes Iris slashed at him, he added, "I used a condom."

"Buck," Iris said, "if you do anything to screw this up for her, for all of us, I'm sending you to your father."

Buck briefly lost the cavalier attitude he generally wore as his look darkened and he mumbled, "Like you know where he is."

"Buck," Iris said, then crossed over to the bar and poured herself a healthy shot of bourbon. It was rare that she drank anything other than wine, but there were moments when she'd take whatever was closest at hand. Mentions of their father were high on that list.

"Fine," Buck said, pretending to wipe lint off of his trousers. "But I'm just saying it was a bunch of dances, that's all. She may never hear from him again." Then, a little cruelly to his mother, "Guys do that, you know?"

Iris threw back a long swig before answering, "It was over two hours, and he never danced with another girl."

"And they did ask," Kimberly said with a tone of fond reminiscing.

Now maybe you have figured out everything that they were talking about, but I had not. I mean, clearly Kimberly had met someone at the ball who Iris thought she could sink her hopes of redemption into, but there were a lot of really rich people there, and more than a few single men who would be plenty happy to screw their courage to Kimberly's sticking place. So, I said, "I take it Kimberly met someone?"

Iris smiled with a cool pride. "No, she met the *only* one."

Iris and Kimberly shared a giggle, then Kimberly actually waltzed around the room with an imaginary suitor as she said, "I met the most amazing, wonderful, beautiful boy ever. He's smart, and funny, and the only thing better than the way he looked at me was the way all of those bitches looked when he turned them down because he wanted to dance more with *me*."

"Bitches," Iris said.

"So who was it?" I asked.

Kimberly and Iris smiled at each other, enjoying the suspense of keeping me waiting. So Buck stole their thunder by saying in a derisive tone, "The most eligible bachelor alive."

"Who?" I asked, still not getting it.

Buck rolled his eyes. "J.J. Kennerly, you butt pirate."

Obviously, I knew that wasn't possible, so I said, "But that's not possible."

"What do you mean, 'that's not possible?'" Iris said. "He's lucky to find a girl like Kimberly."

"No, I didn't mean—It's just that—I, he, we—I thought. . . ."

"Easy for you to say," Buck said.

Kimberly turned to face me, putting her hands on her hips. "Aren't you happy for me?"

As reality slowly sank in, I couldn't exactly tell her that, no, I was not happy for her, because she had just ruined my life, broken my heart, proven once again that I was a stupid idiot, and, worse yet, that I was evidently one of those gay guys I hated who thought that any man they wanted was secretly gay. Instead I quietly offered my congratulations and excused myself, saying it was late and I had a lot of homework to get done when I woke up.

As I returned to the privacy of my own room to lick my wounds, I was honestly angrier with myself than anything. How had I let myself believe such a ridiculous fantasy? Because that's what it had all been. A stupid, silly fantasy taking place in my silly, stupid head. You'd think a kid who'd never really known his mother and had lost his father to suicide little more than a week before his fourteenth birthday would have learned that life was bitter, and cruel, and hard, but evidently I was too idiotic to even learn a lesson spelled out that clearly.

Perhaps I'd picked up a little drama queen bug in my night out with the drag queens. It took almost an hour of lying in bed beating myself up over my foolhardiness before I managed to fall asleep.

Since it was Sunday, at least I didn't have to deal with school when I woke up still smarting from my self-inflicted folly of the night before. So I would be single and alone for the rest of my life. Big deal. No surprise there. Who needs love anyway?! (I'm not the only one who has these moods, right?)

As I threw off the covers and got out of bed, I resolved to be cheerful throughout a day I would make sure was productive and busy. If you can't beat 'em, distract the hell out of yourself, that's my mantra. I'd pretty much always been the first person in the house to arise, and now that Kimberly only had one afternoon class at NYU and Buck wasn't matriculating anywhere, I usually had time to myself even during the school week. But given the mood I was fighting against, I decided that sitting alone with a pile of homework might not be the best way to begin, so I decided to get some fresh bagels and then pick up some produce at the corner bodega.

As I looked for bananas with just the right amount of ripeness, a voice behind me said, "Yo, homey, where'd you disappear to?"

I turned around to see a slightly thuggish-looking black guy in oversized hip-hop clothes looking at me expectantly. I scanned my memory for a scenario where I might have met him, but I really couldn't think of anything, so I said, "Um, I think maybe you have me confused with someone else?"

He tilted his head. "Don't you recognize me?"

I tried, I really did, but still I drew a blank. Even after he pushed his face closer to mine. Uncomfortably close. Still nothing.

He dropped his voice to a whisper. "It's me. Coco."

I pulled my head back, taking in this entirely masculine, short-haired black guy, dressed in a way that would have made me question if I was being racist or just reasonably cautious if I tried to avoid crossing his path too closely, and I just couldn't see it.

He sucked his tongue, *tch*, leaned in closer and started sarcastically mumbling, "Baby, baby, baby, where did those clothes go," to the tune of "Where Did Our Love Go?"

I would like to state for the record that I did *not* gasp at this moment. But I was still pretty shocked. "Coco? Really?"

He shook his head, chuckling to himself. "Shit, you probably think RuPaul is a natural blonde."

"Is that really you?"

"As real as a drag queen can be."

"You . . . you look so different."

"If I walked around like that all day where I live, my ass would be raped and dead. Trust." Then he looked down at the crisp white tennis shoes on his feet. "Besides, these are much more comfortable."

"I'll bet." I lifted the produce in my hands and said, "I need to pay for these."

He walked with me to the cash register, and as we approached he gave a curt nod to the cashier, saying, "'Sup." The cashier nodded back, and I suppressed the desire to laugh. It was just so hard to wrap myself around the idea that this tough-guy pseudo-thug was *Coco*.

Once we got outside and were headed back to my place, I immediately began to apologize for my disappearance. "Coco, I am so sorry—"

"Duane."

"What?"

"My name. It's Duane."

"Duane?"

"Yeah, Duane."

"Not Coco?"

"Not when I'm dressed like this. Not most of the time, really. I'm only Coco when . . . well, when I'm Coco."

"So how do I know which one I'm supposed to call you?"

"Dawg, you didn't even know I was Coco until I made your bitch-ass believe me. Is it really that unclear? When I'm like this, I'm me. When I'm like that, I'm Coco. Clear enough?"

And, actually, it was. The only hard part was wrapping my head around the fact that both extremely different personas existed in the same person. There was just one more thing I wanted to know. "But which one is the real you?"

Duane shrugged. "They both are."

I nodded, accepting this, then asked, "Does this mean you're bi?"

The right side of his mouth curled up in a smile he was trying to restrain, and giving just a bit of Coco-tude, he leaned in and said, "Child, the only fish I eat is at Red Lobster. Can I get an amen?"

It took me a couple seconds to realize that it hadn't been a rhetorical question. "Oh, uh, amen?" I said.

He shook his head. "So what happened to you?"

I was still too embarrassed to tell anyone about what I'd mistakenly thought had gone on between J.J. Kennerly and me, so I just told him I'd freaked out when I heard my stepsister coming while I was waiting for them after the show—and trying to put a little guilt on him by asking what had kept them so long, especially when I knew that eventually in the narrative I was going to have to let him know that I was missing one of those very expensive shoes—and I apologized if he'd left the ball early because of me.

He looked at me confused when I said that, and I said that since he was here with me so early I figured he must not have gone to bed too late, and he laughed. "I haven't been to bed yet. But Kevin—that's Special Kaye's real name—borrowed those shoes from work and needs them back before ten."

I looked at my cell phone and saw that it was 8:32. Ugh.

"You know," I said trying to deflect, "if you hadn't thrown my shoes away, I could have worn them home. But since you *did* just toss them into that trash can—"

"Kevin has a motto. Two things should be used once and then thrown away or given to charity—shoes and men."

"That seems kind of wasteful."

"I know. Good shoes are so hard to find."

We'd reached the brownstone, and once we walked up the front steps and through the front door, I was surprised by the sight of Kimberly, Iris, and Buck all sitting in the living room in their pajamas and bathrobes. And they were surprised by the sight of me with company.

"Uh, hi, this is Co—Duane. This is my friend Duane."

Kimberly and Buck exchanged a significant big-eyed, knowing look. Iris just looked terrified.

"What are you guys even doing up so early?" I asked.

"We couldn't sleep," Kimberly said, motioning at Iris.

"They woke me up," Buck said. "I was sleeping fine." Then he brightened up. "But I'm sure glad I didn't miss this." He looked at Duane, tilted his chin and said, "'Sup."

"'Sup," Duane said.

I cleared my throat. "Um, we just have to get something from my room. We'll be right back." After tossing the bags of food to Buck, I pushed Duane up the staircase, but we hadn't even made it one flight when Iris called in a voice straining with absolutely no success at sounding nonchalant. "Chris, could we see you down here for a second?"

I stopped, desperately wanting to simply ignore her, flee upwards to my room, and slam the door shut. But when I remembered that only one of two expected shoes was up there, I told Duane I'd just be a moment.

Trying for casualness, I leaned my head through the doorway to the living room. "Yes?"

"Come on in," Iris said, taking a long sip from a glass of orange juice which was almost certainly actually a mimosa or a screwdriver.

I took a couple steps in.

"Who is that?" she asked.

"That's my friend Duane. I introduced him, remember?"

"Chris has a friend," Buck said.

"What *kind* of friend?" Kimberly said.

Iris jerked her head at them with annoyance. "Would you two stop that?! It's preposterous. I mean, that fellow is . . ." She searched her mind for the word she wanted that wouldn't get her in trouble if the PC Police were listening. She settled on a term she still felt the need to whisper: "African-American."

Kimberly rolled her eyes. "Mother, even you've heard of jungle fever."

"Bow-chicka-bow-bow," Buck said.

"Stop it!" Iris said, putting her hands up to her ears. "I won't even hear of it!"

With a rare flash of irritation, I asked heatedly, "Do any of you have a legitimate question? Otherwise, I have a guest waiting for me upstairs. We'll be right back down, I promise."

Suddenly Iris had an even more panicked expression on her face. "You sent him up there alone?"

Disgusted with them, I turned around without responding and dashed up to the third floor. Duane was sitting patiently on my bed with his hands folded in his lap. "White people are *so* uptight," he said.

"Sorry."

Embarrassed by my family, whether he'd heard any of it or not, I reached into my closet and pulled out the suit jacket, presenting it to him with overly-solicitous pride. "See, as good as when you put it on me."

"Great. But where are the shoes?" He took the jacket from me and lay it over one of his thighs.

"Right. The shoes." I turned back to the closet, bent down, picked up the one shoe I had, stayed bent down hoping lighting might strike me dead so that I wouldn't have to admit I'd lost the other one, and then, when a *deus ex machina* failed to save me, finally faced up to what I'd been avoiding and turned to him with the one shoe held out.

"Yeah, so here's the one I have."

Duane took it. "The *one* you have?"

"Yes, the one I have."

"Shoes, as you know, come in pairs."

"Yes, that I do know."

"But this is only one."

"Yes, it is."

"So where is the other one?"

"Well, um, I don't know if you're going to believe this, but I swear it's the truth. I mean, I really, really, really swear I am not making this up, as unbelievable as it may sound."

"Do you realize how much that shoe cost?"

"Yes, I do actually know that, and believe me that knowledge does not make this any easier, but perhaps if you'll bear with me for just a moment. You see, uh, the last time I saw that other shoe it was in the hand of . . . um . . . J.J. Kennerly, actually."

Duane looked down at the shoe in his hand, then around the room, then back at me. "J.J. Kennerly?" I nodded. "Jason Kennerly has the other shoe?"

"Well," I said, "I don't know if he still has the other shoe. But the last time I saw it he did."

"Explain, please."

"As you may recall, on occasion I had just the slightest trouble keeping them on my feet."

"That does sound familiar."

"And then when you guys kept me waiting after the show—"

"So now this is my fault?"

"Do we really need to assign blame?" I asked with what I thought sounded like exceeding understanding and reason.

Then Duane did something that truly shocked me. He shrugged, said, "Eh, that'll teach the bitch to lend out shit he can't afford," and stood up. I didn't know what to say, and I just stood there staring at him.

"You going to walk me down?" he asked. "I don't want to get frisked without my escort. Although, damn, your brother is fine."

"He's an idiot."

"Who said I cared about conversation?"

The entire way down I kept apologizing, and he kept telling me not to worry about it, and with a quick wave goodbye to the gawking trio in the living room, we were suddenly at the door, and I realized I really hated the idea of never again seeing the only person to whom I'd ever actually admitted that I was gay.

"Um," I said, keeping my voice low so that nosy ears in the next room wouldn't hear, "I really had fun hanging out with you last night."

Duane smiled. "Me, too."

"I really appreciate everything you did for me."

"Hey, everyone needs a fairy godmother once in a while, right?"

I nodded, starting to get the sense that maybe I was the only one who wasn't ready for our acquaintance to end. It made me feel sad, and I guess that showed, because Duane drew his eyebrows together and asked, "Um, did you want to hang out again sometime?"

"That'd be great!" I said, no doubt smiling too hard. It sure felt that way, at least. "I mean . . . well . . . you're the only one who knows."

He looked like he was about to say something but then thought better of it. "Look me up on Facebook. Use my Coco page."

"Coco Chanel Jones?"

"There's only one." He smiled with a wink, then turned to open the door, and just as he started to walk out, he SCREAMED at the top of his lungs, jumped back, and slammed the door shut with a *THUD!*

"Wha—" I said.

Duane, a look of confused wonder and disbelief, pointed at the door.

"Chris, what's going on out there?" Iris called from the living room, the urgent fear clear in her voice.

Not feeling like I was going to get a timely answer from Duane, I quickly pushed my eye to the security hole in the door, and almost added my own scream.

Standing on the other side was J.J. Kennerly!

Chapter 5

OHMYGODOHMYGODOHMYGOD

If you've ever thought it was unlikely that someone would look better in a sweatshirt and jeans than in a tuxedo, I can tell you that they can. At least J.J. Kennerly could. But what was he doing here? I made the bold decision to crack open the door and maybe ask him.

"Hi," I said, pressing my face into the crack between the door and the doorjamb.

"Hi," he said back, looking unsure. "It was rude of me to come so early. I'm sorry."

"No, it's fine."

Just as Iris called again from the living room, I noticed J.J. was carrying the missing shoe in his left hand. My savior! I grabbed Duane by the arm, swung the door briefly wide, and stepped out onto the front landing, yanking him out behind me, and pulled the door shut behind us.

"You brought my shoe!"

He looked down at it in his hand and smiled. "Yeah, it didn't seem like just one was going to do me much good. It's nice, though."

I nodded, then looked to Duane for any help he might be able to give with the conversation, but I quickly saw there was no assistance to be found there. He was staring at J.J., eyes not blinking, literally with his mouth open. I realized my hand was still on Duane's arm, so I quickly removed it.

Pointing to the shoe in Duane's hand, I said, "I'd actually borrowed it from him, so you've really saved my skin."

"Oh, that was nice," J.J. said, holding his hand out for Duane to shake. "I'm J.J. Good to meet you."

As he haltingly put his hand out to shake, Duane said something along the lines of, "Neh-shem-meh-heh."

J.J. smiled, rolling with it, then held out the shoe in his other hand. "Then I guess this goes to you."

Duane's head bopped up and down like a tacky dashboard toy as he took it.

At this point we all heard another scream, but this time it was muffled because we were on the outside of the closed door. Urgent voices, running feet, and general panic were suggested by the noises coming from inside the house. J.J. and I tried to act like we hadn't heard anything, and, well, I'm not sure Duane was capable of taking in much, all of his senses other than sight seeming to have been momentarily suspended.

"Thank you so much," I told J.J., making my pathetic claim for admittance into the Quick Thinkers Hall of Fame.

"My pleasure," J.J. said, looking awkwardly down at his now-empty hands.

I looked desperately again to Duane for help, but finding him still pathetically starstruck, the only thing I could think to do was punch his arm. I couldn't exactly do the classic snap-out-of-it! face slap right then.

Duane's head flicked to me, outrage briefly flashing in his eyes, then realizing the stupor I'd just arm-punched him out of, he quickly remembered his street mask. "Yo, whaz up?" he said to J.J., jerking his chin up toughly.

J.J., to his credit, suppressed a smile. "What's up?"

"Didn't you have to get those shoes back to your friend before ten?" I asked Duane.

He looked down at the shoes and suit jacket in his hands. "Oh, yeah. Yeah, I do. I should go."

The top half of his body got the message and started moving forward, but unfortunately the lower half was apparently still in shock. He began to pitch forward, and both J.J. and I reached out to keep him from toppling down the front steps. Luckily Duane's feet finally started moving, and he tried to play the whole thing off by adopting an exaggerated pimp-stroll. He held up two fingers, saying, "Peace out," as he left. I couldn't swear to it, but I think his knees might have buckled once or twice on the way. But maybe we'll say that was intentional.

Then I realized getting rid of Duane maybe hadn't been my best impulse, because now J.J. and I were alone. All of the ridiculous fantasy I'd indulged myself in the night before flooded through my mind, and I could feel the heat rising on my cheeks. As the shock of J.J.'s reappearance began to wear off, the miserable awkwardness of my situation began to overwhelm me. Luckily he found something to say first.

"I couldn't sleep last night."

I nodded, focusing my eyes on the landing, wondering if its molecular composition might benevolently manage to alter just enough to swallow me up. "Kimberly was saying the same thing."

When he didn't say anything in return for a long time, I finally ventured a look up to find a questioning expression.

"I couldn't think of any other way," he said.

"You—waithuhwhat?" I said, confusion complicating the struggle between my heart and mind, as a tiny pulse of hope began to radiate in my center while arrows of reason and doubt shot down from my brain, cautioning me to remember how foolishly I'd let my imagination run mere hours before.

But there he was, once again, staring into my eyes, longingly, questioningly, and I'm fully certain that mine could only have been mirroring his.

Was this really possible?

And then the door opened, and Buck, still in his bathrobe, spread his arms wide and said, "Dude, don't you sleep?"

Having gotten themselves dressed and presentable in record time (and all by themselves, as I pointedly pointed out to them later), Kimberly sat with her legs demurely crossed at the ankles, knees together, in a sweater-set and skirt, on the couch cushion next to J.J., and in the wing chair close by, Iris draped a silk-slack-covered leg over her knee while she fondled her long pearl necklace like worry beads. Buck sat back on the couch on the other side of Kimberly, while I trembled (sadly, I don't think that's even an exaggeration) and perched on another wing chair a bit closer to the door.

In answer to a question from Iris, J.J. was telling them something about how his mother thought he should practice law for a few years before running for office, but I was far too discombobulated to follow any trains of thought outside of my own head. There was enough of a traffic jam in there. It was crazy, right, to even entertain the thought that

The J.J. Kennerly could be thinking anything in the same universe as I was, right? Those long stares could be . . . because he thinks I'm a special needs child . . . and, wait, is eye contact good or bad with those? Well, if I don't know the right answer, then maybe he doesn't either? No, wait, the Kennerlys are famous for their work with special needs people, so he probably does know. So, that's probably the right thing to do, make eye contact. Unless. . .

I practically hopped up from my chair. "I'm going to go make some breakfast for us all." I said a little too loudly, and from the looks I was getting from Iris and Kimberly, I'm guessing in the middle of J.J. talking. But I didn't care; I just had to get out of there.

"Buck," I asked, "where did you put those bagels?"

"Uh, Mom told me to hide them."

Iris shot daggers at him until J.J. turned to look at her, then she brightened right up into a smile.

"So, where'd you . . . put them?"

Buck's face twisted uncomfortably, not sure if he should answer.

"That's okay, I'm not really that hungry if you're just worried about me. My mother would be appalled by my breach of etiquette, just showing up like this."

Kimberly reached out and placed a hand on his. "Hush. We're flattered you wanted to spend even a minute of your Sunday with us. What's better than Sunday brunch, after all?"

Buck looked at his watch. "It's barely even nine thirty. That's not brunch, that's full-on breakfast."

Well, at least when J.J. left I wouldn't be the only one killed, if the looks on Iris's and Kimberly's faces were any indication. I crossed over to Buck, excused my rudeness to J.J., then whispered into Buck's ear to tell me where he'd hid the food I'd bought hardly an hour before. Even though I knew everyone was watching me, as casually as possible I walked over to the antique Louis XIV armoire and found the two brown paper bags amongst the assortment of CDs, cassette tapes, and, oh, look, empty wine bottles. And I'd just cleaned it out a couple days ago.

I'd almost managed to escape the excruciating circumstances of the living room, when, just as I was crossing the threshold, J.J. said, "At the very least I must insist on helping."

I stopped short, almost dropping the bags in my hands, and looked over my shoulder to await Iris's cue.

"Oh, you," she said, as if he'd just told a naughty joke. So, I started to move again.

"No, I'm serious," J.J. said. "I'd love to help." So, I stopped again.

Iris waved me away. "Really, J.J., how would it look if I let a guest in my home fend for himself?" So, I started to move again.

"Like you wanted me to feel welcome and like one of the family," J.J. said. So I stopped.

Not quite willing to admit defeat yet, I could see Iris scanning her brain for a way to prevent him from going to the kitchen with me, and as I saw her running into dead end after dead end, I felt a fluttering in my stomach as I realized I might actually find out what the heck was going on between J.J. and me. And the way he was acting was certainly tipping the scales in my favor, or so my heart tried to convince my logic. Hope tingled through me, and I was beginning to feel a giddy burst of adrenaline when—

"Actually, J.J.," Buck said with bro-ish intimacy, "Chris *hates* for anyone to go into the kitchen when he's in there. It's like it's his private sanctuary or something. How gay, right?"

Although I suddenly wanted to throttle him around the neck even if it was too late to stop him from saying what he'd just said, technically, Buck wasn't exactly wrong. The kitchen *had* been my stronghold since my dad died. It was the one place where I knew more than anyone else in the family, and regardless of how they might dismiss me in other matters, it was the one area where I felt I had some control. But that didn't mean *now* was the time for him to have one of his moments of clarity. Not to mention using the word "gay" in that generic, anything-not-cool way.

J.J. looked to me for verification, and I couldn't think of a way to contradict the usual truth of what Buck had said fast enough, and Iris jumped on her advantage.

"It's settled!" she said.

I continued on my way to the kitchen. As exciting as the possibility of learning that J.J. and I were thinking the same things was, I'd be lying if I didn't admit that mixed with my disappointment that Buck had unknowingly blocked my chance at some alone time with J.J., I was also relieved. Not only was I not ready to give up the fantasy of the possibility of it again so soon, but, honestly, knowing you're gay, even saying you're gay, and actually being with another person who might be gay in an intimately gay way—and I don't even necessarily mean a sexual way—was raising the stakes exponentially. While in some ways it felt like I'd been secretly struggling with these feelings for such a long time, in other ways I wasn't entirely sure I was ready to deal with the reality of them. Maybe that seems naive for a seventeen-year-old male, but every flower blooms in its own time. Or so said some motivational card I once saw at a Duane Reade.

But I'd hardly emptied the bags when J.J. peeked his head tentatively through the swinging door and asked, "Do you really not like people to be in here?"

I waved him in urgently, looking to see if anyone was behind him.

"How did you convince Iris?"

He shrugged. "I asked if I could use the bathroom."

"But there's one in the hallway."

He shrugged again, putting up his hands in faux-innocence. "I didn't know."

Have you ever had that moment you really wanted right in front of you, and then not known what to do with it? Well, that was me at that moment. So, true to form, I used productivity as a distraction.

"Bagels or fruit?" I asked.

"Pardon?"

"Do you want to do bagel prep or make the fruit salad? Or eggs. You could make the eggs."

"Shouldn't we do the fruit first? That takes the longest, and the bagels and eggs will get cold."

"You've done this before." I had not expected that.

J.J. rolled his eyes. "Yes, and I also know how to tie my own shoes and wipe my own ass."

I laughed. And it wasn't just nerves (although, maybe partially). Suddenly I realized that since we'd met, I'd been looking at him as more of a myth than a person, and what I thought he was telling me with his joke was that he really just wanted to be known as the guy he really was. I handed him a knife and a bowl. "Start with the melon while I rinse the other stuff."

Full confession: I'd initially offered him the two jobs (bagels and fruit) that required using a knife because my hands had started shaking, and I was afraid I might cut off a digit. I figured I was unlikely to do too much damage with the egg beater, but as J.J. and I talked while I rinsed and organized and he chopped, I forced myself to take a few calming breaths as subtly as possible, and I got the worst of it under control.

"So, did Buck make that up about the kitchen?" J.J. asked.

"No, not really. I mean, it's not like I have land mines hidden to keep people out or anything, but it's sort of how I contribute."

"That's nice. Everyone does their share of the chores, and you cook."

"Well, no, I do those too, actually."

He looked at me with a confused expression, so I explained, "Iris and my dad got married when I was ten. Before that he and I had lived very differently, and I was very self-sufficient. And then when . . ." I trailed off, because I never knew how to handle the next piece of my history. As I struggled for the right wording, J.J. came to my assistance.

"I think my mom mentioned something about a family tragedy."

Afraid that my voice might betray the wave of longing for my father that surged up—no matter how many years went by, I never knew when these moments would hit—I nodded and kept my eyes down on the blueberries I was rinsing.

"We've had a number of those in my family, too," J.J. said.

We worked quietly for a bit, then trying to change the mood, J.J. tossed the last of the strawberries he'd pared into the bowl and jovially asked, "What's next?"

"You're a good assistant," I said.

"This is fun. I hardly ever have time to cook anymore."

"Well, then I intend to take full advantage of you."

Then, as soon as the words were out of my mouth, I heard the unintended double entendre and just about died.

As my eyes dropped to the ground, I caught the slight surprise on his face as he looked to see what exactly I'd meant by those words. *Ohgodohgodohgod, whywhywhy, killmenowkillmenowkillmenow*, was about all my brain was capable of thinking.

"Chris?" J.J. said in a voice so soft it was almost a whisper.

I looked up to find his eyes unwaveringly focused on mine.

"Yes?"

Neither of us blinking, possibly neither of us even breathing, we stood there for what felt like forever, until he finally said, "Is there anything you want to ask me?"

"Like what?" I said, afraid of the painful awkwardness ahead of me if I asked the wrong question, no matter how badly I wanted the answer, any answer, just let this intensely cruel not-knowing end.

"Like . . . anything."

I wasn't conscious of it at the time, and later J.J. said he hadn't been either, but somehow our faces were drawing closer to one another. I didn't even realize it, but somehow we were finally close enough for me to feel the warmth of his breath on my cheek. (So I guess at least one of us was breathing.)

Swallowing, he gently licked his lips.

Then I did the same.

And finally, as my neck tilted up, I gently parted my lips and—

"Yoo-hoo!" Kimberly burst through the swinging door.

The heart that had been beating faster than the wings of a hummingbird inside my chest just about burst from terror and panic as I jumped away from J.J. and spun to face our intruder.

Apparently oblivious, Kimberly beamed at J.J. "We were wondering where you'd got lost to. There's a bathroom in the hallway, silly."

Looking far calmer than I felt, J.J. coughed and ran a hand over his brow. "Yeah, Chris said so, but since I was here, I decided to go ahead and offer to help."

Kimberly shook a finger as if the scolding she was giving me was just a joke, although I certainly knew that it was not, "Chris, shame on you. He's our guest."

"I insisted," J.J. said firmly.

"He insisted," I said, nodding my head with emphatic agreement. "It seemed rude to argue."

J.J. added his own nodding. "Yes, that would have been very rude."

Then Kimberly surprised me by throwing up her hands and saying lightly, "Oh, heck, I don't care. Mom is the one who's all Emily Post about everything." She came over to where we'd been preparing the food. "So what are we having?"

"Well, um, we just finished the fruit salad, and J.J. was about to cut the bagels."

"And Chris was about to make the eggs," J.J. said.

"Well, what can I do?" Kimberly asked.

It took me a couple seconds to realize she'd really, actually, not-just-in-my-fantastical-imagination said those words, but the shock didn't wear off fast enough for me to come up with anything more than, "Ummmm," in response.

"How about I set the table?" she said.

J.J. looked to me for approval.

"Uh, sure," I said. I began to point, "The plates are over—"

"I know where the plates are, silly." With a roll of her eyes, Kimberly proceeded to open a cabinet door that revealed mixing bowls and cake pans. "Oh, someone moved the dishes."

Sure, three and a half years ago. But I didn't say that. I merely pointed to the correct cabinet. Kimberly took out enough plates of every size for a Thanksgiving dinner, then opened a few drawers until she found the silver utensils, and once she'd amassed enough tableware to serve Bolivia, she marred her brow with overwhelmed confusion and asked J.J. if he could help her get everything into the dining room.

"I can take care of the bagels while the eggs are cooking," I said. Once the two of them left the kitchen, as I crossed to the refrigerator for eggs, I was finally able to look down and confirm that I hadn't peed my pants when she'd burst into the room.

Holy shit. What the hell was happening here? I was 99.4% sure that I had just almost kissed J.J. Kennerly, somehow forgetting that my family was only a hallway away, and, oh yeah, my stepsister was under the impression that he had come to see her, and Iris—

The door to the kitchen swung open with a pound, and before I knew what was happening, J.J. had raced across the room, pulled me roughly to him, and with only the minutest of pauses to check my eyes for confirmation, put a hand on the back of my head, drawing it closer to his, and pressed his mouth to mine. Somehow both firm and gentle, hot but cool, the soft pillows of his lips sent shockwaves through my entire body, and my brain finally understood what it meant to relax, let go, and simply surrender to a moment.

Then, just as quickly, he pulled away from me. "I just had to do that," he said, and looked for something to take back with him. Still not saying a word, I handed him the salt and paper shakers, and he was gone.

I slumped back against the counter and immediately relived the moment for the first of what would be thousands of times. Although I hadn't gasped, I'm not going to claim my knees didn't buckle. Because they did.

Of course, I have no idea about what your idea of the perfect first kiss is, but I do know that mine will forever be the one I got that morning from J.J., standing with a carton of eggs in my hand, as the sun continued to shine, the world continued to spin, and no lightning smote me just because I kissed another boy.

Chapter 6

Camelot Reborn?

I doubt it'll surprise anyone when I say I didn't eat much at that breakfast. But since almost all of the attention was being paid to J.J., it was pretty easy to get away with just pushing around the food on my plate with a fork. He tried repeatedly to bring me into the conversation, but my own distraction and nervousness, plus the enthusiastic focus of everyone else on him, gave my well-practiced talent for avoiding the spotlight the chance to shine.

Soon after we'd finished eating, when J.J. said he'd taken up enough of everyone's time and should go, he managed to stand firm against Iris and Kimberly's protestations and made it to the front door. I'd started to clear the table out of habit, but Iris called me to "come join the family" as everyone said goodbye. Obviously, I knew it was just for J.J.'s benefit, and some people will probably say I'm an idiot for admitting this, but it actually gave me a little swell of emotion to hear her include me. And that little swell of emotion would be called happiness. Maybe that makes me a sentimental fool, but to quote E.M. Forster, "Do we find happiness so often that we should turn it off the box when it happens to sit there?"

I mostly kept my eyes to the floor as we all said goodbye, but just before he and Kimberly slipped out the door for a moment alone, I did raise my glance long enough to catch J.J. looking at me. And he smiled.

Once the door shut behind them, as Iris and Buck went into the living room, I went back to the dining room, but not to clear the dishes just yet. Hiding behind the curtains and sheers that covered the windows that looked out onto the street, I carefully drew the fabric aside just enough to see if J.J. would also be kissing Kimberly on this oh-so-eventful Sunday. They appeared to chat awkwardly (in my possibly biased opinion), and then he leaned in and gave her a quick hug before darting down the front steps. As I watched him jog away from the house, I saw something that would quickly become a fixture in our lives. Across the street, partially hidden by a tree, a chunky, stubble-faced man in jeans and a sweatshirt stood with a large digital camera to his face. Our first paparazzo.

And so began the part of the story that the world thought it knew.

The rest of that Sunday was pretty uneventful—I spent most of it doing homework—except for two small things. First, when Kimberly came in after saying goodbye to J.J., she did something I'd never known her to do before. Instead of joining Buck and Iris in the living room, she came into the dining room and asked if I wanted help with the dishes. I guess I looked pretty surprised because she said, "Don't look so surprised. I can be helpful."

Finally, I made some sense of it all. "Did J.J. put you up to this?"

Her defensive look turned to one of barely suppressed annoyance, so I was pretty sure he'd at least somehow suggested it. She moved to the table and began collecting the dirty silverware as she said, "You do a lot of nice things for us which you really shouldn't have to, and I for one appreciate that."

At this point I almost dropped the china serving bowl of scrambled egg remains. But I recovered in time to save the dish, as well as to mumble, "Thank you." We made pretty quick work of clearing the table, but when I saw her overwhelmed look when faced with all the dirty dishes on the kitchen counter, I sent Kimberly on her way. I decided if she were going to be dating the guy I was maybe sort of possibly going to fall in love with, I might have more respect for all of us if I didn't ask if she were aware that we *did* have a dishwasher. I took the road that leads many a Type A to ruin—I decided it was just easier to do it myself. Was it in any way possible that I was partially responsible for how spoiled she was?

The second thing of note during that stretch of aftermath following my first kiss was looking up Coco Chanel Jones on Facebook. By nightfall, Duane and I had exchanged phone numbers, email addresses, and had even started texting and Facebook messaging. He'd gotten everything back to his friend in time and slept most of the day. When I started to ask if that made him worry he wouldn't be able to sleep that night and make him tired in school the next day, I realized I didn't even know how old he was, or what he did in his normal life. I then learned that he was 20, so our ages weren't all that far apart, but he'd gotten his GED when he was 16 because kids at school had been really rough on him. He took courses at Parsons School of Design (and had made all of the costumes I'd seen Saturday night, so I knew he was talented) and worked at a Starbucks on Broadway. It was such a tepid reality compared to what I'd expected for my fairy godmother.

Now, before, when I said there were two small things of note over the course of the day, I was being slightly misleading. Because there was also one very big thing that happened that night. About eight o'clock, once Kimberly had gone up to her room after dinner—a meal, I might hasten to add, after which she did not even *offer* help to clear the dishes—an incredibly loud and high-pitched scream rang throughout the house. I thrust my head out of the dining room to see what was the matter. Across the hallway, Iris brushed at a fresh white wine spill on her blouse, presumably but not necessarily having been startled by the loud cry, and Buck looked at me from where he was stretched out on the couch in front of the TV and belched. "What's her damage, Heather?" he asked me.

Before I could even shrug, Kimberly's head popped over the stair rail and crowed victoriously, "*I'm on the internet!*"

I looked to Buck, and he rolled his eyes at the ceiling, calling back, "Yeah, duh! You've been on Facebook since you were, like, a zygote!" If I could only express to you the glow of pride Buck got anytime he used a word that suggested he truly *had* graduated from high school.

Kimberly flew down the stairs carrying her laptop. She waved a hand for me to join them as she ran into the living room. I followed, curious but cautious. The first thing I saw when I entered the room was the look on Iris's and Buck's faces.

"Holy scrotums," Buck muttered.

Although no words came out of her mouth, Iris's expression said the exact same thing.

I walked around the back of the couch and looked over their shoulders to see, covering the entire expanse of the screen of Kimberly's laptop, a webpage to the online gossip site TheRumorMill.com. The main photo was of Kimberly and J.J. saying goodbye on our front landing just hours before. Smiling, she was reaching out, doing something to the collar of his sweatshirt, probably one of those things we make up so that we have an excuse to touch a person we want to be touching, and he was laughing at something. They both looked beautiful, and happy, and ideal. And the caption, in big, black, bold letters read, "**CAMELOT REBORN????**"

And that was the moment I realized my life had gotten really, really complicated.

School. Although I was an academic star in a highly competitive atmosphere, I'd managed to burrow my way into a pretty low profile at McVities Prep. I was too respected by the faculty and administration, too well-connected via marriage, and too happy to let others grab the attention for anyone to feel like they needed to pay much attention to me in any way other than to get answers to homework questions.

I guess this will sound pretty pathetic, but I really only had one friend there, Vibol, a former Cambodian refugee, who was so closed-mouthed about everything, we rarely talked about anything other than schoolwork. Which might be why we were only school friends and had never even once done something social off campus. Not a baseball game, a Broadway show, not even a walk in Central Park. I can't even honestly say that "friend" is the right word to describe our relationship. We were study buddies, we were competitors as well as encouragers (one of us was most likely going to be valedictorian), and I'd always wondered if maybe we were both scholarship recipients. Because if anyone worried about his grades more than I did, it was Vibol. But I now wonder if what really bonded us was that we both felt like outsiders. He because he'd lived in another country and culture until he was eight, and I because, long before puberty, never felt like I quite fit in with most of the other boys.

Anyway, suffice it to say that when I arrived at school on Monday, very tired after a night of more tossing and turning than dreaming and snoring, I had no expectations of finding myself the recipient of innumerable stares accompanied by hand-covering-mouth mumbling. I did all the basic things—checked to make sure my zipper was up, nothing was hanging from my nose, no bird crap in my hair—as I walked down the hallway to my locker. Just as I reached it, Vibol came up from behind me and said, "So, is it really true?"

"Is what true?" I asked. "Why is everybody staring at me?"

"Is your sister really going to marry J.J. Kennerly? I mean, shit."

I don't know what was more shocking—the question, Vibol indulging in gossip, or him swearing—but I was so taken aback by it all that my reaction was to laugh. Maybe it was painfully obvious to you why everyone had been staring, what with Kimberly's picture appearing on the internet the night before, but that hadn't been why I'd lain awake most of the night. The things I'd been concerned with had run the gamut from how was I going to get in contact with J.J. (his number and email were beyond unlisted), to when would I see him again, would I get to kiss him again whenever I did see him, and did he want children or just a dog? (It was a long night.)

I said to Vibol, "They met for the first time Saturday night. I think marriage might be jumping the gun a little bit."

Vibol's face fell. "Are you sure?"

"Why would you care?" I asked. This was coming from the guy who usually greeted me with stats on anyone in the world he'd learned had received a perfect score on their SAT. (He'd missed it by ten points.)

"Do you know how much a letter of recommendation from a Kennerly could help my college application?" As absurd as that may have sounded, I found it oddly reassuring. At least Vibol was talking like himself again.

"Vibol, you're going to get into any college you want no matter what."

He bit his lip as his eyes dropped to the floor, his head shaking gently back and forth, looking more like someone at a funeral than a seventeen-year-old walking to class. "I don't know, man, it's competitive out there," he said before he walked off.

"And how was your weekend?" I asked.

He waved a hand dismissively as he said, "What does it matter?"

I started to laugh until I realized I was still being stared at. Definitely not my favorite thing. But then, as I busied myself with my locker, a perverse little idea popped into my head, and I decided to have some fun. Grabbing my books and shutting the locker door, I turned to head to my first period class and started humming "Here Comes the Bride." I swear Shoshana Goldberg almost peed her Pradas.

After school, I took the crosstown bus through Central Park, and before walking up Broadway to the Starbucks where Duane worked, I stopped at Levain Bakery to buy two of their chocolate peanut butter chip cookies for us to eat on his break. Obviously, there were baked goods where he worked, but when he told me he'd never been to Levain, I figured that if he was the first person who had gotten me to say that I was gay, then I should be the first person to introduce him to the best cookie in the world. Yes, in the world. No hyperbole.

As I waited for Duane to go on break, I sat at a table, dipping my mind into Madame Bovary and my nose into the bag of cookies, flirting with a contact high from the intoxicating aroma of chocolate and peanut butter. (Whoever thought of it first deserves a Nobel Prize or something. Seriously.) Soon enough, he arrived with two containers of milk and sat down. "Is that some shit about your sister, or what?"

"Good God," I said, "does everyone in the world know?"

"Uh, yeah, pretty much."

I blew out a long breath through my lips.

"Is that all you've been hearing about all day?" Duane asked as he took the bag of cookies from me.

"Uh, yeah, pretty much."

"These things weigh a ton!" He looked into the bag to make sure it in fact only contained cookies. "And there are only two of them?"

"Trust me, one is pretty much a meal."

He reached into the bag. "Ooh, they're still a little bit warm." He drew out one of the cookies, handing the bag back to me, and I watched as he inspected the cookie, broke off a piece, then put it into his mouth. As he chewed, the look which had started out skeptical and critical melted into one of almost sexual pleasure.

"Was I right?" I asked.

He put out a hand to me. "Shut up. I'm in the middle of a food-gasm."

"Cookie *interruptus*?" I joked.

I wasn't sure if he didn't hear my attempt at humor, or just didn't think it was funny, but he was pretty much incapable of conversation until half of his cookie was gone. But eventually he asked, "So, your stepmom got what she wanted, huh?"

I paused before I answered. I'd been thinking all day that I really wanted and needed someone to talk to about what had happened with J.J., and I think I'd basically been planning on making Duane that person. After all, he was the only one who knew my other secret, so it made sense. Except now that I was starting to realize what a big deal anything involving a Kennerly was, and having known Duane for less than a full two days—well, actually, even less than that, since the first night he had been Coco, and the two of them seemed to live pretty separate lives, even if they did exist in the same body—as he watched me eagerly for a full report, I felt myself drawing back. "I guess, sort of," I finally said.

He stopped his hand with another piece of cookie half-way to his mouth, "You don't sound all that happy about it."

I harrumphed. "It's complicated."

"Child, ain't it always." And then he started telling me a story about this guy his mother used to see who didn't know she had children, let alone five of them, and how they would all have to hide and be quiet in one bedroom with the door closed and none of them could use the bathroom when she had him over. As was often the case with Duane and/or Coco, the story got pretty graphic, but besides making me laugh, it took my mind off of my own thoughts for a bit, and by the time he had to go back to work, while I still didn't know how much I could trust him with my really big secret, I did know that I wanted to get to know him better.

Which was a good thing, because life's run of surprises kept right on rolling along when I got home. I had barely walked into the house when Kimberly popped out of the living room and asked where I'd been. There was something both frustrated and excited in her manner. I told her I'd gone to meet Duane for his break, and she said, "Oh, perfect, then you *can* bring him!"

"Bring him? To what? What are you talking about?"

She suddenly turned coy and smiled mischievously. I craned my neck to see if I could find anyone with answers in the living room, but Kimberly said, "Buck's at the gym, and Mom's lying down. It's just the two of us."

Something in the oddly intimate way she said it made my stomach tighten.

"J.J. called me this afternoon," she said.

"Okay, so?"

"So, it seems you've made quite an impression on him."

I honestly thought I might toss my proverbial and literal cookies. Was it possible that J.J. had told her—of all people—what had happened between him and me? That she might be the only person besides Duane, and, well, J.J. himself, who now knew I was gay? And what would she do with that information? Would she use it against me? Would she get me thrown out of the house? Was that why she was looking so cat-that-ate-the-canary? Suddenly I wanted all of the events of the weekend to somehow magically disappear and go back to my closeted little servile-but-safe existence.

"And he told me about meeting Duane out front yesterday, and he thinks you guys both seem really nice, and he wants the four of us to hang out."

"Hang out?" I was on the verge of relaxing slightly, but I didn't want to jump the gun just yet. "You're telling me that J.J. wants to go out with you, Duane, and me?"

"Uh-huh. Doesn't that sound like fun?!"

I don't know if you're ready for this—I sure wasn't—but Kimberly then threw her arms around me in a hug. A hug, I tell you! When she let go, she spun around giddily, stopped short, and asked, "Can you go tonight? I'm dying to see him again!"

I fumbled through a series of excuses—I had dinner to make, I had a Calculus quiz in the morning, Duane was still at work, she had class tomorrow—and she pouted somehow gracefully. "I guess you're right. Besides, I suppose I should try to not look too eager. Ugh, life sucks." She slumped over to the couch and wilted onto it.

I excused myself to the kitchen to get dinner started, but really I just needed some recovery time. Obviously, I was thrilled that J.J. had figured out a way for us to see each other again, but when I'd described the situation to Duane as complicated, I'd definitely not even thought of these possibilities.

Three nights later I found myself on my first date with J.J.

And Kimberly.

And Duane.

Even though it was only over Skype and I was on the third floor, the scream Duane had let out when I asked what his schedule was like because J.J. Kennerly wanted to hang out with us was loud enough for Buck to call up from the living room couch asking if I wanted him to call NYPD for a rape kit.

We eventually all settled on Thursday, and that night Duane showed up at my place an hour early. Although he was totally in his guy-mode hip-hop wear, he said he'd tried on twelve different pairs of tennis shoes, and did I think he'd picked the right ones? When I said I couldn't believe he had twelve pairs of tennis shoes, he gave me a withering look and said, "Child, those are just the ones that went with this outfit." I was about to ask how many pairs of shoes he had, and where did he keep them if his family of six lived in a two-bedroom apartment, but Kimberly called from upstairs.

"What's wrong?" I asked.

"I can't decide if I'm wearing the right thing. Help!"

Duane pushed me aside without missing a beat, saying, "Out of my way, amateur." He did have the good manners to stop at the foot of the stairs and call up to Kimberly, asking if it was okay for him to come up. She eagerly granted him permission, and I had the next forty-five minutes to myself. I'm not saying I hadn't changed my own mind about what to wear a couple times over the last few days, but once I put on my jeans and the button-down navy blue shirt that I fancied brought out my eyes, I was good to go. Part of me felt like I should go upstairs in case I was needed to run interference, but I was too much on edge to try to pretend that I cared, and I had a feeling that they were not the audience to whom to say, "They're just clothes."

I tried reading some of my homework as I sat on the couch, my knees and hands jittery from nerves, but to say my focus was less than optimal would be an understatement. At about quarter to seven, Buck came home, dropping his gym bag loudly by the front door, and waved me to make room for him to stretch out on the couch.

"You know Iris doesn't like you on the furniture when you're sweaty," I said.

"You mean you don't like me on it."

"Well, I am the one who has to keep getting more Febreeze."

He kicked his shoes off and put his smelly feet in my lap. "Give me a foot massage. Please."

Pushing his feet off, I stood up. "You know if Iris hears you made a bad impression when J.J. gets here, she's going to lose her shit all over you."

"Oh, is that tonight?"

Iris had been in such a state since the news of the date that Kimberly told me she'd finally slipped two Xanax into Iris's after-lunch vitamin supplements, and she was passed out in her room. Although I don't know if I would have actually had the nerve to do it, I will say that I was a little ashamed of myself for not thinking of it first.

"Your dinner is in the fridge," I said to Buck. "Just heat it for three minutes in the microwave."

He put on his most pathetic face. "I worked out too hard, and my muscles are all burned out."

"You managed to walk home," I said.

"Barely. Those front steps were like Everest. Trying to lift that plate would make me like Sisyphus with his rock." (See what I mean about the smart-stupid thing? Buck knew I almost always rewarded him when he said something that hinted at hidden depths. I guess Kimberly wasn't the only one I was guilty of spoiling.)

I went to warm up his food, but I was stopped by the sight of Kimberly and Duane descending the stairway. They'd decided on one of those light, loose, flowy halter dresses that still managed to show off her great body, with a light, cashmere shrug and ballet slippers. It was the perfect blend of casual, girly, and super, super flattering. It suddenly occurred to me in a very big way that if J.J. were bi and not gay, I was in serious trouble. I realized that there was so much I didn't know about him, and I began to feel it overwhelm me, almost like a panic attack or something, and barely managing to mumble something about Buck's dinner, I raced for the kitchen.

Once there, I forced myself to take long, deep breaths, and while the food heated up, I first tried to figure out an excuse to get out of going, then I beat myself up for giving up too easily, and by the time the bell on the microwave dinged, I think I'd changed sides of the argument about fifty times. As I told myself I had a future in politics with that much flip-flopping, I grabbed a lap tray, poured a large glass of milk, and lifted Buck's supper.

Forcing my best attempt at a calm smile, I entered the living room to find Kimberly standing by the mirror checking her makeup, Buck still lying on the couch with his feet now in Duane's lap, and Duane looking at Buck adoringly as he massaged said feet. I almost dropped the tray.

"Careful!" Buck said as he sat up quickly. He didn't actually get up or anything, but he did reach out his arms, as if that would help from ten or fifteen feet away. Duane just looked pissed at me for a second, before he caught himself.

"Pardon my interruption," I said.

Duane rolled his eyes, then smiled at Buck, "casually" patting him on his admittedly beefy shoulder. "This man needs to eat to keep him big and strong."

Buck made some sort of Neanderthal noise, and Duane acted like that was just about the funniest thing he'd ever heard.

The absurdity of it all finally turned my forced smile into a real one, and as I chuckled, a world of dark stress lifted right up off of me. I even managed to tell Kimberly she looked beautiful, but when she said thank you, she was looking with concern at Duane and Buck. She waved me over to her discreetly, and once I got there, asked me, "Doesn't that bother you?"

"What?" I asked, really not a hundred percent sure what she was objecting to and not willing to risk a guess.

But before she could continue, her cell phone rang, and it was J.J. Naturally, she answered it, and although I was, of course, dying to listen, I stepped away to give her privacy. As soon as I did, Duane stood up and steered me into the hallway.

"What's up?" I asked.

Still peering around the doorway to watch Buck eat, he said, "Sookie sookie now! Seriously, he is one piece of Grade A beef."

"He's straight."

"You never know. Sexuality is genetic. It might run in the family."

"He's my stepbrother, remember?"

"Then maybe it is environmental. Who's to say?"

"Uh, science."

"If the Fundamentalists can ignore science, then why can't I? 'Cause right now I feel like praying. Or at least dropping to my knees."

"This is making me uncomfortable," I said.

Duane finally tore his eyes away from Buck, turned his head to me, and knowingly responded, "The truth makes most people uncomfortable."

I began to laugh, but Kimberly interrupted me.

"That was J.J. He says that some paparazzi are hiding across the street, and I told him that wasn't a problem for me, but he doesn't want them to follow us all night, which, again, I told him wasn't a problem for me, but he wants us to meet him at the subway. Do you guys mind?"

Once we'd gotten outside, we didn't see any photographers at first, but then one of them moved in the shadows, and Kimberly, Duane, and I exchanged looks, feeling oddly exposed. I mumbled that none of us should say anything, and when I looked over my shoulder at the end of the block, the coast appeared to be clear.

J.J. was waiting for us inside the station, and after she'd given him a kiss on the cheek (although I'm not sure that's what she'd been aiming for), he shook Duane's hand, then gave me a casual hug. Even with all of those people around, just feeling him close for that brief embrace was the second-best moment of my life up till then. (Number one being the kiss, of course.)

"So what are we doing for our double date?" Kimberly asked J.J. perkily.

Was *that* why she'd asked if Duane's attentiveness to Buck had bothered me?

Duane and I shared split-second looks that combined surprise, confusion, and panic, then I looked at J.J. and saw his own doubt register, and then I saw him look unsurely at Duane.

"This is going to be so much fun!" Kimberly exclaimed as she clutched J.J.'s elbow.

CHAPTER 7

PAPARAZZI

The word "awkward" comes to mind to describe the lengthy silence between us as we all stood on the platform waiting for the train headed downtown. Well, Kimberly was chattering at an impressive clip, but J.J., Duane, and I all seemed to be momentarily stumped for conversation.

Once Kimberly had put out the notion that we were all on a double date, not just hanging out, suddenly everything gained an unanticipated weight and meaning. I ran through my mind everything that Duane and I had said to each other, and especially given his behavior with Buck, I was pretty sure he wasn't thinking of this as a date between the two of us. Unless he was trying to make me jealous? Could my visit to see him at work the other day have been misconstrued? I mean, I *guess* it was okay if Kimberly had interpreted it that way, but that had never been my intention. Although, since I'd decided I wasn't ready to confide in him about what had happened between J.J. and me, it wasn't impossible for him to have misunderstood my visit.

I kept darting my eyes over to see if I could tell what Duane might be thinking, but he looked as perplexed as I felt, although he did seem to focus on the way Kimberly was holding on to J.J. Oh god, did that mean he was wondering if he and I should also be holding hands?

As the train arrived, and J.J. and Kimberly queued up with a group of people at one of the car doors, Duane tugged my elbow towards the group waiting for the other door of that same car. As we waited to board, he whispered into my ear, "I thought you said your family didn't know you were gay."

"They don't," I said. "Or, at least, I don't think they do. Or didn't think they do. Did? I don't know."

"Sometimes girls have better gaydar?"

I craned my neck to see Kimberly looking up at J.J. and immediately discounted this argument. I briefly met Duane's eyes for the first time since Kimberly had used the "date" word and shrugged. Passengers had finished getting off the train, and as our group surged on, Duane kept whispering to me as we were pressed together by the crowd. "Because I thought you said we were just going to be hanging out tonight."

"That's what I thought."

"So this is not a date?"

He was behind me, so I couldn't see his face to tell if he wanted it to be or not. "Uh, I guess for them it might be, but I didn't—for us—it wasn't—I thought we were just hanging out."

"Okay, good, because, no offense, you're adorable and all that, but you're a bit clean cut and boyish for Coco Chanel Jones."

As we took our places standing in the aisle, reaching up to hold onto the bar near the top of the subway car, I was finally able to see his face, and he looked concerned and apologetic. I suppressed a laugh. "No offense taken. You're a good-looking guy and all, but . . ."

"Too much of a woman for you?" Duane said, rearing back slightly as if taking mock offense.

"Without a doubt," I said with a laugh.

Then letting out a sigh, relieved that at least one thing was now clear, I had just the slightest wonder at the back of my head—I know this is stupid, but just tell me you've never done the same and I'll call you a liar—well, wait, why wouldn't he want this to be a date? That unproductive thought quickly took a dive into more troublesome self-doubt as I caught sight of J.J. a little further down the car and couldn't help thinking to myself, well, hell, if a twinkish drag queen isn't interested in dating me, how in the world can I imagine that someone as gorgeous and amazing as J.J. Kennerly would ever want to? I started getting a slightly sick feeling in my stomach as I realized I'd committed myself to spend the evening as one of the main ingredients in a recipe for self-torture.

"Why does he keep looking at us?" Duane asked.

"Who?" I looked around, glad for the distraction.

"Kennerly. Freaking homophobic, patriarchal asshole. We have as much right to be on a date as he does, the fucker."

"But I thought we just established that we're not on a date."

"*He* doesn't know that."

And then, just as I caught J.J.'s eye, Duane leaned in and kissed me.

By the time we arrived to the "fresh" air of Bleecker Street, I'd had to twist my hand out of Duane's four times, back away from three kisses, and twice had him pinch my ass as we were walking up the stairs, each and every time only when J.J. was looking, of course. And J.J. was looking over at us more and more, no doubt just as Duane intended. I kept mouthing "I'm sorry" to J.J., but it didn't seem to do much good at removing the darkness from his brow.

Duane had been the one to suggest the East Village, but once we realized that only he and Kimberly had fake IDs, the bar he'd had in mind wasn't going to work. (Although I had a heck of a time stopping myself from shouting out that they should go get a drink, and J.J. and I would just go find someplace else by ourselves.) We found a cafe, and as soon as we'd ordered beverages and desserts, Kimberly announced she needed to visit the powder room, and I suggested to Duane that maybe he needed to go, too.

"Nah, I'm good," he said, dashing my hopes at a moment alone with J.J.

But then he changed his mind, and I felt such relief I almost wanted to cry. He and Kimberly stood up . . . and didn't take a single step away from the table for at least two minutes, which felt, to me, like two hours. They'd spent forty-five minutes alone together in her room, so did he really need to keep telling her how fabulous she looked—and getting confirmation from J.J.—while I was waiting for just a few seconds alone with the only person in the world that mattered?

But just as they began to step away from the table, a guy seated closer to the bathroom got up, entered the men's room, and locked the door. Kimberly made a face and whispered to Duane that she really had to go and the ladies' was empty. He shrugged, saying he could wait and sat back down as she walked off. Argh.

He turned his head to find a vaguely annoyed look on J.J.'s face (and I can only imagine how obvious my annoyance must have looked). "What's the matter, J.J.?" Duane asked as he put his hand on top of the one I had resting on top of my paper placemat. I yanked back my hand, but Duane grabbed it, putting it firmly back on top of the table. "Don't be shy, puddin'. We have every bit as much right to show public affection as anyone else."

I wanted to die, or for the ground to swallow me up, or *some* form of Biblical distraction to occur. But, of course, those things never happen when you need them to, do they?

J.J. gave a slight shrug. "Do whatever you like." But his eyes flicked briefly towards me, as if asking me if that was what I really wanted.

"But I don't like to hold hands," I said to Duane, then turned back to J.J. and blustered, "I mean, in public. I mean, I guess I would under certain circumstances, maybe, if, you know, the circumstances were right."

Duane leaned in, looking deeply into my eyes, and said in a way that sounded like an attempted seduction, "You're so eloquent." He still firmly held my hand on top of the table, so I brought up my free hand and roughly pinched the skin on the back of his as soon as J.J. looked away.

"*Ow!*" Duane mouthed, looking peevishly at me, but I looked back at him with at least equal irritation. Then he smiled towards J.J., and I made the naive decision to take a sip of my water.

"Then again, J.J., I guess as good-looking as you are, I'm sure you're used to girls—and guys—throwing themselves at you all the time."

In the nanosecond I realized I was about to spit the water in my mouth across the table, I managed to sort of suck it back it with a gasp, which led to me coughing convulsively as I'd almost managed to drown myself right there in the dry flats of the East Village.

Finally, the door to the men's room opened. "Bathroom's free!" I practically shouted through my coughs, pointing so emphatically I almost hit Duane with my thrusting finger.

With a look that suggested I was acting oddly, he moved towards the bathroom, and as soon as I was sure he was out of earshot, I leaned over the table and told J.J., "He's just doing all of that to piss you off."

"Doing what?" J.J. asked.

"Making it look like he and I are on a date."

J.J. looked panicked as he sat forward. "What did you tell him?"

I backed away, not expecting that. "Nothing."

"Then why would he think that would make me jealous?"

"No, he thinks you're homophobic. He said you kept watching us, so he thinks he's freaking you out by being all over me."

Looking slightly offended, J.J. said, "Does he know anything about my family's support for the LGBTQ community?"

"Seriously? Is that what you guys call it in your house?"

J.J. smiled guiltily. "Pretty much. It's a very PC atmosphere."

"Well, you might want to let him know that before he feels the need to molest me again for your benefit."

J.J. shook him head, amused. "Kimberly definitely thinks it's hysterical."

As little as I expected from Kimberly in the way of kindness, I have to admit it still hurt to hear she was laughing at me. "She does?"

I guess my expression revealed something of what I was feeling, because J.J. clarified, "No, I mean, she thinks it's adorable."

"She does?" And now I was kind of touched.

"Mm-hm," J.J. grumbled.

As I tried to get by mind around the fact that Kimberly seemed to not only know that I was gay, she also accepted it, another thought dawned on me. J.J. had asked if Duane thought I was making him jealous. I had never used that word. Did that mean it *was* making him jealous? Was it possible that the idea of another guy touching me was making J.J. jealous?

Unfortunately, before I could ask that, or any of the other thousands of questions I'd wanted to put to J.J. since Sunday, Duane and Kimberly returned to the table.

"Hey J.J.," Kimberly said as she squeezed into the side of the booth she was sharing with him, "remember those drag queens that performed at the ball last weekend?"

"Oh, yeah, they were great," J.J. said. Then, with a glance at Duane, he added, "I mean, for a bunch of fags."

I almost dropped the glass from which I was taking a sip. No sooner had I thought I'd bought myself a few minutes of relative calm, then this happened.

Kimberly looked surprised, but Duane looked ready to throw down. Then J.J. let out a laugh. "I'm just messing with you, dude. Chris said you think I'm a homophobe, and that's so not my message. Love is love."

Duane squinted his eyes at J.J., trying to decide if he was still being played with, when I tugged down on his arm and told him to sit down. He did so slowly, still looking at J.J. suspiciously, then finally lifted a hand to wag a finger at him. "You are not funny."

Still smiling, J.J. turned to Kimberly and asked, "What were you saying about those drag queens?"

Kimberly pointed at Duane proudly. "He's one of them."

J.J. looked dubiously at Duane, not sure who was fooling who now. "Shut up."

"No, you shut up, bitch," Duane said, as he snapped a napkin over his lap. "Coco hasn't decided whether or not to forgive you yet."

"*You're* Coco Chanel Jones?!" J.J. asked, genuine surprise clear in his voice and on his face.

Suddenly with his own share of disbelief and wonder, Duane sat forward. "*You* know who Coco Chanel Jones is?"

The night had finally taken a very positive turn.

I would have sworn we had been there less than an hour, sharing each other's desserts, talking, laughing, just, hanging out, but when I looked at my watch, I was shocked to find out it was after ten o'clock! I had to get up for school in the morning, and I still hadn't finished all my homework. Regretfully I announced this to the group, and J.J. immediately signaled to the waitress for the check. But when she came over with the bill folder and J.J. reached out for it, waving away our attempts to figure out our shares, a slightly annoyed look came over his face as he opened it.

"What's wrong?" I asked.

He hesitated, then apologetically looked at Kimberly before saying, "Sorry, this happens sometimes."

"What?" she asked, trying to see what was in his hands.

"Someone has picked up the bill," J.J. explained to us.

"And the problem with that is?" Duane asked dryly.

J.J. turned to show us what the folder contained. On a blank page from an order pad in a woman's flowing cursive was written, *Please allow me. Suzanne. 917-555-9878.*

We all slowly turned to look around the cafe and saw a very attractive redhead in her mid-twenties wave with a smile.

"Redheads are such sluts," Kimberly said.

"Kimberly," J.J. said, "it's never a good idea to jump to conclusions. She could be in politics, or a reporter, or just a fan."

"Or a slut," Duane said.

"I hope you won't think this is rude, but I really should go over and say thank you. In fact, maybe we all could? Safety in numbers and all that."

"Are you serious?" Kimberly asked.

"You know I'm going into politics someday, right? She could be a future constituent."

"Is that the euphemism they use on Capitol Hill?" Duane asked.

J.J. laughed. Before he could say more, I tried to help him out by telling him he should go say thank you and we would wait where we were. He waited for Kimberly's acquiescence, which she finally gave with a shrug of her shoulders. All of our eyes followed him, and not a word was said at our table until he returned, which was in less than a minute.

As we stood, Kimberly shot another dirty look over at the redhead, who held up the slip of paper with her number on it to show that J.J. had returned it. This made Kimberly very happy.

But as he was opening the door for us, J.J. said, "Shit."

"What's wrong?" Kimberly asked.

He nodded to a spot across the street where a number of paparazzi were waiting. "Someone tipped them off." He closed the door, and turned to face us.

"Does this happen all the time?" I asked.

"Pretty much," he said.

"Damn, I have been living my life all wrong," Duane said.

"Do you guys mind if I call a cab? My treat, of course."

"The subway's not that far," I said.

"They'll follow us. They might even follow us in a cab, but less likely."

"Of course, do what you need to do," Kimberly said.

He stepped away to make the call, and Kimberly looked peevishly across the street. "It's just rude, really," she said. "So invasive."

Duane gave her a slow burn up-and-down as he said, "Well, you better get used to it, Miss Thang, because you're dating him."

Kimberly then turned surprising shy. "I am?"

"Girl, you should see the way he looks at you when you turn away from him. It's all just so deep and . . . complicated."

That word again. If he only knew.

Once the cab arrived, we darted out of the restaurant and into the waiting car, having been cautioned by J.J. to look as casual as possible. Don't make eye contact with them, don't smile, don't cover your face or head, just look as boring as you know how. Evidently that kind of picture brought the lowest price, and would likely never see print. Duane had asked, "What if I wanted it to see print?" but J.J.'s look reprimanded him into his best behavior.

Once the car drove off with only one of the photographers running a few steps beside us to get a few more shots, J.J. apologized again for the inconvenience. Duane turned around from the front passenger seat and said, "The only thing you need to apologize to me for is not letting me show them how fabulous I truly am."

J.J. laughed. "Well, maybe we'll have to think of a bigger media setting, so that Coco really has the chance to shine?"

Duane looked at Kimberly as he pointed to J.J. "This is a really, really good man. I approve."

Kimberly, who sat in the middle between J.J. and me, beamed as she leaned against J.J., putting her head on his shoulder.

As she did, J.J. looked over her head at me, and said, "It's not easy dating me. There's constant attention, and you have to be very careful, and very secretive. Our security people do electronic sweeps all the time, but even a text, or a phone call, or an email might be intercepted and made public, so everything has to be very innocuous. We might even want to make up codes, so that only we know what we're trying to say to one another."

"I don't mind," Kimberly said.

After a long moment of J.J. and me holding each other's eyes over the top of Kimberly's head, I gave him the smallest of nods. As we continued uptown, I at first felt an almost overwhelming weight of fear and guilt and self-doubt. But then as I replayed in my head what he'd said about the difficulties of dating him, I finally stopped and focused on one word: dating. I was officially (if secretly) dating J.J. Kennerly.

Chapter 8

A Little Less Conversation

I doubt anyone who has been in love would argue that the process of falling is pretty ridiculous. You're exhausted because you can't sleep from thinking about the person, and then the second you see them it's like you just drank thirty Red Bulls in one gulp.

After that first date, which had been a Thursday, I hardly slept at all. Since I had school, and I figured he was always busy, I didn't really expect to see J.J. until the weekend. But when he didn't show up on Saturday, obviously, the world was over. He'd realized he wasn't gay, that I was heinously ugly and awful, and he was never coming near the Fontaine brownstone again in anything less than a hazmat suit, if even then.

I didn't feel quite that desperate and dark in the morning, but by noon I was decidedly on edge. And Kimberly just slept, and slept, and slept. Since I didn't have J.J.'s phone number, and knew I couldn't text him anyway, she was my only source of information. I couldn't concentrate on my homework for the life of me, so I made myself busy rearranging the kitchen pantry. And because I was in it, I managed to miss Kimberly leaving the house. It was dinner-time before she returned from shopping, my mood was full blown fatalism, and when she blithely answered my question about J.J.'s whereabouts with, "Oh, he had a family thing," I wanted to both strangle her—why couldn't she have told me that earlier?—and hug her.

After not sleeping well Thursday or Friday nights, Saturday night was even worse. By seven o'clock Sunday morning, I gave up even trying and decided the kitchen shelves needed fresh lining. Around ten-thirty, I was in the later stages of the task when the door swung open and J.J. entered in a rush and grabbed me up in a kiss. It probably lasted somewhere between thirty seconds and a minute, but it somehow felt both instantaneous and eternal. Then, as quickly as he'd entered, he ran out calling to Kimberly that of course he was ready.

I, naturally, now entered one of those thirty-Red-Bull highs. I completed the shelves while dancing around and making up lyrics to an absurd secret little ditty with the refrain, "Mr. Man just kissed me, oh, yeahyeahyeah, Mr. Man just kissed me."

The next month or so was for me a period of exquisitely torturous highs and lows. I mean, I was falling in love for the first time with, arguably, the most sought-after man on the planet—that would be the high part—but it was all in secret and while my sister and the world thought he was falling in love with her. That would be the low part.

Now, while I can't exactly defend lying to Kimberly, in my . . . well, defense . . . I really didn't think she would mind that much. As the paparazzi presence outside the house increased and the papers and magazines and blogs made her a daily fixture, and friends she hadn't heard from, or girls who had barely paid her any attention started getting in touch, and charities started asking her to attend as their guest, and fashion designers offered her exclusive showings, sometimes even sending things right over to the house—all of that and more—well, it was pretty clear to me that she was having a great time. And to be honest, J.J. wasn't with her for a lot of that, so I eased my guilt with the comfort she was getting what she most wanted from dating J.J., even if he and I were the ones who were actually falling in love. And, truly, it was quite a love fest between Kimberly and the media. She adored them and they adored her.

While we did go on a few more "double dates"—only Kimberly thought of them that way—almost all our time together was spent in our living room with Kimberly, or since she went to a lot to society things that J.J. begged out of, with Buck and/or Iris right there with us or close by, and it was all actually pretty Victorian and chaperoned. Not that they had any idea they were acting as such.

The advantage of this was that J.J. and I got to know each other very well in a quite old-fashioned way. We talked about what was going on in the news, politics, literature, what we were learning in our classes, our beliefs on what determined morality, kindness, spirituality, all sort of things. I probably don't need to mention that Iris and Buck added little to these discussions, but she seemed happy enough with a glass of wine in her hand, and he happy enough with his Xbox controller. When Kimberly was around, she would sometimes try to participate, but usually a text or a picture of herself in a newspaper or magazine would distract her soon enough.

But being that we were also two teenage boys, even as we were discussing the merits of the latest Nobel Prize recipients, we were also always trying to figure out a way to steal a few moments alone together, so that we could honor the wishes of Elvis Presley and have a little less conversation. It didn't take long before that included more than just kissing. J.J. was quite fond of grabbing my ass. After the first couple times of pretending it was an accident, neither of us needed the pretense.We both knew we wanted it.But we still hadn't managed to find a long enough moment of privacy to get further. Which is why I came up with a plan.

J.J. usually spent about two nights a week over at our place, not including the nights he actually accompanied Kimberly to events and social commitments. It didn't take me long to notice that on the nights Kimberly went out without him, Iris and/or Buck would always hang out with J.J. until just before Kimberly walked in the door, then they would suddenly need something upstairs and would hightail it out of there, pushing me along with them. Since neither of them had ever struck me as having particularly keen hearing, I had a feeling it wasn't just the jingle of keys that tipped them off as to when to dash out of their starting blocks.

A little further observation and I noticed that about fifteen minutes before she arrived, one of them would always get a text. Part of me was hurt that I hadn't been included in the plan, and another part of me worried that was because maybe Iris suspected what was up between J.J. and me. Because now part of Iris's breakfast ritual was to read Kimberly tips on how to make your man happy in bed. Kimberly would seethe. So far J.J. had been a perfect gentleman, and she didn't appreciate the extra pressure being put on her. One morning, before Iris could even start to read, Kimberly pulled out a purple fedora with a long feather tucked into the band and tossed it on top of Iris's plate. I'm not sure if the glare Kimberly received was because of the hat implication or because it had almost knocked over the waiting mimosa.

If I'm being completely honest, I'm not exactly sure what I thought we were going to get accomplished in fifteen minutes. I knew that was enough time to take care of things on my own, but the stolen seconds and minutes—two at a time at most, so far—I'd shared with J.J. were the sum total of physical intimacy I'd ever experienced. All I knew was those moments were amazing, and fifteen minutes were exponentially longer, so I would take what I could get.

On the day I'd picked, knowing Iris and Buck charged their phones while they slept, I'd little by little been burning through their battery power when they weren't looking. Then, when J.J. arrived and he was helping me make popcorn and drinks (and grabbing my butt, because that's what he did when we were alone), I mentioned I was annoyed about how much Iris and Buck were on their phones and how I hoped it wouldn't distract from our enjoyment of the movie we were about to watch. I think J.J. caught on that I was up to something, because his right eyebrow raised ever so slightly. But that didn't stop him from walking into the living room and telling Buck and Iris about a dinner he'd been to the night before where everyone had to put their phones in a stack on the table, and the first person to check their phone had to pay the bill.

"Chris got the movie from the library, and the popcorn and sodas are paid for," Buck said, his tone suggesting that J.J. needed to step up his mental game.

Iris, however, was having none of that. In the Fontaine household, J.J. would get what J.J. wanted. Obviously, she hoped that would mean Kimberly sooner than later, but in the meantime, phones would have to set the precedent. God love Iris's ambitious, manipulatable heart. She was playing into my plan just as I'm hoped. I volunteered to collect everyone's phone, and then once the movie had started, I discreetly burned through the rest of the power on both of their phones.

As the movie ended, I reached under the pillow I'd put over the phones and then acted surprised to have received a text from Kimberly. (A total lie, of course.) "Huh, odd, Kimberly texted me that she's on her way home. Oh, and she sent it almost fifteen minutes ago."

Well, Iris and Buck lunged for their phones, then both looked exasperated to find them out of power.

"That must be why she texted Chris," Buck said.

Iris badly faked a yawn. "Oh, I'm so tired. You'll forgive me, J.J., if I head up to bed, won't you? Kimberly will be home any second." She headed for the door as she spoke, pulling Buck and me each by an arm. Buck went along willingly, but I twisted free, blaming it on my need to take the dishes into the kitchen. "Okay," she said, "but then it's right to bed for you."

"Of course," I said, putting on my most respectful voice.

I hadn't been in the kitchen for half a minute before J.J. was pushing through the swinging door. "What was that all about?" he asked as he pulled me into him and kissed me, his lips still tasting of lingering butter and salt.

"We might have more than fifteen minutes," I said. "Or less. I really don't know. But hopefully more."

"What are you talking about?"

I'd been super antsy during the movie, filled with as much nervousness as excitement at the thought of what we were about to do if my plan worked out, and so far, it was working perfectly. While my heart had started racing once I got to the kitchen, knowing that J.J. would follow me as soon as Iris and Buck were safely upstairs, once he held me and kissed me, it was all I could do not to rip his clothes off. My nerves were gone, and my hands were wandering all over him.

"Whoa, what's going on?" he asked.

"I figured out how to get rid of them early enough so that we could finally have sex."

"What?"

I began to unbutton his shirt, but he took each of my hands in his, stopping me.

"Don't you want to?" I asked, immediately feeling the flash of heat that comes from soul crushing embarrassment.

"Of course I want to."

"So, let's—"

"Kimberly could be home any minute."

"So, we'll hurry." I tried to free my hands, but he held on firmly.

"I don't want our first time to be rushed."

"You don't? Why not? Who knows how long it could be before we'll get another chance?"

J.J. raised my hands to his lips and kissed them. "I want our first time to be amazing."

"It will be. Everything's amazing when I'm with you."

He let go of my hands so that he could use his to cup my face. "You are the sweetest person I've ever met."

And that's when it made sense to me. I was the sweet guy. The one admired and respected, but that no one ever wanted to have sex with.

I looked down at the buttons of his shirt, the ones he hadn't let me undo, and something of what I was thinking must have shown in my face, because J.J. asked, "Wait a minute, what's going on in there?"

"I'm sorry," I said softly. "I just thought . . . you wanted to, too."

A deep hollow chuckle came from low in J.J.'s belly. "Okay, you cannot seriously think that I'm not dying to make love to you right now."

"You are?"

He nodded.

"Then . . . then why don't you?"

He blew air from between his lips, moving slightly away from me so that he could hoist himself up to sit on the countertop. "I'd been hoping to put this off a little longer, but things are maybe about to get a little weird."

Rather than say anything, some instinct told me to shut up, to get close to him, but to let him say what he needed to in his own way. I turned my back towards him, leaning back to rest in between his legs, putting the back of my head against his chest. Not only was I giving him the freedom to tell me whatever he needed to say without having to look me in the eye, I was giving myself the freedom not to have to cover up what I was feeling. If I couldn't see his face, he couldn't see mine.

"Obviously, you know my life is not like most people's. And that I have to be careful about everything I do—to a ridiculous level." I nodded, and since I could feel the top of my head brushing against his chin, no matter where he might be looking, he knew I heard him. "I like you, Chris. In a way I've never liked anyone before. And I, oh my God, I want you. But because of what I'm feeling, I also want to protect you."

I reached for his hands and pulled them close to my chest. And maybe it was this gesture, but suddenly the words started flowing out of him. "I have every advantage a person could think of, but that doesn't mean my life is always easy. You've seen it, how public it is, no matter what I may try to do to keep something private. And I don't want you to get hurt by that. Or hurt by me if I realize I can't . . . love another guy. I mean, publicly. I don't have any doubts I can do it emotionally. But there are a lot of things expected of me. And I've been brought up to always consider the possible public consequences of my actions. Let's say, even if I thought I could run for office as an out gay man, if it came out that I'd had sex with you while you were underage, it could ruin everything I'm supposed to accomplish. And I realize how incredibly fucked up and weird that sounds, but that's my life. That's how I've been brought up to think. If you want to run screaming, I get it. I really, really do."

Confession time. While I heard all of what he said on some level, on another level I was kind of distracted by the realization that he had clearly been thinking a lot about having sex with me. A lot. In a far more complex way than I'd been thinking about having sex with him. Another confession. This was a super-hot realization to have. J.J. Kennerly had been spending a lot of his time thinking about having sex. With. Me.

"My birthday's next month," I said.

"What?" He leaned forward, his chin resting on the crown of my head.

"I turn eighteen next month. Legal adult." I turned to face him, smiling, feeling a kind of confidence I don't think I'd ever felt before. "No more excuses from you."

My smile spread onto J.J.'s face as we looked intensely into each other's eyes.

"So you have a month to decide if you want to deal with the many, many, *many* limitations of my life," he said.

"And you have a month to make sure you live up to your promise," I said.

"Which promise?" he asked.

"That our first time will be amazing."

The kiss that followed sure was.

CHAPTER 9

KIMBERLYGATE

So now we're up to the incident which became known in the media as Kimberlygate. Although I didn't actually have anything to do with the events of the scandal as they occurred that night, I do still feel partially responsible, because J.J. was supposed to have gone with her. But when he arrived that evening to pick her up, he was the only person who caught on that something was not quite right with me. J.J. was always like that, very attuned to peoples' energies, and especially to mine.

About a week before had been the fourth anniversary of my father's death, and while Iris had marked it in her own way by never getting out of bed that day, I knew that keeping busy was always the best way to distract myself, so I had gone to school as usual. Although I'd said nothing about it to him, when I woke up that morning I'd found a subtly but encouragingly worded card slipped under my door from J.J. It wasn't signed, of course, but I knew there was only one person in my life who would ever think of doing something that considerate. He and Kimberly had been out late the night before, so he must have figured out a way to get it to me when they got home.

Anyway, even though it was a day I was prepared to soldier miserably through, the card had made it far less awful and had me feeling much less isolated than I usually felt on that anniversary. I guess maybe my guard was down a little bit because I was thinking about J.J. and the card when I exited the school building, when a guy around thirty years old called out, "Christopher!" I stupidly responded to him. All I said was, "Yes?" but that was enough for him to join me as I walked home and start asking all sorts of questions about Kimberly, and J.J., and how the family was observing the anniversary of "your father's tragic suicide." I felt trapped, because I figured if I ran he'd just run with me, and if I told him to eff off he'd have a quote that would be made to reflect badly on the family and therefore on J.J. I opted to keep my head down, staring hard at the sidewalk as I walked as quickly as I could while he kept asking me the same questions over and over again. Finally, he gave up, and not a moment too soon, because as hard as I'd been trying not to cry, I was on the verge of losing the battle. It was his saying, "Do you think your father would have tried to stay alive if he'd known the Kennerly fortune might be in your family's future?" that had really gotten to me.

I didn't say anything about the reporter to anyone, because sometimes it's just easier to keep pain to yourself. But a week later, the day of the night that would become known as Kimberlygate, I'd had another unsettling interaction with the media. This time it actually happened inside school, not while I was walking home.

The first few days after the Autumnal Ball, when the news of Kimberly and J.J. had first made a splash, I'd gotten a lot of extra stares in the hallways and in class, but it quickly became old news. It was not all that surprising that someone associated with McVities Prep would be dating someone as high profile and powerful as a Kennerly, and by the end of the week I was blessedly allowed to sink back into the shadows. So it had immediately struck me as odd when this squirrelly-looking blond kid sat down in the lunch seat that Vibol had just vacated in order to go buy a second ice cream sandwich.

"So, brah, what's up with your sister and that Kennerly dude?"

"Excuse me?" I asked, surprised to have a schoolmate I'd never noticed before being so nosy.

"You're Christopher Bellows, right?"

It was the use of my full name that made the hairs on the back of my neck stand up. Since only the press referred to me as Christopher, and anyone who actually knew me at all called me Chris, at the very least this kid's only "close source" must be what he read online or in the papers. "Who wants to know?" I asked, keeping my eyes fixed on my Coke.

"Shit, brah, it's cool, you can trust me," he said softly, almost in a whisper. "It's not like I'm going to go tell anyone."

I looked up and into his eyes, and he fixed me with the most sympathetic and intimate expression that I totally would have fallen for . . . a month ago. Instead, I said, "You didn't tell me your name."

"It's Brandon." He held out his hand to shake.

I didn't take it. "I've never seen you before."

"Yeah, I'm new."

"May I see your school I.D., please?"

He laughed.

"I'm serious," I said.

"Uh, they haven't given it to me yet."

"They give everyone an I.D. first thing. If you don't have one, you shouldn't be in here." I reached across the table, and he jerked back his arm.

His pale skin growing pink, he said, "Relax, I'm just saying hello—"

Standing up I looked around and yelled, "Someone call for a security guard! This kid's not supposed to be in here!"

Squirrelly, blond "Brandon" took off running around the table, racing for the door. I don't know what got into me, but not seeing anyone from the Security Team close by, I took chase. He had a good lead and knew the fastest route from the lunch area to the front door, because by the time I reached it, he was saying something to the reporter standing on the sidewalk across from the school—the same reporter who had harassed me the week before. So now it looked like even school wasn't going to be a safe place for me.

And that's why I was in the mood that J.J. noticed that evening. I kept telling him I was fine, and that Kimberly was really excited about their date, but he kept watching me. Trying to distract him, I asked how his European policy paper was going, and he said he had a first draft, but it needed editing and proofing.

"Chris is really good at that, you know," Kimberly said as she entered the room, looking amazing in an emerald green wrap-dress.

"I'm not surprised," J.J. said, winking at me.

Kimberly sat on the couch beside him, resting her hand on his forearm. "Yeah, I had a paper due for my comp class, and he totally saved me. I, or should I say we, got an A."

Although she was only taking a single class at NYU, with the busy life of a media-star socialite, Kimberly would have failed on that paper if I hadn't helped her out. But considering she didn't know that her boyfriend and I were falling in love with each other, I figured it was the least I could do. I realize that might sound flippant, but it wasn't something I took lightly, and J.J. and I had spent a good chunk of our alone time discussing how I felt bad about lying, and him agreeing but saying he didn't know any other way for us to see each other. Some might say the solution was obvious, but a lot of things are obvious when you don't actually have to live them.

"Hey, Kimmy," J.J. said, "Would you hate me if I said I was too tired to go to this thing tonight?"

Kimberly and I both looked at him, she trying to cover up her disappointment, and me trying to see if he was doing this because he'd noticed my mood.

"But you love Klimt," I said.

"Yep, that's the guy," Kimberly said. "You said he was one of your favorites."

"He is," J.J. said. "And I'd love for you to see some of his paintings in person. I'm just worn out."

Kimberly looked torn, sort of motioning to herself as if to say that she'd gotten herself all dolled up, and while I think I was trying to encourage both of them to go, it's also possible that I was really just trying to make her want to go more when I said, "That dress will photograph really well."

"It certainly will," J.J. said.

Kimberly sighed. "Oh, they won't want just me."

"Are you kidding?" J.J. said, "They hardly even notice me anymore. You're the one who's selling papers these days."

Kimberly blushed, unable to suppress a smile for long, "You're just saying that."

"I'm serious. If you want to go, you should totally go. Don't stay because I'm tired and boring."

Kimberly stood and began to recite as if she were giving a report at school. "Gustav Klimt was a Symbolist painter

from Vienna, Austria. He is most famous for," she winked
at J.J. suggestively, "*The Kiss.* Although that's not at the
exhibit tonight, I don't think."

"Probably not," J.J. said. "We saw it in Austria a few
years ago, and it's the Belvedere's top draw, so I doubt they'd
lend it out. It's amazing."

Surprised to hear her so informed, I said, "You've been
doing some research. I'm impressed."

She shrugged. "I only Googled it, but J.J. has been
encouraging me to figure out what I'm interested in, so I
figured getting a little more informed before we go to all of
these cultural events was as good a place to start as any."

"You're a good influence on her," I said to J.J., trying to
look merely admiring and not the full-on adoring that I felt.

Kimberly nodded her agreement. "He says that privilege
is a responsibility, and that good works are how we give
back."

Burying his head in his hands, J.J. said, "That sounds so
pretentious when I hear it said back to me."

"But you're right." Kimberly said, putting her hands on
her hips with sassy determination. Then, with something of
a pout, added, "I just haven't figured out what I want to do
yet."

J.J. said, "You will. Don't worry."

She held out a hand to him and asked, "You sure you
don't want to go have our picture taken?"

He first took her hand and kissed it, then shook his head.
"I really just want to chill. Do you hate me?"

"Of course not." She leaned down to pick up her purse,
and he gave her a quick peck on the lips.

As soon as she was out the door, I let out a soft groan.

"I know what you're going to say, Chris, but I really
don't like it any better than you do, I swear."

"I just . . . couldn't we at least let her know she's acting as a beard?"

"And what if she doesn't want to, or worse yet, tells the whole world?"

"Would that be so bad?" I asked. I knew that I still hadn't even officially talked to my own family about being gay, but somehow knowing that I had J.J. to support me meant I finally felt like I could do it.

"You know what's expected of me." By that he meant that basically the entire world expected him to be president of the United States someday, and while his own party supported the rights of gay Americans, that didn't mean they were ready to elect a homosexual when a personal issue such as sexuality was still such a divisive issue. Not that anyone but me knew he was gay. But having grown up in a family expected to serve, it had been ingrained that self-sacrifice was part of their burden, and to him his own happiness was not a terribly important factor when he believed he could do so much good in the world. I'd told him I understood. Which I did. In theory. But that didn't make it any easier emotionally.

"Do you want me to leave?" he asked.

"You know I don't."

He looked around the room, empty of people other than the two of us. "Do you want to make out?"

I couldn't help but smile. "Always. But I'm not sure where Iris is."

He frowned exaggeratedly. "Maybe we could get her some sort of cow bell or something."

"Put it in a Tiffany box, and she'd probably wear it."

He laughed, then stood up, crossed to the chair I was sitting in, and bent down. "Kiss me."

I guess it was the conversation we'd just been having, because I suddenly flashed back on what had happened

114

earlier that day at school with the undercover reporter, and the seriousness of J.J.'s position, our position, loomed over me darkly with intense immediacy. It must have shown on my face, because J.J. asked what was wrong, and after I told him about what had happened, he slumped back to his place on the couch.

"I'm so sorry," he said. "This is so unfair to you."

"Don't worry about me."

He looked over at me pensively. "How can I not? I love you."

Although I'm pretty sure I appeared calm hearing this from him for the very first time, inside my head I did a major gasp. I couldn't remember anyone other than my father ever saying those words to me with true intimacy and seriousness, and parental love was such a different thing, and I don't know that anyone who hasn't felt it themselves can ever understand the wave of joy that comes with hearing those words from someone for whom you feel the same thing. I'm not sure how long it took me to find the wherewithal to take in a halting breath and whisper back, "I love *you*."

We both stood up at the same moment, ready to throw caution to the wind for at least a brief kiss.

But just then we heard the front door open. Buck was home from the gym.

We ended up watching a Harold & Kumar movie that night (Buck's selection), with Iris looking horrified by what was happening on the TV screen and saying to J.J. no less than fourteen times, "We can change this to something else." But neither he nor I were really paying much attention to the movie, because we kept stealing glances and catching each other's eye, and whenever our eyes locked, the goofiest smiles would blossom and we'd look away quickly to hide them. This love thing was a seriously stupid drug. Even when I thought of Kimberly—which I did numerous times—I can't say I was capable of feeling bad for her right then, because I simply felt too good.

That's what we were all doing while she was out unlocking Kimberlygate. Not that she was aware of it that night. Because when she got home, she said it had been a fine night, only wrinkled slightly by one rude woman who had called her a bitch when she had offered some help. J.J. assured her sometimes that happened. No matter how good your intentions were, some people were simply determined to be jerks.

The next morning we would all wake up to the other side of the story.

CHAPTER 10

SKINNY BITCH!

I knew something was amiss when I woke up a little before seven a.m. and found I had eleven text messages from Duane. He'd been planning an all-nighter to finish an evening gown for his class at Parsons, and the first text had come at 3:17 in the morning. "OMG, have you seen the *Post*?! What was K thinking?!?!?!?!" The last text from 6:44 said, "Bitch, wake the fuck up! I'm on Skype. We must discuss!!"

I briefly struggled with whether to go to the *Post's* website first or to log onto Skype, but I decided to let Duane break the news. I had this vague notion that getting bad news from someone who cared for you was easier, so I thought I'd test the theory. Except that Duane wasn't there. His Skype was still on from our conversation the night before, his cam showing the gown he was working on fitted onto his dress form, but the room was Duane-less.

With growing dread, I went to the homepage and saw the headline in bold, black writing—**SKINNY BITCH!!!!**

—over a picture of Kimberly looking lovely (and, yes, skinny) in her green wrap-dress as she entered the museum the night before.

According to their "sources," she had told an overweight woman named Wanda Cartwright that fat people shouldn't use elevators because they might break them, and then if skinny people got stuck in the elevator with them, they risked being eaten like the Donner Party, because fat people couldn't go long between feedings.

I knew that some pretty outrageous things had come out of Kimberly's mouth, but this comment seemed a bit much. But then I realized the only way I'd be able to get Kimberly's side of the story was to wake her up before I went to school, and since she generally slept well past my departure time, I was trying to decide if it was cowardly of me to consider leaving for school a little early today just to be safe. Because, after all, wouldn't it be nicer to let her sleep a last few peaceful hours in ignorant bliss than to wake her up with this kind of news?

That's what I was thinking when Duane spoke from the Skype window behind the Post article. "Would you like cream and sugar with your scandal this morning?"

I clicked his window to the front to find him sipping from a steaming cup of coffee. "What the hell should I do?" I asked.

"Just make sure you do something with your hair before you open that front door, you hear?"

"I just woke up," I said.

"I'm just saying, you don't want that bed head being the family's next embarrassment."

"Duane, I'm serious. Should I wake her up or not?"

He looked momentarily surprised. "Oh, shit, she doesn't know yet?"

"You know they all sleep in late."

"I just thought—oh, hell, honey, pack a bag and RUN!"

"Yeah, that helps."

"That's what I'd do."

"And miss out on the drama? Really? You?"

"Hmmmm, good point." Duane looked at his creation on the dress form before continuing. "If it weren't for *this* travesty, I'd hightail it over there to get a front row seat to watch *that* travesty."

"I'm sure she'll appreciate the sentiment."

"So what the hell happened?"

I shrugged. "I have no idea. She seemed fine when she got home last night."

"So you don't think it's true?"

"Do you really think Kimberly knows what the Donner Party was?"

"Good point."

"Do you know if anyone else has picked up the story?" I asked.

Duane froze with his coffee cup halfway to his mouth, then clearing his throat, took a sip before answering, "Child, you really did just wake up, didn't you? It's everywhere."

"You mean like Perez Hilton or whatever?"

"I mean like the *New York Times.*"

Oh. This was bad.

But before my stomach had time to twist itself into a tighter knot, I heard a tapping downstairs. Someone was at the front door. I looked at the clock, then said to Duane, "It's barely seven o'clock. Who would knock that early?"

"My money's on the grim reaper or Jenny Craig with an Uzi."

"You're a big help. I'll be right back."

I grabbed my robe, and although the floor was cold against my bare feet, I left my slippers, because I didn't want them making any noise that I could possibly avoid. I'd only reached the second floor when I heard the tapping at the front door again, so I tried to speed up my descent while still trying to be quiet. Once I reached it, I put my eye to the security glass, and I was surprised to find J.J. No sooner had I turned the doorknob than he burst in, grabbing onto me to keep me from falling over, and pushing me behind the door to keep me out of view from the camera flashes outside.

"What's going on out there?" I asked, putting my eye back to the glass of the closed door, now realizing there was an entire sea of people outside.

"You guys don't know?" he said, running a hand through his short brown waves and looking filled with dread.

"I just found out about five minutes ago, but everyone else is still asleep."

"I've been texting her for over an hour."

"She's started turning her phone off at night, or else it wakes her up at all hours."

I sighed. "I wish you felt you could text me."

"You know why I can't."

"We could be careful. I swear I wouldn't say anything incriminating."

"Chris, please, not now." He began to pace the front hallway, rubbing his hands together and looking very tense.

He was right. This was not the time to bring up the complaint I had the most trouble suppressing. I tried to remind myself that back in the day, people hadn't texted, and a few years before that, they hadn't even had cell phones. To my generation, that's like not having the wheel, or fire. I mean, seriously, how did people even live like that? If not being able to text with J.J. was any indication, it was a life arguably not worth living.

As J.J. took off his pea coat, he said, "My mother is so pissed."

"Why is your mother pissed?" Kimberly's voice said from above us she stood at the top of the stairs. J.J. and I both froze.

"J.J., Chris, what's going on?" she asked, her voice still rough from sleep.

It's probably going to sound very shallow of me to admit this, but at that particular moment, with the world seemingly crashing down around us, the only thing I could think of as she walked down the stairs, still tying her silk robe closed over her short nightie, was that this was the first time J.J. was seeing her without makeup, without her hair done, without any of the polish that countless hours in front of the mirror usually provided, and the girl still looked ravishing. It made me suddenly aware of what I must look like, especially after Duane's comments about my bed head, and I had the quickest flash of jealousy. And, then, even less flattering to myself, the thought passed through my mind that she deserved whatever the hell this mess was into which she'd gotten herself. That brief feeling of superiority didn't last long, though, because I quickly reminded myself that if anyone was responsible for whatever situation she was in, it might very well be me.

With her cheeks flushing (making her even more attractive, naturally), Kimberly stopped halfway down the stairs and repeated, "Why is your mother pissed, J.J.? Does it have something to do with me? Why are you here so early?"

They say women have more sensitive hearing than men, and at that moment I definitely believed it, because while I couldn't hear anything but the thoughts raging in my head, Kimberly tilted an ear towards the door, heard something, then rushed the rest of the way down the stairs and put an eye to the security lens. She spun around, asking us, "What's going on?" But before either J.J. or I could answer, she ran into the living room, grabbed Buck's laptop from beneath the couch, made a noise of disgusted annoyance at his vagina screensaver, tapped a few keys, waiting for whichever website she'd picked to load, and then . . . BEGAN SCREAMS OF EPIC PROPORTION.

With the whole household now awake, Kimberly told us, through broken sobs, her side of the story. She had been thinking about J.J.'s advice to help others on the ride to the exhibition, so when she got there, after stopping to talk to the press and waving to the cameras, she "saw this fat woman—I'm talking Jabba the Hutt fat—waiting for the elevator, and I thought we were both going to the same floor, but then when we got in and she pressed the button, she was only going up one floor, and you know how all the health and diet magazine articles say you should start by doing small things, like taking the stairs if you're only going a flight or two, so I said, 'I find that the magazines are right about those little ways to kick start the metabolism, you know, like taking a flight of stairs,' and then she started giving me this really dirty look, so I said, 'I mean, if you care about what you look like, which is really nobody's business but your own, although if you have a husband or kids, which isn't, like, impossible, different men like different things and all, but for your family it's important to do whatever you can for your health, and you really might want to think about them, right?' And then, thank God, because she was seriously glaring at me by this point, the elevator opened on the second floor, and she got out, and she turned around and shouted,

'Bitch!' at me. I couldn't believe it. I was just trying to help."
And then Kimberly turned her red, streaming eyes to J.J.,
saying, "Just like you told me to."

From the arm of the couch he sat on, Buck stretched
with a yawn and said, "I think it was good advice. She was
just a cunt."

"Buck!" Iris said with as much bark as she could manage
through her Ambien fog. She sat in an armchair, holding her
robe closed at the neck. "You know how I feel about that word."

Buck rolled his eyes. "At least I like them," he said, gesturing towards me.

My stomach dropped as I felt my whole body combust
with heat. Why was I getting dragged into this?

"See, there's another example," Kimberly said, as a fresh
jag of crying started. "I tried for all of those months to let
Chris know it was okay if he were gay, and I think he just
thought I was being mean to him. I'm just not good at
anything!"

"Wait, what?" I managed to sputter.

Since she was loudly blowing her nose, she gave Buck a
look, and he nodded. "Yeah, at the beginning of summer she
told me she thought you were gay and afraid to come out,
so we started saying all of that butt pirate and cock gobbler
stuff. She thought if we joked about it, you wouldn't make it
some national crisis or whatever, since you're such an uptight
little repressed drama queen."

"I am not!" I said.

"Dude, you take *everything* so seriously. Just relax.
Especially, from what I hear, if you're going to take it up
the ass."

"Buck!" Iris and I yelled in unison, perhaps the first time
we'd ever been that much in sync. I wasn't quite sure what
to make of the fact that J.J. guffawed.

Buck held up his hands in mock-surrender, then mimed zipping his mouth shut.

I was once again thinking more about myself than about Kimberly. I was lost at sea, realizing that those comments that had cut so deeply had actually been meant to show support. As crazy as it may sound to some, I believed them. Buck had always given me a hard time, saying I just didn't get how they communicated, and this was the moment when I finally realized maybe it was me. Maybe my expectations were the reason we hadn't been closer.

But that still didn't excuse Buck making such an off-color comment in front of J.J. Disgruntled, I crossed my arms over my chest, and couldn't resist trying to get in a little dig. "Nice screensaver, by the way."

He shrugged. "It's how I like to start my day."

I'd hoped to raise Iris's ire, but she was too busy fighting to keep one eye open to notice.

Kimberly had finally gotten some control over herself and rested a hand on top of J.J.'s. "Do you think your mother will ever forgive me?"

Surprised, J.J. turned to her and put his hands on her shoulders. "She's not mad at you, Kimberly. She's pissed at *me*."

"At you? But because of what that lady said I said, right?"

"No, because she says I should have done more to prepare you."

"Prepare me? For what?"

He motioned to the unseen mob that herded outside our house. "For that."

"Oh. Right."

"She wants you to meet with our media consultant. Today, if possible."

Iris snapped out of her slumber to ask, "Is that expensive?"

"Don't worry about it. We keep her under retainer."

Iris nodded herself back into nodding off.

Since Kimberly was afraid to go alone, J.J. had a major exam, and I was already late for school, I offered to go with her to meet with the consultant. I was feeling a bit responsible for her being in this mess, plus I thought I might be able to learn something. That's how I ended up looking into the heart of darkness and discovering a few things about myself.

When I first saw Kiki Cacciatore as we were shown into her office by an assistant, I had a dark feeling of foreboding. At first I rationalized it by the severe, black and red, minimalist decor of the office, and the all-black clothes and severe cut and exaggeratedly black dye of her hair. But then the look of annoyed disapproval she gave as she watched Kimberly walk over to a chair reinforced my sense of doom.

"Well, you really managed to step in it, didn't you?" Kiki said and then sighed impatiently, waving the assistant out of the room.

Kimberly stared at the floor, nodding her head.

Kiki looked over various printouts of the story covering her desk, shaking her head. "I hope J.J. learns something from this."

Kimberly looked questioningly at me before asking, "J.J.? Shouldn't I be the one to learn something from it?"

"Honey, I realize you're a Fontaine, and that once upon a time that name meant something in this town, but my long-term strategy will be to suggest to J.J. that I prescreen his future dates."

Kimberly swallowed uncomfortably. "What are you saying?"

"What you mean, what am I saying? Don't you understand English?"

Kimberly looked to me for help. "Is she breaking up with me for J.J.?"

I hadn't given Kiki's words such a draconian interpretation, but now that she said it, my stomach dropped. "Are you?" I asked Kiki.

Kiki rolled her eyes. "No. As many things as I've been asked to handle for the Kennerlys, that, so far, has not been among them. Not that I would advise against it."

Maybe it was to compensate for my feelings of guilt, maybe it was the confidence that being in love gives a person, maybe it was Duane's sassiness rubbing off on me, or maybe it was just that subliminal conflict that comes from two opposing natures sensing immediately that there was no love to be lost, but something just rubbed me wrong about this woman, and without even thinking about it, I found myself staking my ground. I still very much doubt I would have done it for myself, but I was starting to question how many ways I might have misjudged Kimberly, and I was apparently ready to act in her defense.

"Excuse me, Ms. Cacciatore, or do you prefer Miss? I'm guessing it's not Mrs."

The way her shoulders tightened let me know I'd hit the sensitive mark I'd suspected lurked below her Armani armor. Then I continued, laying on a purposeful tone of innocence, "I mean, I don't see a wedding ring." Her eyes briefly dropped to her bandless left fourth finger before she lifted them to reconsider me. "Unless J.J. misled me, you're paid by the Kennerlys to advise them," I gestured to Kimberly, "or their proxies, on how best to avoid media mishaps. I'm not quite sure how it's appropriate for you to be talking to Kimberly, the client, so dismissively."

Before answering, she closed her eyes exaggeratedly to let me know I was trying her patience. "You're the little stepbrother, Christopher, correct?"

"Anyone who knows me well enough to use my first name calls me Chris," I corrected her. "Otherwise, Mr. Bellows would actually be proper etiquette." I swear I had never been this snotty to anyone in my life, but something about this woman got my scruff up.

"Well, Christopher," she sneered as she emphasized my full name, "seeing as she's the client, and I wasn't warned that I'd be babysitting two of you, I will expect you to sit quietly with your mouth shut while I advise her. Otherwise, you can wait outside." Then very slowly, she added with exaggerated diction, "Do you understand what I'm telling you?"

Both a little intimidated and a lot outraged, I turned to Kimberly for reinforcement, but what I saw was a look of intense pleading to not make this day any worse for her than it already was. I immediately clamped my mouth shut, crossed my arms over my chest, and burrowed into my chair.

Kiki smiled with bland triumph, standing up to emphasize her advantage. "Now, Kimberly," then throwing a quick, dismissive glance at me, before turning back to Kimberly, "is it all right with you if I call you Kimberly?"

Kimberly nodded.

"Excellent. Here's the deal. I'm not the coddling type." She looked at me again. "Even if she were the one paying. Which she's not." She turned her attention back to Kimberly. "I don't know how long you're going to be in the picture, but if you act like a spoiled blonde with a bigger chest measurement than I.Q. again, I don't think it's going to be long."

I took in a breath to say something, but Kimberly quickly put her hand on my arm to silence me. Kimberly might have been intellectually lazy most of her life, but she wasn't actually stupid. Obtuse would probably be a better way of putting it. But she, at the moment at least, seemed to be keeping a much cooler head than I was. It was a rather unexpected flipping of our usual positions. Then again, sometimes it's easier to take abuse than watch it be given.

Kiki leaned forward over her desk with balled up fists resting on top of some printed reports. "My instructions are going to be very simple for you to follow. You have a nice smile, and you photograph well. You rode your arm candy status to a nice month of free publicity. Don't push your luck. Don't speak. Don't open your mouth. Don't offer any opinions. And especially don't rub your anorexia in anyone else's face. Everyone's already going to think you're a bitch; don't help them out by proving it."

Restraining myself from defending Kimberly was taking such an effort that I began to break a sweat. I cleared my throat, but managed to limit myself to that.

Kiki continued. "Your best defense for this mess is to go into hiding. Anything else you do will just feel like you're trying to manipulate people, and you definitely don't have the savvy to pull that off."

"Don't you even get to tell your side of the story? You were trying to help," I said to Kimberly. Keeping my eyes on the black carpeting, I held up a finger in Kiki's direction before she could scold me. "That was a sidebar to her. I said nothing to you."

"Her side of the story doesn't matter," Kiki said. "The story is out there, and it will forever more be part of who you are in the public's mind. You're a bubbleheaded Barbie doll that managed to get her legs around the man they all fantasize about, and you gave them the excuse they need to think you're the bitch they always knew you were. Do you understand that?"

When I risked a look over to check on her, Kimberly was squeezing her arms around herself tightly, as if willing her apparently undeserving self into taking up less space, biting her trembling lower lip, and losing the fight to hold back tears.

Unrelenting, Kiki continued, "You're every girl who was ever mean to them in high school, you're every skinny, blonde, rich bitch who ever made them feel bad about themselves, and now they have the proof right there in the papers and on their computers. That's the great work you managed to do last night. Well done."

I'm not sure if it was the sound of her sniffling, or maybe it was the almost mewling sound she made when she took in a halting breath, trying desperately not to sob, but something in Kimberly's pain-filled sounds as she fought to control herself set me off. I jumped up from my chair and shouted at Kiki, "Look, I don't know what pain your life has known, or if you are just pissed that she's skinny and beautiful and you're not, but there's no excuse for talking to her that way!"

"HA!" Kiki shot back at me in what could hardly be called a laugh. "Get out of my office, you little shit! I'm this bubbleheaded idiot's only hope for salvaging what chance she has, and I'll talk to her any way I see fit!"

"She's not stupid!" I said. Then pointing at the diploma she had framed on her wall, added, "And even if she were, just because you have a degree from Barnard, that doesn't make you a better person. So just get off your high horse. A good education doesn't make you a better person. No more than being beautiful makes someone a better person. Or being ugly, for that matter. Or being rich, or poor, or a great athlete, or a total loser, or of a certain religion, or being straight or gay. None of that matters. The only thing that makes you a better person is being a *fucking better person.*" By this point I'd worked myself into such a crescendo that I suddenly realized I didn't know what to say next. So, very lamely, I ended with, "So there!"

Already sensing the extreme wave of embarrassment that was welling up inside me, and really, really, *really* not wanting to be in the same room as Kiki Cacciatore when it arrived in full force, I spun on my heel, stepped fluidly to the door, and said, "Come on, Kimberly," as I let myself out without looking back.

As soon as I reached the elevator, I realized I probably should have told Kimberly I'd be waiting outside, because when she stayed to get the advice which J.J. had sent us there for, which I fully expected her to do once I'd returned to sanity, well, I was going to look like even more of a fool than I already did. See, Buck, this is why there's a lot of good to be said about being uptight and repressed, I thought to myself.

But then the weirdest thing happened. Kimberly ran up and threw her arms around me. And although her face was still wet with tears, a huge smile graced it. "That was awesome!"

Gratitude for her support only briefly tempered the mortification that continued to wash over me as I repeatedly hit the elevator button, as if that would somehow make it come more quickly. I kept checking in the direction of Cacciatore's office suite, half-expecting her to come blazing out with some sort of automatic weapon trained on me.

"I'm so sorry," I said.

"What are you apologizing for? You totally defended me."

"But what's J.J. going to say?"

The realization only briefly clouded her brow, before she shook it off and said, "Well, whatever he says, it'll be my turn to defend you, if that's what needs to happen." She smiled at me with a pert, determined nod.

Luckily the elevator came right then, because her response had caused me to feel the first pricks of tears and a tightening in my throat. For maybe the first time in the five and a half years since I'd first met her, I had an inkling of what it felt like to have a sister. Could my timing have been any worse?

As we rode the elevator down, I didn't say much, basically struggling to stay afloat while I tried to process everything that had just happened to me in the last fifteen minutes. Apparently oblivious, Kimberly stood beside me humming "My Favorite Things" from *The Sound of Music*. At first I found this odd, but when I considered that maybe she was thinking of Kiki Cacciatore in place of, "When the dog bites, when the bee stings," I suddenly found it very endearing. Being more the type to worry and stew, I admired anyone who could bounce back that swiftly.

When we exited the building, the Kennerly limousine was still waiting outside for us. Since the throng of reporters and photographers had been so thick outside our house all day, J.J. had arranged for his security people to get us safely to the meeting with Kiki (if only we'd thought to bring them up to her office with us). He usually preferred to take the subway or a cab, not liking the pretensions associated with having a limo and driver, but this day had been far from usual.

No sooner had we settled ourselves in than the car phone rang, and after the driver answered it, he told us to pick up the back extension. Kimberly and I exchanged uncomfortable looks.

"Who is it?" I asked the driver.

"Mr. Kennerly."

"You mean J.J.?"

"Yes, sir."

Caught in a mini Mexican standoff, Kimberly and I each waited for the other to pick up the phone.

Finally, she said, "Fine," and reached for the phone. "Hello?"

I waited torturously through the one-sided conversation of fines, yeses, and mmm-hms until she hung up, her expression unreadable. Her brow furrowed intently as she stared out the window.

About ready to pull out someone's hair if she didn't clue me in on what J.J. had said, I softly said, "Well?"

"That was J.J." she said.

"Yes, I know."

And then she went back to staring out the window. Clearly she was trying to induce a heart attack or stroke or any of those other lovely illnesses triggered by impossibly high blood pressure. Although, quite frankly, at the moment, death didn't seem like such a bad option.

"So what did he say?"

She turned her head to look at me carefully, chewing her lower lip. "He doesn't think we should go home until after the six o'clock news is over, because at least the TV people will probably leave by then."

"Okay." Not quite as informative as I'd hoped, but it was a start. "Did he suggest anything for us to do until then?"

"Yeah."

I waited. Pointlessly, it seemed. I tried to prompt her again. "And his suggestion was?"

"He wants to talk to us. Both. Together. At home."

"But you just said we're not supposed go—"

"His home."

Clearly I wasn't hearing her right. "You don't mean we're supposed to go to the Kennerly Mansion?"

"Uh-huh."

"Now?"

"Uh-huh."

Maybe it was just being in the backseat of a limousine, but I started to feel nauseous. "Does the driver know that?"

"Yep."

Gulp. Oh my. "Kimberly?"

"Yes?"

"Is this a good thing, or a bad thing?"

"I have no idea."

Those were the last words spoken between us for the rest of the ride.

Chapter 11

Meeting Mama Kennerly

As the limo pulled up in front of the egregiously intimidating Kennerly home, in an attempt to lower the tension radiating from both of us, I turned to Kimberly and tried to sound causal as I quipped, "What, they couldn't afford marble curbs?"

She reached out for my hand and squeezed it painfully. "I think I'd rather go home and deal with TMZ."

I couldn't say I didn't totally get how she felt, because I was feeling pretty much the same way. But I also was more the rip-off-the-band-aid sort, because I'd learned that as bad as reality might be, it was rarely as bad as what I could make up in my head. "J.J.'s waiting, though."

She hung her head, then nodded. "I know."

By now the driver had gotten out and walked around to open the curbside door, which was the side I was sitting on.

I thanked him as I alighted but had to wait awkwardly as Kimberly was slow to emerge.

"You are expected, sir," he said. Then he bent down slightly to look into the car. "Are you all right, miss? Do you need my help?"

"No, I'm okay, thanks," Kimberly said. Finally, she appeared, looking pale and wan.

We lifted our heads in unison to take in the large white building that resembled a hotel more than a private residence. Kimberly made a noise somewhat like a half-laugh and said, "I wonder how many Xanax Mom would need if she were here right now."

"That would depend on how much vodka or wine she'd had."

"Think I should call and tell her?"

I checked to see if she was serious, but what I saw was such an odd mixture of fear, resentment, and mischievousness, that for maybe the first time, I considered what had been placed on Kimberly's shoulders from the moment Iris realized that her daughter was going to grow into a great beauty—the responsibility, the expectation, the desperate need for vindication. It made me wonder if maybe I'd had it easier being more of an afterthought.

Kimberly took my elbow as she said, "Let's just get this over with," and took the first step towards the wide marble stairs that led up to the vast, arching double doors.

We hadn't even reached the top step when one side of the doors opened. I guessed that the driver had told the butler, or housekeeper, or whatever the proper names for the staff must be for this kind of house, but instead of a someone standing in the entrance in a black and white domestics uniform like I was expecting, smiling warmly at us in a Chanel or equally as runway-ready suit was the even-more-stunning-in-person Jennifer Kennerly.

J.J.'s mom! In all the scenarios that had run through my mind on the drive over, meeting his parents had somehow not been among them. I couldn't see myself, of course, but when I think back on the moment, I'm embarrassed to say that my jaw likely dropped open and hung that way for several seconds before I recovered enough to snap it shut. Luckily, Mrs. Kennerly was graciously ignoring it and welcoming us into the house.

And, holy shit, what a house. It was like entering the most exclusive museum in the world. The rugs, the chandeliers, the tables, the chairs, the lamps, all of it subtly suggesting its authenticity by its confidence. (If you didn't know that furniture could exude confidence, take my word: it can.) And if I wasn't mistaken, there was an original John Everett Millais in the entry hall. I'd done a paper my sophomore year in Honors English about Shakespeare's influence on other artists, and Millais's *Ophelia* painting had been a major component. This one wasn't quite as stunning as that, but it was about as close as anyone was likely to see in a private home, or most museums for that matter.

"Kimberly, I am so sorry for what you've been put through today," Mrs. Kennerly said kindly, giving her a warm hug. "Jonas and I have given J.J. a stern talking to, don't you worry. He forgets sometimes that his life isn't exactly normal." Then she turned to a handsome, older woman in a muted yellow cashmere sweater and gray wool shirt who lingered not far away, and said, "Celeste, could you please let J.J. know that his guests are here? Thank you."

Celeste disappeared as Mrs. Kennerly turned back, this time beaming the warmth of her benevolence on me. "You must be Chris. I knew your sister was gorgeous, of course, but why do you always seem to be keeping your head down and avoiding the photographers? You're adorable."

Do you ever have three or four thoughts go through your head at seemingly the exact same instant? Well, that's what happened to me. First off, she knew my name. And she hadn't called me Christopher, as the press always did, she called me Chris, which meant that she knew about me from . . . J.J., right? Had J.J. actually been talking to his parents about *me*? Obviously not about our being in love or anything, surely. Right? Right. Of course. And she just called me adorable. *Me*. And this from one of the most beautiful women I had ever seen. Oh my god, what a great nose. And her eyes. So brown. Those weren't contacts, were they? No, real. Pretty sure. And, wow, did she even know how rich and famous she was? And the life she had lived, and the history she'd seen. And now here she was not only talking to me but being super, super nice about it. See, Kiki Cacciatore, *that's* what class looks like.

Oh, fuck. Kiki Cacciatore. And suddenly I remembered the events that led up to my standing in front of Mrs. Kennerly, and I realized I'd been shaking her hand and nodding, and I hadn't said anything while all of that stuff was colliding in my head, and with panic I knew that I needed to say something gracious and complimentary, and even as the words came out, before I had any idea what I was saying but hoping it would sound all right, I heard the tones of awe and desperation drip, "You look like Julia Ormond." Then realizing how stupid that sounded, I somehow thought I was making it better by adding, "Or, uh, I mean, she looks like you."

It was painful.

But she smiled modestly, even blushing slightly—I swear—and said, "J.J. warned me how charming you are, so don't think I'm going to fall for that too many times. But maybe just this once." She winked, then led us further into the house and to a "small" sitting room where a formal tea had been laid out. The weird thing about all of the exquisite surroundings and the precise rightness of everything—from the leather-bound classic books lining the walls to the cut-off crusts of the finger sandwiches—was somehow it all felt unexpectedly casual and comfortable. I thought to myself that *this* was what self-acceptance looked like. And then I thought about how ridiculously far from that I myself was.

Apologizing that she had a meeting at the mayor's office and that she hated to make others wait, she asked us to forgive her for leaving so rudely but indicated that J.J. would be right down. No sooner than she had disappeared from the room, I had a profound certainty that we had just been bamboozled. She was the good cop, making us feel relaxed and welcomed, and J.J. was going to be the bad cop, letting us know that in less than twenty-four hours, we had shown why, in the grand scheme of the universe, the Fontaine-Bellows and the Kennerlys were never really meant to mix. They had salmon finger sandwiches, and we told fat people to take the stairs and Barnard graduates that they weren't all that smart.

I will say this about that moment when you realize your worst nightmare has proven to be reality—it can be oddly comforting. After all, once you've hit rock bottom and lived, there's only one place you can go, and that's up.

Kimberly leapt from her seat as J.J. entered. She'd fallen for the act, hook, line, and sinker. I mean, was I really supposed to believe Jennifer Kennerly had been making the mayor wait while she schmoozed with us, and then just *happened* to have to leave before J.J. came in to deliver the bad news? Please. Kimberly at least had enough sense to not throw herself at J.J. as he walked in. She still had enough doubt to wait for him to come to her.

Although he was doing a pretty convincing job of carrying on the defense-lowering welcoming act, beaming a smile at both of us, kissing her cheek as he gave her a hug, and looking at me while proudly saying, "Kiki *loved* you."

Kimberly and I made eye contact, both not sure if we'd just heard what we thought we'd heard and looking for confirmation from the other. Not noticing, J.J. let go of her and stepped towards me with his arms wide open for a hug, then catching himself, lowered his left arm and held out his right hand to shake mine.

"You don't understand," he said, "she hates everyone, so whatever you did to impress her must have been amazing."

And then I caught on. I'd been right about the good-cop-bad-cop thing, and this was where he tricked us by starting with praise, and just as we started feeling confident, he would pull the rug out from under us by throwing one of the Ming vases against the wall, shattering it into a million pieces, and ranting, "Of course not, you morons! You've ruined everything!"

Now that I was onto him once again, I said, "Oh, really?"

"Yeah, really. She said Kimberly had such genuine vulnerability that enough people would begin to doubt what the media said, and that if they got ugly with her, you could come to her defense and make another one of your great speeches. Everyone likes a guy, especially a brother, who sticks up for a woman, and that would make people think she must be a good person after all if someone as genuine and all-American as you were willing to defend her." He cocked his head slightly to one side as he looked at me with amused curiosity. "What kind of speech did you give in Kiki's office anyway? That seems so unlike you."

My eyes flew to Kimberly for help as I said, "I wouldn't call it a speech, really. Would you?"

"J.J., he was amazing!" Kimberly said, clapping her hands together and giggling. "Although, honestly, I actually thought she might be kind of pissed."

Thanks, Kimberly. Nice show of support. Good to know you've got my back.

"Pissed?" J.J. asked. "Why would she be pissed?"

"It's really not important," I said. "Would anyone like some tea? I'll pour."

I busied myself with serving, and we all settled in on the overstuffed couch and chairs, loading our plates with finger sandwiches and decadent desserts. My stomach still wasn't quite sure it was ready for food, and my mind still had doubts that this was really not a trick, but as J.J. happily informed us of Kiki's strategy for returning Kimberly's reputation back to the pedestal from which it had so recently tumbled, I began to accept that we had seemingly dodged a bullet.

"So Kiki doesn't want you to go anywhere without either Chris or me as an escort from now on," J.J. said.

"For how long?" I asked, already freaking out a little bit about having missed a full day of school. I figured it was going to take me a couple days as it was just to catch up on all of the work I hadn't done this one day.

"It could take a while for this thing to fully blow over."

Kimberly brushed a scone crumb off her blouse. "When you say anywhere, you mean, like, to society events or whatever, right?"

"No, Kiki said she doesn't want you leaving the house without one of us. At least for the next couple weeks until the worst of it is over with. If you're photographed alone, it makes you look like you've been abandoned, and that people are embarrassed to be seen with you, which reinforces the negative image. If you're always with someone, it looks like people are sticking by your side, and therefore, you must not be as bad as it seemed, and it's just another case of the media trying to make money by tearing you down. Things could blow over pretty quickly if she can get that narrative going."

"So, I can't even go to . . . the gym by myself?" she asked.

J.J. shrugged. "So the three of us will have a great reason to hang out a lot for a while. That's not so bad, right?"

Being in high school, I actually had the least time flexibility. I was out of the house a little after seven thirty in the morning and rarely home before five in the evening, and then fixing dinner, picking up the house, and homework began. But J.J. suggested that other than classes he needed to attend, he would try to study and do as much as he could from our house, so that he would be available to get her out of the house enough. He told her this, glancing at me a lot, and I realized he sounded kind of happy about all this because it meant he and I would see more of each other. And when I envisioned coming home from school and finding him in my living room, basically waiting for me, even if Kimberly or any of the rest of the family were there, it made me smile.

But.

Damn it!

I realized there was a fly in the soup. And a really big one at that. While it would be great to spend more time together quantity-wise, the highest-quality time that J.J. and I had been sneaking for ourselves had almost exclusively been while Kimberly was attending events without him. If either J.J. or I had to be with her at all times outside of the house, and it had to be the three of us together inside the house, that meant J.J. and I would never have any time together alone. While that wasn't all that much different than the way things had basically been for more than the last month, my birthday was just over a week away, and that was the day we had promised each other that we were finally going to have sex. And sex was not something I wanted to have with Kimberly (or anyone other than J.J.) close by.

I put down my tea cup and plate, and cleared my throat. Giving J.J. what I hoped was a loaded look, I said, "Um, next week is my birthday."

I could tell by the way J.J.'s smile slipped away that he caught my meaning. "Oh. Right."

"So, we'll all go out together," Kimberly said as if we were idiots and she'd just solved the issue of world peace. "Maybe Mom and Buck will even come. That way, Chris, you won't have to cook your own birthday dinner for a change. Won't that be nice?"

I painted on my best attempt at a smile and nodded.

"Oh, shit!" Kimberly exclaimed. "That's next Tuesday, isn't it?"

"Yeah, why?" I answered.

"J.J. and I are supposed to go to that whatchama-callit dinner. You know," she said, nudging J.J., "for that foundation."

"We'll miss it," J.J. said.

"But aren't you the honorary Chair?" she asked.

He squeezed his eyes tightly shut. "Shoot."

"It's okay," I said, trying to hide my disappointment. It looked like I wasn't going to get the birthday present I'd really, really, really been looking forward to after all. For most of my life I'd trained myself not to expect much on birthdays anyway, first because my dad and I had never had much money for anything but necessities, and since his death because I just tried to remind myself to be grateful for anything I had. I guess it might seem silly, or shallow, or immature, or just like teenage boy hormones that this little disappointment hit me so deeply, but it did. Happiness can be a dangerous thing; it can make you greedy for more.

"We'll just do it the night before," Kimberly offered.

"Or the night after?" J.J. suggested, I knew thinking of his stupid legal/political concerns about my still being under-age the day before my birthday.

"Whatever," I said. Again, I knew the way I was feeling was stupid and selfish. After all, at issue was a fundraising event for a charity that did really amazing work, and here I was feeling sorry for myself. Obviously, the actual day didn't mean anything compared to the dual significance of the personal milestone and the relationship advancement, but I'd been looking forward to the symbolic neatness of doing the deed on my eighteenth birthday. I mean, becoming a legal adult and having adult relations with the love of my life on the same day. How cool would that be? Like something in a movie or a novel or something otherwise artistic. Why, oh, why was life always messing up my attempts to get some order and some metaphorical poetry into it?

"So you're sure you're okay with that?" J.J. asked, watching me closely. "I promise I'll make it up to you."

Kimberly rolled her eyes and took his hand. "You have nothing to apologize for, silly. Right, Chris?"

"Right."

"Isn't he the best boyfriend ever?" She leaned over with puckered lips, and after an uncomfortable glance at me, he gave her a quick peck.

"That's it?" she asked, unsatisfied.

"In front of your family?"

"Oh, Chris doesn't care." Then she got an idea that clearly excited her. "Hey, he should invite Duane to join us all for dinner! Don't you think?"

J.J. nodded his agreement. "Sure, why not?"

"There, it's settled," Kimberly said.

"Well, I still have to ask him," I said. "He might have a school project, or rehearsals, or a show, or who knows what."

Kimberly frowned.

"But I'll ask him."

She smiled.

J.J. did his best to follow suit, but I could tell he was worried that I wasn't really happy with the situation. Which, of course, I wasn't. But what could I do?

If I'd only known then what a roller-coaster ride my birthday would turn out to be.

CHAPTER 12

PERSUASION

A week and a couple days later, I found myself sitting on the floor of Kimberly's bathroom while Duane experimented with her make-up. When I'd invited him for the celebratory dinner planned for the day after my birthday, he'd happily accepted, but when he asked what I was doing on the actual day, and I said nothing, he insisted we spend it together.

Between school and having to escort Kimberly around when J.J. wasn't available, I'd been even busier than usual for the last week, so when the day arrived, I asked if it would be okay if we just ordered pizza and stayed in. He said it was my day so if that was what I really wanted, then that's what we'd do. And that's what I really wanted. I figured it would be easier acting like I wasn't depressed if we were just hanging out than trying to pretend I was having an amazing time somewhere supposedly "fabulous."

When Duane had first arrived, he'd almost immediately gone up to help Kimberly get ready for her date, as he usually did if he was around on a night she was going out. I'd never have predicted it, but the two of them got on like a drag queen afire. It never failed to bemuse me the way they both got so much pleasure from powders, creams, exfoliants, and all of that stuff, and how much they enjoyed sharing the passion. It was like they'd found the sister they'd never had. (Duane did have two biological sisters, but from what he'd told me, they were less, um . . . polished? glamorous? civil? . . . than Kimberly was.)

When the doorbell announced J.J.'s arrival, I'd left them to continue their preparations and raced downstairs hoping for a moment alone with him. But Buck beat me to the door. The one time he actually got his lazy ass up off of the couch was the one time J.J. held a dozen red roses, which I could tell from his expression were meant for me, but he had to pretend he'd brought them for Kimberly. From her place on one of the wing chairs, Iris oohed and ahhed over how beautiful they were. Then motioning her wine glass at me, she told me to go put them in some water.

"Oh, let me help," J.J. said.

"Chris can manage," Iris assured him.

Reluctantly I nodded my agreement, but J.J. wasn't going to be deterred. He stuck his head into the living room and said, "Mrs. Fontaine-Bellows, how many times do I have to tell you, I like helping. My mom says hello, by the way." He did this whenever he wanted to distract her.

This perked Iris right up. "She did? Why that's so kind of her. Give her my love."

Before she could ask him to come tell her more, he pushed me towards the kitchen, throwing a fake punch at Buck as he passed. After flinching, Buck compensated by playfully threatening, "Don't fuck with me, Kennerly, or I'll beat your bitch ass into next week." This, of course, got him called into the living room for an admonishment from Iris, which, knowing the way J.J. was always thinking two or three steps ahead, was probably what he'd intended.

As soon as we were through the swinging door, J.J. spun me around, took me into his arms, and gave me a passionate kiss. I blindly reached out to put the roses onto the closest countertop, and then reached my arms around him.

"Happy Birthday," he said, once we finally came up for air.

"Thanks."

"You know those flowers are really for you, right?"

"I suspected they might be. And I should probably get them into some water."

"But then I'd have to let go of you."

As I pushed him away—and some people say climbing Mount Everest is hard, how little they know—I said, "Well, if some people didn't have charity dinners to attend, some people could have held onto some other people all night."

He dropped his arms, letting his head slump forward like a rag doll. "Cruel, cruel man."

I laughed. "Yep, that's so me."

I picked the roses up and moved over to the cabinet where I kept the crystal vases. I turned to look at J.J.—it was always such a pleasure to be able to look at one another with our true emotions in our eyes, not having to pretend we felt nothing in case anyone was watching —and found him smiling at me with a certain secret pleasure.

"What?" I asked.

He slipped his hand into his suit jacket pocket and pulled out a beautifully wrapped package about the size of a small book. "I didn't want you to have to wait until tomorrow for all of your presents." He slid it into a corner of the counter. "Open it later. If you should happen to miss me at some point during the night."

"As if I'll be thinking of anything else."

"I love you."

Every time he said those words it was like a supernova of joy exploding inside me. I just didn't yet know that supernovas burn so brightly because a catastrophe is taking place. That lesson would come later.

"Yoo-hoo, I'm ready!" Kimberly's voice called from down the hallway.

"You'd better go," I said. "I'll be right there."

J.J. pointed at the package he'd tucked into the corner, and blew me a kiss before disappearing out the door. As I filled the vase with water and arranged the flowers, I tried to get all of my emotions under control, but I still had to wait at the doorway for a few breaths before I was ready to push through.

Looking as beautiful as ever in a strapless midnight blue gown, the diamond choker that was one of Iris's very last pieces of serious jewelry sparkling wildly at her neck, Kimberly laughed at something Duane had just said. Or, given how much makeup he himself was wearing, maybe I was supposed to switch-over to calling him Coco. I'd find out soon enough, no doubt.

"There's the birthday boy," Kimberly said as I approached with the vase of flowers.

"But these are for you," I said, handing her the bouquet.

She held her arms out for them, admiring their beauty, but then said, "Nope, it's your birthday. Why don't you keep them?" She drew her hands back and smiled with satisfaction.

One of the reasons to analyze everything from every possible angle, to imagine every possible reaction, to try to predict every possible thing that can go wrong, is so that you're never taken off guard. And her unexpected generosity definitely took me off guard. The vase almost slipped out of my hands as I found my throat tightening and my eyes stinging. Maybe it was being in love making me a more emotionally sensitive person, maybe it was finally starting to feel like I was developing a real relationship with her, or maybe it was old-fashioned guilt over using her as a beard without her knowledge. While I knew for her the flowers were just a way of saying thank you for defending her in front of Kiki, Kimberly's unanticipated kindness almost ruined my birthday.

Luckily, J.J. noticed my distress and quickly diverted everyone's attention away from me, and quickly got them out of the house. But not without one last look of loving concern over his shoulder as the door shut.

"So now that the Spice Girls have had a musical on the West End, does that make them retro enough for me and the girls to build an act around them?" Duane was still straddling that undefined line between himself and Coco, but as he applied more and more eyeshadow, I knew that a pronoun shift was not far off.

This was when I was sitting on the floor of Kimberly's bathroom, and he was playing with her makeup, as she openly encouraged him to do. I still hadn't recovered my spark since Kimberly had suggested I consider the roses mine, so I tried to bring my focus to Duane's question.

"Hm. Would this be Coco Chanel Jones and the Spice Girls?"

"Or I could just be Scary Spice," he said, considering several packages of different sized false eyelashes. "That might be easier."

"Are you thinking four-member Spice Girls or five-member Spice Girls?"

He looked at me as if I'd just kicked a kitten. "As if the spice rack was ever truly full without Ginger!"

I held up my hands in surrender. "Sorry. Who would Aphra and Special Kaye become? And what about the other two spots?"

"Special Kaye is so tall and lean, so that could work for Sporty, and Aphra has been known to wear a diaper in certain clubs, so she could be Baby. I mentioned it to my friend, Lolita Falana, thinking she could be Posh, but she wanted to call us the Spic Girls, which I said would get us beat up by some *chollos*, but she says it's okay because she's Latina, but I don't know. First we have to figure out if changing acts is a good idea, although I'd really miss the outfits we have now. Life it too complicated, I swear." Then he perked up. "Although, Anne Frank-Margaret would make a fierce Ginger!"

At that point I may have stopped listening for a bit. It wasn't that he wasn't being his usual entertaining self, but I had a lot on my mind. For just a moment I got obsessed with the idea of telling him everything, realizing it would be a relief to not have to keep it all in to myself, and even as I knew it was the worst idea I'd ever had, and that it would be such a betrayal to J.J. that he would have no choice but to turn his back on me forever, almost against my will, I found myself interrupting him. "Duane——"

"Child, please, can't you tell I'm Coco now?"

I looked up to see Coco glaring down at me with one raised eyebrow, a pair of very thick false eyelashes now waving like little bats with each blink of her eyes.

"Well, what did you want to say?" Coco said. "Child knows better that to interrupt Ms. Chanel Jones when she's brimming over with creativity."

"Oh, sorry, it's nothing. You're right; this is much more important."

"That's what I thought. Do you have an opinion or not?"

Since I hadn't been listening to whatever it was that he was asking for my opinion about, I said, "Not really."

"Good. We'll see how Buck reacts."

Buck? How had Buck come into a monologue about the Spice Girls? Or had he changed subjects? I suddenly felt very uncomfortable, because although Duane had never been subtle about his crush on Buck, I wasn't sure if Coco had designs as well. And if that was about what she'd been asking my opinion, I may have just passed up my one chance to avoid a messy situation.

The doorbell downstairs rang, which would probably be the pizza guy. It occurred to me that if I were fast enough, and if Buck miraculously got up to answer the door twice in the same night, maybe I could shove him out of it before Coco came down. I, of course, had no basis for this irrational fear of what Coco might have in mind; it was just a feeling. Of dread.

"You'd better go get that," she said. "And pick out the DVD. I'll be right down."

Afraid to leave her to her own devices for even a second now that I knew something was up, I had no choice but to go when the doorbell rang again. As I raced to the door, passing by the living room to see Buck lying on the couch watching TV and Iris flipping through a thick fashion magazine, I grumbled to myself the question of whose birthday was it exactly?

Once I'd paid the delivery guy, I carried the two pizza boxes to the kitchen, even though Buck had called out to leave them with him. I told him that I wanted to make sure there would still be some pizza left by the time I got the plates and napkins, and he called back that I was just selfish.

I still hadn't had the chance to open J.J.'s gift, and as I collected plates and utensils and the like, my eyes kept being drawn to the beautiful, orange, almost papyrus-like wrapping paper and the simple yellow cloth bow. I was dying to open it, but part of me also wanted to save the surprise. Partially because I didn't want to feel rushed by Buck's waiting to feed, but also because the tantalizing secret it held for me was almost sensual in its teasing.

But when I heard the unexpected sounds of high heels walking down the steps from upstairs, my stomach lurched, and afraid of what Coco might be up to, I grabbed the dinner necessities, and without another thought of J.J.'s gift, pushed my way through the door.

Coco was just gliding to the bottom of the steps. She wore a snug, black-and-white polka dot cocktail dress, actually rather tasteful and demure, black high-heeled shoes, and a sassy short wig. Where the heck had she hidden all this stuff without my noticing? Duane's backpack was not big enough to carry it all, was it?

"What the hell are you doing?" I asked.

Coco looked at me like I was crazy. "You said you didn't have any opinion, so I'm following my instincts."

Before I could say anything else, she disappeared through the living room doors as I stood frozen and mortified in the hallway.

Then I heard Buck say, "Dude, you make a *hot* girl!" and panic thawed my freeze, sending me stumbling desperately into the breach.

Buck had sat up and was making room for Coco on the couch, and Iris looked as if she was trying to make her eyes focus. I didn't have the heart to tell her that, for once, it wasn't the wine or the pills; her eyes were actually functioning properly.

"What movie did you decide on?" Coco asked.

Knowing Iris and Buck's preference for the colorful and mindless, I took a stab at scaring them away by quickly picking a classic. "*Casablanca.*"

"What's that?" Buck asked with his lip curled, doubting my choice would be one he would like.

"Oh, it's fantastic," Coco said. "Ingrid Bergman never looked more gorgeous. World War Two, 'Play it again, Sam,' it's so romantic and sexy."

Buck shrugged. "If you say so."

"I do," Coco said.

Iris sat up in her chair. "Wait, isn't that in black and white?"

"Yes," I answered, maybe a little too quickly.

"Uck, I hate black and white." Then, looking back and forth between me and Coco, she stammered, "Um, I didn't mean, you know, I mean, well, you know—I'm going to my room." She stood up so fast I was surprised she didn't get woozy. Trying to cover a laugh, Coco asked, as Iris passed by, "Don't you want to take a piece of pizza with you?"

"Carbs are the devil's candy," Iris said with a wave of the hand holding her carb-filled wine glass. As soon as she was out of the room, Buck motioned for me to put the pizza down on the coffee table. As I did, Coco frowned. "We need drinks."

Giving her an annoyed look, I answered, "I didn't have time to get them before I heard *high heels* on the stairs."

Having suddenly decided that a Southern accent would go with her outfit, Coco said, "Do ya'll have any sweet tea? I just *love* me sweet tea with my pizza."

"There's a pitcher of *regular* iced tea in the refrigerator," I said. "But if that's not good enough, there's surely a flight to Atlanta leaving from LaGuardia soon, and you could make it there in no time."

"He's so dramatic," she said, winking at Buck. "I can turn what ya'll have into sweet tea in two shakes of a lamb's tail. Want some, Buck?"

"Sure," Buck said, moving the plates off the pizza boxes and opening them to check the toppings.

As soon as the click of Coco's heels had faded down the hallway, I turned to Buck who was enraptured by the pizza. As clueless as he was, he couldn't really be obtuse to what Coco was up to, could he? Discord between my new friend and my family was the last thing I wanted to promote, but I just didn't feel like I could take any further misunderstandings or complications, so being beside myself with frustration, I decided to trust in what I hoped was Buck's good sense of humor.

"You know he—she—totally has the hots for you, right?"

After taking an annoyingly long time to tame a dripping string of cheese into his mouth, Buck said, "So what? You don't really think he's the first guy to throw himself at me, do you?" He waved the pizza in his hands at his pecs and biceps. "I mean, look at me. And it's not like it's hurting anybody. So why not let him enjoy his fantasy?"

Although it's usually really tempting to shoot down anyone so confident in their looks, however justified they may be, for a beefy jock airhead like Buck to be that comfortable with his own and everyone else's sexuality . . . what could

I really say? It was another of the moments where I questioned what actually went on inside that head of his. I know, I know, I go back and forth on whether Buck is an idiot or a secret genius, but I can never decide!

"Besides," he continued, "it's so much fun to watch you squirm." He took another huge bite of pizza, held up a finger to make sure I was paying attention while he slowly chewed and eventually swallowed, and then added, "Let's just be clear on one thing. There will never be any three-ways between us."

"What?" Were my ears bleeding?

Buck laughed so hard he had to drop the rest of his slice onto a plate, then held his hands to his stomach, the belly laugh seeming to grow in volume and intensity.

"What's so funny?" Coco asked as she sashayed in with the pitcher of iced tea and three glasses.

"Nothing," I answered with a surly glare at Buck. Which seemed to make him laugh even harder. Finally, he started coughing—dare I hope he was choking on something?—and Coco quickly poured him a glass of tea, telling him to drink it to clear his throat.

"Mmmmmmm, that's good tea," Buck said after he'd drained half the glass.

"Thank you," Coco said. "You know what my secret is? Brown sugar."

"Oh really?" Buck asked.

"Yes, honey. I just stick my finger in and stir."

Buck looked me right in the eye just to make sure I was listening when he told Coco, "Sounds delicious."

"Mm-mm-mm, child. It's so hot and humid on this sultry Southern night," Coco said, acting as if perspiration were dripping from her brow.

"It's November in New York City," I said.

"Hush you," she said. "Make yourself useful, and just go stick it in."

"What?" I choked, not believing the things that were being said to me, on my birthday of all nights.

"The DVD," Coco said. "Go stick the DVD in the player so that we can get on with the movie."

One hundred and two of the most uncomfortable minutes of my life followed. While Ilsa and Rick tried to deny their great love for each other, and he eventually sacrificed his heart for the good of mankind, I ate my pizza without tasting it, Coco played the role of a Stepford wife, and it would be hard to say which Buck enjoyed more—the pampering, or my discomfort at watching it. And on top of all that, my boyfriend was out on a date with my stepsister, and there was a wrapped-up surprise waiting for me in the kitchen.

The credits had barely started rolling before I was pushing Coco upstairs to get her things, and because I didn't want to have to wait through the lengthy process of *her* turning back into *him*, I tucked a portion of the grocery money into her bra, and said I'd call a cab. I was aware I was being rude, but it was taking everything I had in me to get through one of the worst birthdays ever, and I just wanted to get J.J.'s present, escape to my bedroom where I could be alone with it, and fall into the blissful oblivion of sleep as quickly as humanly possible.

That was why I found myself alone by ten o'clock on the night of my eighteenth birthday, feeling about as low and lonely as I'd ever felt. I sat on my bed, holding the still-wrapped present, which should have made me feel better, but the way the day had gone, I suddenly had a fear that the present might be a disappointment. Then the one piece of hope and happiness that I'd been holding onto would tip me over the edge into an even deeper and darker abyss.

But the thing was, even if it turned out to be something awful—have I mentioned I liked to prepare for things, I liked to know what was going on, and that I hated surprises?—I would never get to sleep if my mind was just thinking up all the things I would most hate to get. So maybe it was better to get it over with.

I'd felt the package and knew with about ninety-nine percent certainty it was two smallish hardback books. Unless it was one of those things made to look and feel like something it wasn't, in order to trick thieves or whatever. And I loved books, so at least he hadn't gotten me a video game, or a hockey puck, or whatever else would suggest that he didn't really know me.

After pulling the yellow bow loose, I slid my finger through the flap where the wrapping paper ended, breaking away the double-sided tape that hid underneath, and slowly unfurled it, revealing the backs of two very old but pristine books. I turned them over and had a curiously mixed reaction when I saw a two-volume copy of Jane Austen's *Persuasion*. Yes, it was my favorite novel, so it showed that J.J. had been listening when I'd said that, and that, of course, was a good thing. But he also knew I already had a copy. I'd even shown him a couple of quotes I'd underlined in my edition. True, mine was a paperback copy, and these were hardback, so maybe he was trying to help me start building the library I told him I someday dreamed of having, and suddenly I felt very happy. The fact that his gift had a symbolic meaning to my future, possibly our future, lifted me up and made the day melt away. Today might be rough, but there's always the potential for better in the future. At least, that's how I decided to interpret it.

I opened the front cover of the top book, and that's when my new happiness grew even greater. It wasn't just any old hardcover copy of Jane Austen's *Persuasion*; it was the first edition—from 1818! The title page said, "Northanger Abbey and Persuasion, In Four Volumes," and although I briefly wondered if he'd gotten the entire set and was planning on giving me the other two books tomorrow, almost as quickly I thought to myself, as much as I loved Jane Austen, I didn't care anything about books compared to what I really wanted from J.J.—HIM!

Feeling a little lightheaded from my quick ascension from depressed to euphoric, mixed in with a healthy dose of hormonal and horny, I decided a little fresh air might do me some good. Pushing the books aside and leaving them on my bed, I stepped out onto my balcony, shrugging on a hoodie against the chilly November night air. I leaned forward, putting my elbows on the ledge, hugging my arms around myself, and luxuriating in the perfection of J.J.'s gift, the crazy way that just thinking about him could make my heart pound, and this may sound weird, but also almost relishing the delicious torture of not being able to be with him right now, when I wanted nothing more in the entire world than that. I don't know if it's this way for everyone, but other than actually being with your beloved, sometimes the best part about being in love is the anticipation of seeing them again.

I lost track of time thinking about J.J., allowing my imagination to linger on his smile, and his laugh, and his lips, and his eyes, and his hands, and the dark hairs on his muscular forearms . . . if you know the word tumescence, you could apply it here.

But then something happened which confused me, because everything about him had been so crystal clear in my mind, it confused me when I thought I actually heard his voice whispering, "*Psssst*, Chris."

I shook my head, stood up straight, and decided it must be time for me to go to bed. The punishing schedule of my usual schoolwork, keeping the house in order, and escorting Kimberly was evidently getting to me.

"*Pssssst*! Chris!"

There it was again.

I looked around, and then over the ledge, and what miracle should I find smiling up at me from the shadows of Kimberly's balcony below other than J.J.

CHAPTER 13

A PUDDLE

"J.J.?" I asked, still not quite sure if he was really standing on the balcony below mine, or if my imagination was simply taking another flight of fancy. Although the night was dark, the whites of his eyes and teeth sparkled familiarly.

"'But soft,'" he said. "'What light through yonder window breaks? It is the east, and Christopher is the sun. Arise, fair sun, and kill the envious moon, who is already sick and pale with grief, that thou her maid art far more fair than she. Be not her maid, since she is envious. It is my Christopher, oh, it is my love!'"

Kimberly's balcony was much longer than mine, and he was standing at an angle where we could see each other's forms decently enough, but it was still a flight below, and the ten or fifteen feet between us seemed like the cruelest distance ever conceived by man or deity.

"Aren't you impressed?" J.J. asked.

"I'm a puddle."

"Then maybe I should come up there and wipe you up." He cleared his throat. "I wonder if that would have sounded less cheesy if I hadn't just quoted Shakespeare?"

"What are you doing here? Those charity events usually go on forever."

"I slipped out as soon as I saw a chance. But Buck said you had gone to bed."

"You didn't leave Kimberly, did you?! Kiki will kill us all!"

"No, she's in the bathroom."

Although we'd been whispering to each other, I lowered my voice, worrying that maybe we hadn't been whispering softly enough. "You let her take you to her room?"

"I don't know if you realize it—I had not, but Kimberly seemed pretty sure—but this is the first time since she and I met that either you or Iris hasn't been waiting for us when we got home."

"So why didn't you say you had to leave? You know what she has in mind, right?"

"But this was my only hope of seeing you tonight."

If I hadn't already been a puddle from his Romeo interpretation, I would have been now. As it was, I was basically whatever liquid state followed. Distilled puddle?

"You've got to get out of here," I said, saying the thing furthest from what I wanted.

"Shit!" J.J. said, reacting to a light going on inside Kimberly's room.

"Is that her?" I mouthed.

Somehow he must have been able to read my lips in the faint light, because he nodded.

Then the most amazing thing happened.

I don't know if you've ever noticed how certain old buildings have a pattern of bricks sticking slightly out, almost like a little ladder of hand and foot holds. I guess maybe because back in the day, chimney sweeps or someone needed them, but our house had these, and before I could even comprehend what was going on, J.J. climbed up the wall of our house like Spiderman.

"What are you doing?" I asked, panic making me forget to keep my voice as low as I should have.

Too preoccupied to answer, J.J. continued up from Kimberly's second floor balcony to my third floor balcony, all on the exterior wall of our house, without any sort of safety harness or anything that might have prevented him from plummeting to his death. Because that's about all I could think about. That, and how was I going to explain to the world why I was basically responsible for the death of J.J. Kennerly?

Although his ascent probably took less than half a minute in real time, to me it felt like one of those movies where the ticking red digital clock attached to the Bomb-That-Will-End-Civilization goes into slow motion, and the last fifteen seconds of humanity takes up most of the third act. But then, somehow, miraculously, J.J. was swinging his leg over onto my balcony, and I was reaching out to pull him to safety.

"Are you crazy?!" I asked him, the pitch of my voice about two notes higher than a dental drill.

"What? I climb the rock wall at the gym all the time," he said. Which could have been really annoying, but *he had just climbed up the wall of a building to be with me on my birthday!*

This time I would forgive him. I threw my arms around him, hugging him fiercely to me, and immediately I felt the reassuring strength of his hands on my back, each of us trying to pull the other closer than was physically possible, our mouths meeting desperately. But then the sound of Kimberly's anxious and confused voice calling his name below, "J.J.? Where'd you go?" tore us briefly asunder.

I grabbed J.J.'s hand and pulled him off of the balcony and into my bedroom. We'd have to figure out an explanation for Kimberly soon enough, but at that moment I cared only about one thing. It was my birthday, and for once I was getting exactly what I wanted.

As I lay beside J.J., watching him sleep as the first whispers of dawn began to waken the city, a numb, sleep-deprived happiness might be the best way to describe my state of mind. Sometimes in life I felt like the most boring, milquetoast, asking-to-be-walked-over nonentity in the world. Other times I felt like I must be the most painfully obvious freak who could never hope to be accepted or esteemed or loved. But lying in J.J.'s arms I just felt like . . . me. And whatever "me" meant, that was perfectly fine and absolutely enough. Everyone should feel that kind of peace and self-acceptance far more often than I think most of us do.

I can't say I'd gotten much sleep that night, an hour or two at most. Besides multiple "physical expressions of our love," while J.J. seemed to be easily able to fall asleep in between, every one of my senses was hyper-alert, and every minute that passed was almost excruciating in its wonderfulness. Every moment I wanted to drink in the sight, taste, smell, feel, and sound of him, and although even when I tried to close my eyes knowing that I needed to get some sleep, my other senses just seemed to become even more alive, and my eyes would pop back open. Sometime after four o'clock in the morning, I drifted off for a little while, but now here I was thinking how badly I wanted the sun to come up so that I could see this beautiful man more clearly, but also knowing that light would mean the end of the night's miraculous dream.

"Are you watching me?" J.J. mumbled, his eyes still closed.

"So conceited," I said, dipping my head onto his chest, not really even embarrassed at having been caught.

He opened one eye. "I like the idea of you watching over me while I sleep."

"Are you a little lamb lost in the wood?"

He smiled at my Gershwin reference and nodded. "I know I could always be good to someone who'll watch over me."

"Oh, you could, huh?"

So about thirty minutes later. . . .

Morning sun brightly lit the room, and we were both frantically dressing while trying to figure out how J.J. was going to explain his disappearance to Kimberly. (I'd also been worried how he was going to explain not coming home to his parents, but he said he'd just tell them he'd slept over here, and they weren't likely to pry further.)

"Would it be too lame to act like I sent her a text?" he asked as he slipped on a shoe.

"Well, since you've never been able to text me, I wouldn't know if that would be believable. And stop putting on your shoes. Carry them until we get to the front door."

"Right. Quieter." He took off the shoe and stood. "And, actually, hackers are why you and I can't text, so maybe I can blame them for her not getting hers?"

"Why wouldn't you have just told her through the bathroom door? Or at least written a note?"

"Does Kimberly even have paper in her room?"

"Good point. Okay, but why'd you have to leave in such a rush?"

"Family emergency? She'll think I mean mine, but it was kind of an emergency that I get up that wall to you."

As he said this, he leaned over the bed, his puckered lips offered, and I, of course, had no choice but to meet him for a kiss. "Yes, it was definitely a four-alarm fire," I agreed as I stood back up.

And then the LOUDEST ALARM IN THE WORLD WENT OFF!

Okay, so it was just my regular morning alarm, but at that blissful-but-jittery-from-fear-of-getting-caught moment, J.J. and I both jumped high enough to give LeBron James a run for his money.

After I'd lunged to turn it off and J.J. had checked to make sure that his heart was still beating, we knew that if we didn't want to push our luck any further, we'd better get him out of the house. In stockinged feet, we tiptoed down the two flights of stairs, not too worried but still cautious since no one else would likely be up for hours, but we did take some time to survey the areas across the street where photographers tended to hang out. Luckily, since I was the only one who was ever up early in the morning, and pictures of me sold for practically nothing at that point, we were pretty sure the coast was clear. Which didn't mean we weren't careful to kiss goodbye with the front door still closed, or that I didn't make sure that no part of me showed when the door briefly opened for J.J. to slip out.

I only momentarily panicked over how we'd explain a picture of J.J. slipping out of our house early in the morning showing up in any gossip sites or newspapers, because then that panic was replaced by the one I felt when I realized I needed to hurry or I'd be late for school. Even as adrenaline pumped through me as I rushed on my way, I worried about the sleep deprivation crash that was no doubt going to hit soon after I sat down, and Mr. McGully started droning on about cusps and ellipsoids. It was going to be a long day.

But my two most pressing worries of that morning never came to be. If anyone photographed J.J. leaving, they never posted the pictures, and somehow, although I'd hardly gotten any sleep, I was pretty much a beacon of glowing energy and clarity all day. So much so that I began to worry that people might notice that something was up with me and then begin to speculate on why. I don't think it's uncommon to wonder if you look or act differently when you're in love for the first time, or after you've finally had sex for the first time, or even, since it had happened on the same day, wondering if I looked older now that I was eighteen and legally an adult. But, for good or for bad, no one seemed to notice a thing all day. Not a one.

That is, of course, until that night, when I opened the front door for Duane and, with Kimberly, Iris, Buck, and J.J. waiting in the living room mere feet away, his eyes first looking confused and then growing huge, said, "What's going on with you? Something's changed. Don't try to deny it. *Gasp! You've finally had sex!*"

Although I'd shushed him with adamant disavowals, Duane kept glaring at me accusingly the entire limo ride to the restaurant J.J. had picked to surprise me with for my one-day-late birthday dinner. I knew Duane didn't care in a judgmental way if I'd had sex, but for me to not tell every juicy detail was highly, highly offensive to him. But since I was afraid of slipping and saying too much, I rolled my eyes and shrugged my shoulders, continuing to play innocent.

Iris tried to cover her disappointment when J.J. said the limo ride would be a relatively short one, but when Duane exclaimed, "Shut up!" as the limo stopped in front of Douglas on E. 64th Street, she tried to act casual. "Oh, yes, I've been meaning to try this restaurant."

"You and everyone else since it got three stars from Michelin, honey," Duane said. Then he cut his eyes at J.J. "Are we going Dutch?"

J.J. laughed. "It's on me. Order whatever you want."

Duane pointed at Iris. "You're getting the wine pairings and sharing."

"Good luck with that," Buck mumbled. Kimberly covered a giggle, explaining to Iris that she was just so happy we were all together to celebrate my birthday.

Once we had been solicitously seated and were looking over menus, Duane's eyes grew big at the prices, then he leaned over to J.J. and whispered, "When you say you're treating, you really mean your very rich parents are treating, right?"

J.J. smiled and repeated, "Order whatever you want."

"Mm-mm, I should have worn looser pants," Duane said as he disappeared behind his menu.

As everyone read through the selections, J.J. and I kept stealing glances at each other, and as much as I tried, I just couldn't keep what I knew was a shamefully stupid smile off my face. I don't know that I'd ever been as happy. Here I was in an exclusive, highly regarded restaurant with my family, flawed though they may be, a good friend, and the man with whom I was in love. Does it really get much better than that?

And that's when I felt a sharp kick on the side of my calf. Duane, who was seated beside me, leaned over, very unsubtly holding his menu in front of us as if that didn't broadcast to the rest of the world that he was saying something "private" to me, and hissed, "You told *him,* and you won't tell *me?*"

Realizing that my effervescent giddiness was making me careless, my stomach clenched, but luckily I managed to bluster through faux annoyance convincingly enough to shut Duane up. "Would you stop it? I don't know what it is you're imagining you see, but if I can't be grateful to the person who is about to buy *you* a very expensive dinner, well, then something is really messed up in your world."

Only looking half-chagrined, Duane slit his eyes and pursed his lips. "Hm." But he sat back and returned his attention to the decision at hand.

"Mr. Kennerly, we're so pleased you've honored us with a visit," the restaurant's chef and owner said as he arrived at the table. I'd seen the guy on one of those cooking shows on TV, and at that time I wouldn't have thought "obsequious" was a word that could have ever been used to describe him, but standing in front of J.J., it was definitely what I was seeing.

"Thank you so much for accommodating me at short notice. It was my friend's birthday yesterday, and I wanted to do something special since *my* schedule forced the delay in celebrating." J.J. shot me a quick smile intended to be loaded with secret meaning, but I tried to warn him away from any such displays by darting my eyes to Duane with a distressed look. Then realizing how that must have looked to the chef, I tried my best for an appreciative smile directed at him. (Duane, by the way, stared slightly drop-jawed at our celebrity host, so I need not have worried about him seeing J.J.'s look that time.)

"Happy birthday," the chef said to me, somehow implying with the two words how lucky I was to know someone like J.J. Kennerly or I never would have been allowed to even eat out of the trash cans in his restaurant. This was much more like what'd I expected from the personality I'd seen on TV.

But then he turned to Kimberly and told her she was even lovelier in person than in the many beautiful pictures he'd seen of her. I guess as the second most famous person at the table, she got the second-best treatment.

"Do you all know what you want, or do you need more time?" he asked J.J., back to his most gracious.

J.J. looked expectantly to me. "You're the guest of honor. Do you know what you want?"

I couldn't exactly answer, "You," even though that's what I was thinking, but since I hadn't understood half the foods and preparations listed on the menu, I asked him if he would order for me. Almost in unison, Kimberly, Iris, and Buck asked if he'd order for them too. Duane held up a finger, "I'll order for myself, thank you."

Per Duane's instructions in the limo, Iris did request the wine pairings, but then she also ordered a separate bottle of a favorite wine she hadn't had in ages. (Maybe because it cost $700.) And then she actually acted surprised when it arrived and she "realized" she was the only one at the table of drinking age. "Oh, how silly of me. And I'd been thinking we could all enjoy it together."

"I guess you'll just have to enjoy it all for us, Mom," Buck said with a tone that could have been called supportive . . . or patronizing, depending on which side you fall on the question of Buck's I.Q. Then he added, "Although I am going to be twenty-one soon."

"Soon," Iris said, patting his hand. "But not yet. We don't want to get anyone in trouble with the paparazzi lurking around every corner."

And as if by divine design, at that exact moment, a news van could be seen pulling up outside, and a photographer began yelling that he'd gotten there first.

"Someone must have tipped them off," J.J. said, resigned.

"A wolf in chef's clothing?" I suggested. J.J. nodded.

"Photographers?" Duane said, looking almost overwhelmed with anxiety.

"Yeah, so?" I said. "You love having your picture taken."

"But I just ordered enough food for three people. If I eat all of it—which I am entirely capable of doing—I'll look fat in the pictures. Oh my God, I suddenly understand *Sophie's Choice* in an entirely new way."

J.J. burst out laughing, but then when he realized from Duane's look that he'd been serious, he tried to cover it by coughing.

"Who's Sophie?" Buck asked.

As Duane began to explain the plot of *Sophie's Choice* to him, I surveyed the table and realized that although she sat smiling next to J.J., Kimberly had said almost nothing all evening. I caught her attention and mouthed, "Are you okay?" She nodded, then leaned over the table and whispered, "I'm just so happy." Her eyes moved from Iris, to Buck, to Duane, to J.J., and then back to me. "Isn't this great?"

Although I did at first have a pang of guilt that she didn't know the entire story, as I looked around the table I found myself flirting with optimism. Nothing about it was what would classically be called "perfect," but it was as close to happy as I'd ever been.

The meal was every bit as delicious as anyone could dream, we all had a great time, and somehow Buck's saying, "Don't make me choose," over every little decision stayed funny throughout the entire meal. Even when Duane hand fed him samples of each of the desserts he'd ordered and asked which one was the best. I guess Iris really believed that Duane and I were dating, because I don't think the wine would have been enough on its own for her not to notice the black guy trying to seduce her beefy, blond son. Instead, she just laughed at everything. Which was actually nice to see, because Iris laughing had been a pretty rare sight since my father died.

Incidentally, the paparazzi photo I mentioned at the very beginning of this story was taken that night as we were leaving the restaurant. And if you happen to remember that I didn't mention Duane in the picture, it's because he'd been Photoshopped out. He made such a fool of himself trying to get in the center of every frame as the throng of photographers swarmed us, that they all either only used pictures taken from angles he wasn't able to throw himself into, or with digital magic they made him disappear. We all got a good laugh over that the next day. Well, except for Duane, of course.

There was a lot of laughter in my life at that time. In fact, the next seven or so weeks were some of the best of my life. But happiness seems to always be a ticking clock, and time ran out soon enough.

CHAPTER 14

A Big Deal

The holiday season started out pretty great. Since the night of my birthday dinner had been the first night with some bite to the cold, it was the first night I'd worn my too-small winter jacket since the previous year. And although even Iris had commented we needed a new coat for me when she saw the picture in the paper, before we could do it, the next time J.J. came to take Kimberly out, he had a present for me. He acted like it was an old jacket of his that he never wore and was going to get rid of anyway, but even though it wasn't wrapped, I could tell it was new. For starters, I was a few sizes smaller than J.J., and even someone as fashion illiterate as myself could tell that the cut was very much current. But also, tucked deep in a pocket, he had included a gift receipt so that I could return it for something else if I didn't like it.

The lie about the gift was just to avoid having to come up with an explanation for my family as to why he was giving it to me, of course, but J.J. had actually conceived a one-two punch of distraction for them, just in case. Because just as Iris reached out to touch the fabric, he sprang a whopper on them. His parents were inviting us to their home for Thanksgiving.

I think Iris's reaction might best be summed up by what Buck mumbled dryly to Kimberly, who sat next to him on the couch. "Who knew a dinner invitation could hit someone's G-spot."

Kimberly turned slowly to him with a look of disgust. "Gross. That's our mother you're talking about."

"Doesn't make it any less true."

Surprisingly, I don't have any good stories from the actual event. Other than china and silver expensive enough to send an Ethiopian village to Harvard, Thanksgiving dinner at the Kennerlys' wasn't really much different than Thanksgiving anywhere else. Sure, there was a table long enough for forty people, almost all part of their extended clan, but Buck behaved, Iris didn't drink (although I'm not sure how many Xanax Kimberly slipped her in the days and hours leading up to that Thursday—even Calculus has its limits), and Duane considered it all "disappointingly boring" when I gave him my full report over Skype when I got home.

And, since their entire extended family was expected at Livia Kennerly's compound in the Berkshires for the Christmas holiday, Christmas wasn't any more eventful. J.J. did manage to make contact by calling Kimberly and having her pass the phone around to all of the members of my family so that he could wish me Merry Christmas (and tell me he loved me). For those keeping score, the other two volumes of the Jane Austen set he'd given me for my birthday were just the start of the gifts he slipped me before he left town. (I don't mean that as dirty as it sounds. Although, thanks to Kimberly having bragged about my proofing and editing skills, he had managed to get me over to his house alone a number of times, and while somehow neither of our grades suffered, there were lots and lots of "study breaks.")

Like I said, the weeks following my birthday, with a few momentary exceptions, were pretty much one long miracle of bliss. It wasn't until the stroke of midnight on New Year's Eve that it all began to fall apart.

The Kennerlys' annual New Year's Eve party was the most important unofficial event of the New York society calendar. Since there was no charity to fundraise for, or sponsor to help coordinate, or anything but Jennifer and Jonas deciding with whom they wanted to ring in the New Year, it was the most desperately whispered—and schemed—about invitation imaginable. It was also an unspoken law among those who had a legitimate chance to even aspire to attend that if you didn't get an invitation, the last thing you would ever want to do would be to mention it to Jennifer Kennerly, let alone plead for one. That would not only get you blacklisted from the event for life, it would most likely increase what you would have to donate for the "privilege" of attending even lesser events in the subsequent years. High society works that way.

What I'm saying is, it was a BIG DEAL. And because it was such a BIG DEAL, Iris hadn't felt secure enough of Kimberly's status in J.J.'s life, even after being included for Thanksgiving, to actually allow herself to hope she might receive an invitation. (Full disclosure: on one of my visits to J.J.'s house to "help him with his homework," Mrs. Kennerly had asked if our family had plans for the night, but I'd chosen not to tell Iris. Partially I enjoyed the secret, but also self-preservation helped me keep it, because I wouldn't have wanted to be the focus of Iris's ire if the invitation had failed to arrive.)

I had just gotten home from school, and luckily Buck was at the gym when the thick-papered envelope with embossed printing arrived, because if he'd thought Iris was excited when we'd gotten invited to Thanksgiving dinner, I don't even want to imagine what he would have said about the pleasure she took in opening that envelope. Although, as pure as the look of almost religious redemption on Iris's face was as she read the invitation, it was curiously short lived. Within a minute, her breaths began to shorten, and her face and chest burned flush.

"What's wrong?" Kimberly asked, concerned.

"We're running out of time," Iris told her, grabbing her arm urgently.

"What are you talking about? Mom, this is exactly what you've been saying you wanted most in the world."

Iris swallowed dryly, then looked around in distress. "Where's my glass?"

Although it was on the small table right beside her chair, she seemed too perplexed to see it, so I walked over, picked it up, and handed it to her. Since it was only half full and I'd been able to read Iris's expression as needing more than that, I had the bottle ready to refill the wine glass as soon as she moved it away from her lips.

"Kimberly, I'm running out of things to sell. That diamond choker you've been wearing everywhere is just about the last thing we have."

"But we get a quarterly check at the beginning of next month."

Iris looked miserably at the glass I'd just refilled. "That's already spent." She downed the wine, then turned to me expectantly. Holding up the empty bottle, I motioned towards the kitchen and left to get a fresh one.

As I stepped out into the hallway, out of the corner of my eye I saw Iris lean in towards Kimberly. Suddenly suspicious that I'd been sent away on purpose, I eased myself back against the wall to eavesdrop. Not an honorable thing, perhaps, but my guilt was quickly assuaged by what I overheard.

"How many times do I have to tell you? The fate of our family is in your hands," Iris said.

"Mom, I've been trying."

"It's been almost three months. No one waits that long anymore."

Kimberly made a frustrated noise, then said, "How many times do I have to tell you? He's Catholic."

"Kimberly, Catholic men do not wait until they're married to have sex. Ask an altar boy."

"Well, so what if we want to take things slowly? Is that so wrong?"

"We don't have time for you to take this slowly. Don't you get what I'm telling you?"

"Mom, would you stop it! This is my life, not some . . . trade agreement! You're like one of those women on CNN who tries to sell off her daughter's virginity."

"You haven't been a virgin since you were sixteen!"

"*Not* the point!"

"Maybe not, Kimberly, but do you think he's really going to want to keep dating you when they realize we're broke? You need to make something happen and fast, because your time is running out. Do you understand me?"

Kimberly said, "I've tried everything you've told me to, Mom. Showing cleavage, wearing lingerie, making suggestive comments, trying to get him drunk. Maybe he's gay and just doesn't know it."

And then my guilt was back.

But as I rushed as quietly as possible towards the kitchen, rage, relief, and fear battled through me. The rage from the thought that they were just using J.J. because of his family's money, the relief because that meant keeping the secret of our love wasn't hurting anyone, at least not emotionally, and fear from the realization that if things were really that serious financially, I had managed to fall in love with the one person everyone else was looking to as our savior. Rock + hard place = nausea.

When the doorbell rang right then, I was at first extremely annoyed, but when I remembered I'd asked Duane to stop by in anticipation of the party invitation, I was extremely relieved by the thought of a distraction in the house.

As this was all a couple weeks before Christmas, it was only somewhat odd that I opened the door to find him wearing a Santa hat.

"Nice hat," I said.

"Ho, ho, ho. Out of my way, bitch, this shit weighs a ton." He pushed past me, lugging several garment bags over his shoulder. "You couldn't have had an emergency on a day when I wasn't carrying all of my class projects from the entire semester?"

"You didn't just have to take in the final piece?"

"No, that bitchass Tim-Gunn-wannabe said he wanted to see our 'progression over the entire semester.'"

Not even noticing Kimberly wiping away her tears, he practically fell into the living room, shrugging his heavy load onto the couch, and greeting Iris with a, "Hey, Mrs. F."

He and Kimberly exchanged cheek kisses, and just as he noticed her eyes looked puffy, she asked, "Are these your designs?"

He nodded, then proudly announced, "I got an A."

"Can we see them?"

He had one of those oh-I-really-want-to-show-off-but-I'm-going-to-play-shy looks on this face, so I said, "Well, if you don't want to—"

"Okay, fine! If you insist."

"I do," Kimberly said.

Iris had that look of smelling moldy cheese, as if she didn't know how she would ever be able to pretend she liked whatever ghastly rags he had created, but as he began pulling clothes out of the bags, she at first looked confused, and then entirely mystified. Standing up to get a closer look, she said, "These are really good."

"Duh," Duane said, but then smiled sheepishly and added, "Thank you."

Kimberly held up a white gown with a silver and blue tulle layer floating over it and gushed, "This is gorgeous!"

"That was my final project. Clinched the A."

"Duane, would you let me try it on?" Kimberly asked, as if she were suggesting something scandalous.

He beamed. "I thought you'd never ask."

As soon as Kimberly swept out of the room holding the dress up to herself, Iris inspected the remaining items a little more closely. She'd gotten in the habit of keeping some of the castoff clothes that designers sent over but that Kimberly didn't want. Although, even with Kiki's deft handling of Kimberlygate, there were markedly fewer of those than there had once been.

"Too bad you don't have any gowns for more sophisticated women," Iris said.

Duane looked offended. "You don't think the dress she just took is sophisticated?"

"She means older," I whispered into his ear, and Iris pretended not to hear.

"Oh. Well, what do you need it for? I can dress *any* kind of woman," he said, motioning at his own male body significantly.

A curious expression came over Iris's face as she mumbled to herself, "Well, it would be cheaper."

Duane looked at me for an explanation. "What's going on? Does she need a dress for something?"

Afraid to open the wrong can of worms, I caught Iris's eye and asked her, "Are you thinking of . . .?"

"What do you think?" she asked me.

"He's really good, as you can see."

"*What are you two talking about?*"

Ignoring him, Iris continued to look at me, "I guess if he wanted to draw up some sketches?"

"Are you sure?" I asked.

Right then Kimberly walked in wearing the dress he had made, and even with casual hair, day makeup, and no jewelry, she possibly looked more beautiful than she ever had in her life.

"I'm sure," Iris said.

"Duane," Kimberly said, "I will kill you if you do not let me wear this."

Duane waved his hand in front of his face as if the room were stiflingly hot. "Damn, she going all gangsta on me."

"Well, can I?" Kimberly asked, running up to him and tugging on his arm pleadingly.

"Precious, nothing would make me happier than to have you wear one of my dresses, but doesn't it seem a little dressy just for dinner?"

Suddenly Kimberly realized that she was now the one with the power. "Silly, I don't want it for just any dinner. I want to wear it . . . to . . ."

Duane leaned further and further towards her until it was a marvel that he didn't tip over. "To where?" he finally said.

Kimberly held her silence until we all could tell Duane couldn't take the suspense any longer, and then finally told him, "The Kennerlys' New Year's Eve party."

My hands flew to my ears in anticipation of his screams, but all he did was blink three times, turn his head slightly to look at Iris and ask her softly, "Is that what you need a dress for, too?" Iris nodded.

I cleared my throat. "Actually, Duane, they don't know this yet, but depending on if you wanted to go as yourself or as Coco, you might need a third dress."

Kimberly was the first to catch on and asked, "J.J.'s inviting him, too?"

I nodded.

An expression of intense bitterness and jadedness came over Duane's face as he looked disappointedly at me. "Do you really expect me to believe that *I* have been invited to the most exclusive party of the year? Jay-Z can't get into that party."

"Fine, don't believe me," I said.

And *that's* when the screaming started.

Because of all the noise, none of us heard Buck enter the house, and it wasn't until we saw him standing in the doorway that we realized he was back.

"Women," he said, shaking his head. "Can't live with 'em, can't have sex without 'em."

"*You* can!" Duane said, leaping towards him with the fervor of a man who had just seen almost all of his dreams come true and wasn't going to miss his chance at one more.

"Duane!" I threw myself across the room to get in his way, but because my foot caught on the edge of a rug, tripping me, I ended up tackling him.

From the floor where I lay crumpled on top of Duane, I looked up at Buck, and warned him, "One of these days I'm not going to be around to stop him."

Buck shrugged. "Promises, promises."

I'm not sure how to describe the noise Duane made from underneath me.

Bliss passes quickly, so before I knew it, New Year's Eve was upon us. Sure, I'd returned many times to the conversation I'd overheard between Iris and Kimberly, but because at the center of their discussion had been J.J., and every time I thought of J.J., I was suddenly happy no matter what . . . Well, if that doesn't explain my lack of focus, I'm guessing you've never been in love.

J.J. had been back from the Berkshires for several days, and both of us being on winter break had made it both easier and more difficult to see each other. Easier in that he was spending a lot of time over at our house, but more difficult because we weren't able to use studying as an excuse to be alone over at his house.

Because their house was such a whirlwind of activity New Year's Eve day, J.J. was due to show up at our place by nine that morning to avoid as much of the chaos as he could, and although he and I had purposely not told anyone he would be over early so that we could have some time alone together, Kimberly unknowingly foiled our plan by waking up hours before her usual time. When, wrapped in her bathrobe, she came into the kitchen where I'd been preparing an elaborate breakfast in anticipation of J.J.'s arrival, I looked at the clock, trying to mask my annoyance.

"Shouldn't you get back to bed?" I suggested. "You're going to be up late tonight."

"I can't sleep. I'm too excited." She picked up a piece of bacon to nibble on as she looked over the fruit and pastries I'd bought earlier and the potatoes I was preparing to sauté. I also had French toast waiting to go, a plate of lox and bagels, and a quiche in the oven. (Yes, it's possible I'd overdone it. But I'd really, really been looking forward to spending some time alone with J.J.) "Do you eat like this every morning while we're asleep? How do you keep so trim?"

"Usually I'm lucky if I have time to make toast. But since I'm on break, I thought I'd do something special."

"You're always so good about taking care of us."

I looked up from the onions I was chopping, and while I could lie and blame them for the rapid blinking I suddenly found necessary, it was really the sincerity in her voice and in the way Kimberly was watching me. I shrugged. "It's nothing."

"It's not nothing," she said, pushing herself up from the counter she'd been leaning on and coming to stand beside me. "I mean, look at all of this stuff. I wouldn't know how to do any of it."

"Well, I bought some of it." Then added, "You certainly know how to do that."

She smiled, but with an obvious sadness underneath. "Yeah, that's about all Mom ever taught me."

I didn't quite know how I was supposed to react to that, so I busied myself with rinsing off the knife.

"Can I help?"

"You want to help me make breakfast?"

"Yeah. I could learn, right?"

"Of course you can learn. It's just cooking."

"So you'll teach me?"

I studied her face to see if she was serious, and to my surprise, she sure seemed to be. "You really want to learn?"

"I do. I mean, let's face it, you're going to get offered a lot of academic scholarships, and no one could blame you if you wanted to go somewhere far away from here for college, and then who is going to keep us from starving? Mom and Buck certainly aren't likely to be much help."

I don't know for which I was least prepared—that Kimberly was asking me to teach her how to take care of our family or that she had clearly been thinking about the future and that I factored into her thoughts. She took the knife out of my hand and asked, "So what do I do?"

I took the knife back. "Why don't we start you off with grating some cheese?"

"Okay," she agreed, but then a faint knocking at the front door drew her attention. "Who could that be?"

I shook my head, feigning ignorance. "I'd better go see."

"I'll do it. You've got enough going on." And before I could protest, she was on her way.

It wasn't more than a minute or two before she showed J.J. into the kitchen. "Look who is here all bright-eyed and bushy-tailed," Kimberly said.

"Hey," J.J. said.

"I hope you're hungry," I said.

His eyes swept over the array of food I'd prepared, then he turned to Kimberly. "Maybe you'd better go wake up Buck." Then seeing me pull the quiche out of oven, he added, "And your mother."

"Ooh, mimosas!" Kimberly said. "I'll be right back!"

As soon as she was out of the door, I said, "Best laid plans."

J.J. moved quickly to me and gave me a kiss. "I'd been hoping this morning might make up for midnight."

"What do you mean?" I asked, feeling my stomach start to knot.

"Well, you know everyone is going to be watching to see Kimberly and me kiss when the clock strikes twelve. I just don't see how I can avoid it."

I don't know if you've ever experienced this, but sometimes it can be a surprise to realize that inside everyone else's heads are as many ideas, and fears, and hopes and dreams as there are inside your own. Without my ever considering the possibility, Kimberly was wondering where I was going to go to college, and J.J. was trying to figure out a way for us to kiss at midnight to welcome in the New Year.

After giving it a moment's thought, I suggested, "Maybe we can pick somewhere to meet five minutes before and have our own little celebration?"

"My dad's library?"

"Seriously? You're going to kiss me in a room full of books and expect me to stop at one kiss?"

"Are books some sort of fetish for you?" he asked, with an eyebrow raised matched by the raised corner of his mouth fighting a playful smile.

"Is it a problem that I like my men smart?"

"Why would it be? I have a library card."

"Uh, your father also has his own library right there in your house."

"Ooh, yeah. Lucky me."

Just as the kitchen was about to turn into as much of an erogenous zone for me as a library, we heard Buck's feet stomping down the stairs.

"Damn," I said.

"Damn," J.J. said.

By three o'clock, J.J. headed home and the rest of us went upstairs for naps. At five o'clock on the dot, I opened our front door to find Duane wearing something so unexpected, I should have known right then and there that the night ahead was going to end up far differently than I ever would have imagined.

CHAPTER 15

11:55

"You're wearing a tux," I said.

"You're damn right I am," he said as he passed through the door, the garment bag with Iris's dress over his shoulder. "With your sister and mother both wearing my designs, I'm not letting anyone confuse the future of my business with a drag show."

"You're thinking like an MBA."

"I'll take anyone's money, honey."

"Chris!" Iris and Kimberly both called simultaneously from upstairs.

"Iris is really calling for you," I said. Then, with my eyes darting to the garment bag, I asked, "How'd the final alterations go?"

Confident in his work, Duane said with rare understatement, "I think she might be happy."

"*Chris!*" Iris said again, more urgently.

"You'd better get up there," I said.

"Should I take up a bottle of wine just to be safe?"

"I just opened a new one for her. You should be good for a while."

We both headed upstairs, separating once we reached the landing. As Duane went to present Iris with her finished gown, I went to see what Kimberly needed.

"Was that Duane?" she asked when I entered her bathroom.

"Yep."

"And?"

"He seems pretty confident Iris is going to be happy."

"I hope so," Kimberly said, rummaging through her makeup drawer. "She's going to give me a nervous break-down one of these days, I swear." She picked up a stick of black eyeliner and with a slightly trembling hand lifted it to her eye.

"I thought Duane wanted you to use blue to pick up the blue of the tulle?"

"Oh, right!" Kimberly said, flicking the stick back into the drawer with frustration. "I can't seem to do anything I'm supposed to. Maybe I should just let him do my makeup. He knows how he wants me to look."

"Want me to go get him?"

"Give him some time to calm down Mom. But maybe you can help me with my hair for now?"

"Really? You know I'm not really good with that sort of stuff."

She pulled over a vanity stool and sat down. "I just need you to hold it up while I put the combs in."

"All right," I said, with no attempt at hiding my doubts.

Soon enough, and with very little help from me, Kimberly had her hair swept up, secured and hair sprayed into within an inch of concrete. "Would you please go get Duane for me?

I don't want Mom to see me until it's too late for her to tell me what I've done wrong."

I nodded and headed down the hall to Iris's bedroom suite. The door was open, so I didn't have to knock, but when I reached the threshold, I stopped short. Standing in front of her full-length mirror, with a softness in her expression that I couldn't remember ever having seen, Iris admired the dream of a dress Duane had designed for her. Knowing they would be standing beside each other most of the night, he had created a dress that would not only complement Kimberly's, but one which, when seen together, would make them stand out as the two most admired women in the room. Using the same shade of blue that was hinted at in the tulle of Kimberly's dress, he had created a long-sleeved satin gown that could not have flattered Iris's more "sophisticated" form any more grandly, and then to play off both the white of the more youthful dress as well as the tulle layer that floated over it, Duane had designed a high-standing mini-shrug that acted as a subtly dramatic collar and also tied the two gowns flawlessly together.

"Wow," I said. "Iris, you look amazing."

"Thank you." She met my eyes, then turned hers to Duane. "But he deserves the credit."

Duane feigned modesty somewhat convincingly.

Returning to admire her appearance in the mirror, Iris said, "Your father used to love for me to dress up. Do you remember? He would buy us tickets to anything formal, just so we'd have the excuse."

It surprised me a little to hear Iris speak of my father. I'm not implying it was such an incredibly rare event, but it was usually tainted with pain and tiredness. This time it seemed a pleasant memory, almost a tribute.

"I do remember the two of you going out a lot," I said. Even as I said it, I realized that in my memory I'd always imagined they'd done it so much because it was what Iris had wanted, but then as I remembered the way he had always called her "my princess," it suddenly occurred to me how proud it must have made him to show her off. Even now she was still a beautiful woman, and for him I suppose she had always seemed like something from a fairy tale.

"Kimberly wants help with her makeup so that she doesn't mess anything up," I said to Duane.

"I *love* a client who is willing to listen!" Duane said as he rushed out of the door.

I hung back with Iris, hoping to hear what else she might say about my dad. After we'd both stood there for a while admiring her dress, almost without my realizing it, I found myself asking her, "Did you love him?"

Iris looked at my reflection in the mirror with surprise. "Your father?"

I nodded.

She lowered her eyes, smoothing down an imaginary wrinkle on the skirt of her gown. "I loved how happy I made him."

"But did you love him?"

"Why are you asking me this now?"

"Because I want to know."

She turned around to face me, picking up her glass of wine and taking a sip. "Your father was the best man I ever met. He treated me, and every person he came into contact with, with respect and kindness. And when we got married, I was certain that he was going to make me happier than anyone had ever managed to before."

"But did you love him?"

189

She met my eyes. "Honestly?"

"Yes. Please."

She began to straighten up the things on her vanity. "I think I would have grown to. I liked and esteemed him more than any man I've ever known. But love is a very slow thing for me, Chris. I don't know if you can understand that. And he was gone before . . . well, he was gone too soon."

"So why did you marry him?"

"Because he was a good man. And I thought we could make each other very happy. He did make me happy, and, I thought, I made him happy."

"And because he could pay for your children and fix up your house."

Iris moved back to stand in front of the mirror, and holding up panels of her dress, said, "Is it so awful to want nice things for your children?"

I don't know if it'll make sense to anyone else, but our conversation didn't make me angry. I didn't even need to ask if my father had known the truth about her feelings, because I knew he had been the kind of man who believed that what he wanted would come to him if he worked hard enough for it, even if that meant her love. I was also, oddly, feeling relief. I'd finally asked the one question I'd spent so many hours wondering about, and now I knew the answer. It wasn't the answer I would have preferred, but it was the truth. And my dad had always told me that the truth was the best place on which to stand.

"Do you hate me?" Iris asked.

"No," I said. "But I am going to leave you now and get ready for tonight." At least now I didn't have to feel quite as guilty if J.J. and I being in love might keep her from having another meal ticket.

As I walked down the hall towards the stairs, I passed by Buck's room, where he stood in front of the mirror, in boxers and a tux shirt, struggling with his bow tie. Seeing me, he said, "Why can't I have a clip-on tie?"

"I'll help you once I'm ready," I said.

"Duane's here, right? He can help me."

"Not until you put pants on," I said. Just to be safe, to keep Duane from walking down the hall between Iris's and Kimberly's room and seeing anything he'd no doubt spent many hours imagining, I closed the door firmly.

From the moment we all entered the party, as I'd expected, Kimberly and Iris were the most looked-at women in the room, and Duane handed out more business cards than a candidate for senior-class president hands out flyers. J.J. and his parents went to great lengths to keep introducing them to everyone with whom they spoke, and although I didn't really intend to, I found myself hanging back as much as possible, which gave me the view of an observer more than of a participant. Old habits die hard. It was with a mixture of pride and regret that I was really able to take in the picture of all-American perfection that J.J. and Kimberly presented beside each other. They were both so beautiful individually, that when paired together it almost seemed like a golden aura emanated from them in a self-produced spotlight, and everyone unconsciously rotated around their sun.

But then an unexpected flash of anger coursed through me. Why wasn't that me beside J.J. being introduced to the *crème de la crème*, with everyone offering praise, and admiration, and wishes for a glorious future? In fact, if it were me, wouldn't a lot of those covetous looks turn to hate, and judgement, and disgust? It wasn't fair, and it wasn't right. Love is supposed to be the truest and most esteemed emotion in the world, but many of these people would only be willing to admire it on their own terms, under their own rules. Rules which J.J. and I, and even Kimberly for that matter, had had no part in creating.

"Dude, your boyfriend seems to be the hit of the party," Buck said, leaning in and putting a hand on my shoulder.

WHAT?! Buck had caught on to J.J.'s and my secret?!

But luckily I managed to keep myself from screaming out in horror, because then I realized he was looking at Duane. "Buck, do you really think I'd keep dating someone who keeps throwing himself at you?"

Buck shrugged, then waved his hands over himself as if he were a prize on a gameshow. "You might as well accept that it's going to happen with just about anyone you bring home. The gays love me."

"But not as much as you love yourself," I said.

"Maybe we'll call it a draw," Buck said with a "modest" wink.

I rolled my eyes, but even as I did it, I felt grateful that he'd distracted me from my internal rant. To keep myself diverted, I played Buck's wingman for a while as he caroused and flirted with just about every woman in the place under fifty. And as much as it pained me to acknowledge, I had to admire his skills.

I kept checking my watch, not wanting to miss my agreed upon pre-midnight kiss with J.J., and had even gone so far as to have timed the number of minutes (or even seconds) it took me to get through the crowd to the library from just about every point in the house to which we party guests had access. By 11:45 I decided that I was going to sneak two glasses of champagne from the bar under the Millais painting I'd admired, which was between one minute and thirty-seven seconds and two minutes and fifteen seconds, depending on foot traffic, from the library threshold. I wasn't entirely sure if I was supposed to meet J.J. there or inside, but the idea of entering on my own seemed a little presumptuous. Besides, with two glasses in my hands, I might risk spilling the champagne if I tried to open the door myself, so waiting for J.J. was probably best all around.

But then, just as I began lurking near the bar, trying to figure out if the bartender was carding anyone, I felt a hand lightly touch the small of my back and turned around to find Jonas Kennerly, J.J.'s father, smiling politely at me. Busted.

Hoping I might still be able to play off my bar proximity as accidental, I stammered through what I hoped was convincing confusion. "Uh, hello, sir. I, er . . . I was just . . . uh, wondering if, uh, you know . . . the, uh, wait staff needed any help with midnight dispersal. Not for myself, of course, but . . . um. . . ."

"We have enough help, Chris, thank you, but very kind of you to offer. I was wondering if I could speak to you for a minute alone."

"Who? Me? Alone?"

"Yes, you, alone."

"Now?"

"Unless you have something else you need to attend to."

"Uh, well, sir—"

"Please, call me Jonas."

"I can't do that. I mean, I could, I'm not saying no to you, per se, but—"

"Okay, just anything but sir. I realize I'm ancient by your standards, but 'sir' makes me feel like I need to tip, and I do enough of that without having to worry about J.J.'s friends."

"Yes, sir—I mean, uh, yes."

"So can we talk?"

"Oh, right, of course. What did you want to talk about?"

He looked at all of the people in close proximity and made a "follow me" gesture with his head. "Let's go talk in the library?"

NO, NOT THE LIBRARY! That, of course, was only in my head. Out loud I said, "Of course, sir. Not sir. I didn't mean that."

He laughed, then led the way through his guests, telling people who tried to engage him in conversation that he'd be right back. I didn't check my watch, but I'd guess that these slight interruptions added a good thirty seconds to our walk to the library, so we were probably inside with the door closed by 11:50. Which meant I had five minutes until J.J. was supposed to arrive for our New Year's Eve kiss. Because my mind was so full of these considerations, I realized that Mr. Kennerly's mouth was moving, and I wasn't listening to him.

He was in the middle of a sentence as I tuned in. ". . . and with you at the other end of the table, I didn't get to hear your views."

"The table?"

"Yes, Thanksgiving dinner. I really did mean to talk to you more that day, but there was a lot of family to deal with."

"I can relate," I said. "Pardon the pun."

Mr. Kennerly chuckled, nodding his head. "J.J. said you were quick."

"He did?"

"Yes, he speaks very highly of you, and he's been exceedingly impressed with your integrity and intellect."

"He has?" I cleared my throat. "That's very kind of him. But we both know he's really the one everyone looks up to."

Mr. Kennerly cocked his head, one side of his mouth raising in an appreciative smile. "See, it's answers like that which make me think he's right about you." He put a hand on my shoulder, and looked me directly in the eyes with a suddenly very serious expression. "Obviously, he has several years of schooling and seasoning left, but it's no secret that if he chooses to pursue public service as a career, the sky could be the limit for J.J."

I knew he was talking about political offices, and since J.J. had been talked about as a potential president of the United States from birth, he probably really meant that. But what did any of this have to do with me? Since I wasn't quite sure what he wanted me to say, I simply nodded.

"I realize the two of you haven't known each other that long, Chris, but when you grow up in a family like ours, it can be very hard to meet people you really trust. And J.J. trusts you. Now I know that your own interests may lie in another direction all together, so if politics isn't for you, that's totally understandable. Clearly I wasn't really meant to excel in it." He dropped his head, perhaps flashing back on the dark period of his life when he had been close to getting his party's nomination, but then broke into tears during a press conference, and almost overnight his political career was over. He shook it off. "But J.J. is a better man than I am, and he needs to surround himself with other good men. What I'm saying is that if you ever have any interest in being a part of that team, I want you to feel free to come talk to me."

I don't know if you've ever had one of those moments when what is being said to you seems so out of someone else's life that you wonder if you're actually asleep. But I was having one of those. I was an eighteen-year-old high school student, and unless I was just being stupid, this guy was asking me if I had any interest in someday being part of a future presidential campaign or something. Clearly someone had slipped hallucinogenic drugs into the crudités' dip. I just wasn't sure which of us had eaten too much of it.

"You look a little overwhelmed," Mr. Kennerly said. "Sorry, I didn't mean to spring too much on you, but I've never known J.J. to have so much praise for anyone, and I trust his instincts. I thought I'd plant the seed. But it's just between the two of us. J.J. doesn't know I'm doing this."

"I'm beyond flattered, believe me. But, Mr. Kennerly, I just don't quite understand what you would want me to do."

"Chris, I'm not asking you to do anything. I promise. I'm just letting you know that if you ever find yourself interested in politics, you come highly recommended, and I think we could help each other. And even if you have no interest in it—and who could blame you, it's a very frustrating business—we always need smart people we trust to give us honest feedback. Even if you decided to become, I don't know, a potato farmer, you could still help J.J. out by giving us a politically unbiased view into the gay community, what the chattering classes are really saying . . . you know, the things people won't tell someone taking a poll."

Now I don't know if you caught that part about a "view into the gay community," but those were the last of his words that I really heard, because as soon as they were out of his mouth, I was fighting the urge to run for the hills. That meant that J.J.'s dad knew that I was gay, right? What else did he know? Did he know that J.J. was gay? Did he know

that his son and I were doing gay things *together*? Or was—
oh, shit, he'd just asked me a question, hadn't he?

"I'm sorry," I said. "Could you repeat the question?"

"That wasn't a question, Chris, it was an offer."

Not helping me figure out what I missed, Mr. Kennerly.

"Dad?" Although he didn't know he'd be helping save
me from admitting to his father that I hadn't been listening,
J.J. looked equally confused as Mr. Kennerly and I turned to
see him standing in the doorway to the library. "And Chris,"
J.J. added, sounding almost as mystified as I felt.

"J.J.!" Mr. Kennerly said. "Chris and I were just having
a little talk."

"You were?" J.J. said, his eyes going back and forth
between his dad and me. Each time his eyes landed on me,
I tried to let him know with my expression that I had had
nothing to do with this.

"You're right about this one," Mr. Kennerly said, patting
my back again.

"It's 11:55," J.J. said, looking at me.

As overloaded as my brain was from what had just been
thrown at me in the last few moments, I knew with complete
sadness that what he meant was our chances of sharing our
New Year's kiss had been ruined.

"Well, then I guess we'd better get in there, hadn't we?"
Mr. Kennerly said. "Your mother will kill me if I'm not by
her side at the stroke of midnight."

"Yeah, that's why I came looking for you," J.J. answered,
meeting my eyes briefly while shrugging apologetically, as
Mr. Kennerly ushered us both out into the hallway.

We found everyone in the main salon. Iris and Jennifer Kennerly were laughing like old friends, and I'd be hard pressed to say if Kimberly or Duane looked happier at the way their night was turning out. I, on the other hand, had a lot running through my mind. While in some ways it had been nice to have J.J.'s father acknowledge homosexuality in such a casual, non-event kind of way, I was also feeling a little violated that I'd been outed to him. I mean, obviously, J.J., Duane, and my family knew, but beyond that, it had still been my secret, and I wasn't sure how I felt about someone else telling it for me. Had J.J. done it as a way to see how his family would react? Was it his way of breaking the ice, getting them to like me, so that when he told them the truth about us, it wouldn't seem like such a horrible thing? I guess I could see the value in that, even though it would have been nice if he'd asked if it was okay with me. But if it got us what we needed in the end, he knew how to deal with his parents better than I did, and I trusted J.J. to look out for my best interest. So maybe it was for the best. And now that I knew the truth about Iris's feelings for my dad, and I didn't have to feel so bad if things didn't go as she'd planned for Kimberly and J.J., and maybe if we made sure the media kept paying attention to Kimberly, she wouldn't really mind that we kind of used her, and she had, after all, turned out to be surprisingly sympathetic and supportive of my being gay, and she certainly accepted Duane, who was the most flamboyant person I'd ever met, and, well, maybe this wasn't going to be such a bad New Year's Eve after all. Things were certainly looking up for the year ahead!

And no sooner had that thought flown through my head, than Buck put his arm around my shoulder and said, "I'll kill you if you ever tell anyone I said this, but that's really sweet. They look so in love."

As the clock stuck twelve, I looked up to see Kimberly lift her face to J.J.'s for their New Year kiss, and at that very moment I realized our house of cards was due to crumble. Because the look in her eyes was one that I had somehow managed not to ever notice before. She was totally, one hundred percent, and irrevocably in love with him. Just like me. And it was all my fault.

Happy New Year.

Chapter 16

Alice in Wonderland

"We have to tell her!" I shouted at J.J., whom I'd dragged into a guest bathroom as soon as I was able to get him away from all of the congratulations and best wishes of the deceived and unknowing family and friends.

"Tell who? Tell what? Why are you yelling?"

As I opened my mouth to vent my dismay, he suddenly lifted a hand to cover it. "Wait." He then leaned in, smiling softly and looking at me with the purest adoration imaginable, and said, "Kiss me. It's a new year."

I realize a person better, or at least stronger, than myself would have resisted the offer of a kiss to first explain our crimes against humanity, or at least against Kimberly, but when faced with J.J.'s mouth and dark brown eyes, I melted just long enough to meet his lips. But, really, I swear, I kept it short, because I knew what I needed to say was too important to think only of myself, and I pulled away with

J.J. craning his neck to chase my lips with expectations of continuing.

"Kimberly."

'What about her?"

"We have to tell Kimberly."

"About what?

"About us."

"What are you talking about? You know we can't do that."

"We have to."

"Why?

"Because she's in love with you."

He paused, doubt briefly fighting to make an appearance, but getting pushed away. "No, she's not."

"She is."

"She's in love with all of this," he gestured to the nice bathroom fixtures, but I knew that he meant the whole mansion, and the Kennerly lifestyle and fame that went with it.

"Well, if that's true, and that's all she cares about, then telling her the truth won't keep her from having what really matters to her, will it?"

J.J. sighed, slumping back against the wall and sliding down it into a squat. "Chris, we've been through this."

"And it still hasn't gone away. In fact, it's just gotten worse. Oh, and thanks for outing me to your dad, by the way."

"What?"

"Your dad knows I'm gay. That's part of what he was talking to me about in the library."

"I'm not the one who told my parents. That was Kimberly."

"Kimberly?"

"Yeah, and to be honest, I think she's sort of proud of it in a weird way. It's like she thinks it trendy to have a gay relative or something. And she thinks you and Duane are adorable together."

I rolled my eyes. "I keep telling her we're not a couple."

"She thinks you're just afraid of your feelings."

"Well, see, all the more reason we should tell her. She likes the gays. She'll understand. And besides, your parents are, like, the most famous liberals in the world. It's not like they're going to disown you or anything."

J.J. dropped his head and dug the heels of his hands into his eyes, rubbing them. "It's all so easy to figure out from the outside."

It didn't make me happy to know that I was making him miserable, so I lowered myself down to the marble floor next to him and put a hand on his leg. "J.J., if anyone understands how hard it is to come out to your family, it's me. Really, I suspect it's just about any gay person."

He took my hand and moved it to his heart. "If only it were that easy. If I ever come out, it's not going to be my family I have to worry about. At least, I think they'll deal with it . . . eventually. It's the rest of the world."

Having spent the last few months on the periphery of the media feeding frenzy that was his life, I had some idea of what he meant. And when I amplified the troubles I had had coming out in my own little world—and to be honest, I'd only just started, and I'd only told a few people—I began to understand what he was facing. But a part of my own little world was Kimberly, and what we were doing to her wasn't right. I pulled my hand away from J.J. as I said, "I can't keep doing this to Kimberly. It's just not fair."

"And having to deal with any of this just because we were born a certain way is?" he said.

Since there was obviously no good argument for the ugly truth of what he'd said, I kept my mouth shut, but the way I looked into his eyes did not change.

"She could react very badly," J.J. said.

"Well, we have been lying to her," I said.

"Chris, I just can't do it. I can't risk it."

Throughout our entire conversation, a part of me had been allowing myself to believe that if I were patient and relied more on logic than emotion, maybe I'd be able to make him understand that we didn't really have a choice anymore. But then, finally, it hit me like a blow to the gut that in fact we did have a choice. However, the only choice I could continue to live with was at odds with the only one with which J.J. felt he could live. "Well," I said, beginning to stand, "I can't keep lying to her. If someone's heart has to get broken, it's better if it's sooner rather than later. Even if that means it's mine."

Looking utterly dismayed, J.J. pushed himself up from the floor. "What are you saying?" he asked, fear beginning to fill his confused eyes.

"I'm sorry, loving you has been more amazing than anything I've ever known. But you have to decide." Suddenly, as if the enormity of what I was saying overwhelmed me, and not being able to stand another second in that confining space, three feet away from the only man I might ever love and having to see the look on his face as I told him he had to choose between loving me or continuing to live a lie, I couldn't take it anymore. I burst out through the door, leaving him behind.

As I moved through the crowd as quickly as I could, keeping my eyes focused on the front door through which I was determined to escape, desperately afraid that I would lose control of my emotions and sob in front of all these strangers, I had the slight good fortune of seeing Duane close by and mumbled into his ear that I was feeling sick and heading home. I had no idea what, if anything, he said in response, because all I cared about was getting away.

I got the first text of my life from J.J. at 4:12 a.m. that morning. Clearly neither of us was getting much sleep. It read: "Meet me at Alice in Wonderland at 8 a.m.?" I didn't know exactly what it meant that he was actually risking a hacker intercepting the message by sending me a text. Did it mean he was ready to live the truth? Or that he was so distraught with grief that insanity had caused him to forget the danger? Or was it simply that if I were now to only be the brother of his girlfriend, what we texted to each other didn't matter?

Guessing that in less than four hours I would find out, I texted back, "See you there."

As I walked through Central Park in the early-ish morning of the first day of the New Year, it was as empty as I'd ever seen it. There were workmen still cleaning up from the midnight run, and some joggers who had presumably not been a part of the night's festivities, and a few women pushing babies in strollers, but that was about it. So, even from a distance, as I approached the Alice in Wonderland statue, I was pretty sure that the figure leaning against the largest mushroom was J.J. We were both early. The air held a brisk tanginess, and the sun shone through a light cloud cover, but we both kept our hands buried in our pockets as I approached. I chose one of the lower mushrooms and sat down.

After we both sat in silence for at least a minute, J.J. finally spoke first. "Do you wish you were straight?"

I shrugged. "Who wouldn't want their life to be easier?"

"But no one's life is easy. *Life* is not easy."

"I didn't say easy, I said easier. Besides, are you suddenly advocating that all of this is the most perfect way things could ever be?"

"Hardly."

"But I'm not complaining," I said. "Or suggesting we drew the short end of the stick, or whatever. I'm not saying it wouldn't simplify a lot of things for both of us, for anyone really, but they say we learn from struggle, so something good must come out of it, right?"

"Like what?"

"I don't know. I mean, I know my experience is limited, but gay guys do seem to be more fun."

"A million fag hags can't be wrong?"

"I didn't think that word was okay anymore?"

"I think it's like using the 'n' word if you're black." He looked around to make sure no one was close before he whispered, "Fag."

"Faggot," I whispered back.

Finally, we shared our first smile of the day.

"What else do you think is good about being gay?" J.J. asked.

I thought about it for a second. "It seems like gay people are more compassionate and less judgmental. I mean, about big stuff. About clothes, and hair styles, and stuff like that, it seems pretty vicious."

"Duane *can* be a bit bitchy, can't he?"

"You should hear him when he's with the other drag queens. They could probably make war veterans cry."

"Maybe that's why it took so long for the military to allow gays in," J.J. said.

I started laughing. "I suddenly have this picture of Coco Chanel Jones in Iraq telling some woman, 'Oh, hell no, honey, those shoes are all wrong with that burka! You need to tell your man how things are gonna be, 'cause you control the punani, hear?'"

J.J. joined in my laughter, then said, "If only Coco ruled the world."

"Don't let her hear you say that. I don't want you putting any ideas into her head."

"Good point." Then, while not turning serious, he did take on a genuine sincerity. "Why do some guys like to dress up like women? I don't get it."

"You're asking the wrong person. I don't get it either."

"I mean, more power to you if you figure out what really makes you happy, but it seems like so much *work*."

"And expensive."

"And you know what tucking is, right?"

"Yeah, Duane explained it to me. Or was he Coco at the time? I forget. Anyway, no thank you on the tucking for me."

"You know what I really hate?" J.J. asked.

"What?"

"Gay pride. I mean, not the concept, or even the parade, or whatever, and I don't want to sound like I don't appreciate the historical importance of it, and that it's probably more about proving to the world that you're not ashamed, or whatever. But I was brought up to question feelings of pride, to ask yourself if they're deserved, and only if you've worked really hard for something do you then deserve to feel proud. But saying I'm proud to be gay is like saying I'm proud to have brown hair. It's just how I am, how I was born, and I did nothing to earn it, so why should I feel proud of it?"

I took my hands out of the pockets of the winter coat that J.J. had given me as a secret gift and rubbed them together as I considered his words. I completely understood what he meant, and yet I also didn't want to devalue the concept that pride could be a positive thing. "Maybe it's people being proud about accepting who they were born to be and not trying to hide or deny it anymore?"

After a moment's pause to consider, J.J. nodded his head. "I like that."

Feeling encouraged, I dipped a toe into the question that had kept me awake most of the night. "Does that mean you might be ready to show some of that to a person other than me?"

As if the world's largest cloud had just sailed over him, all evidence of our light conversation disappeared from his face and body. He sighed heavily. "Today's a holiday. All over the world. Can't we just pretend for this one day that life is like we want it to be? That no one else matters except the two of us? Just for one day?"

Having spent the last eight hours with a hint of the misery that I knew I was going to feel if J.J. wasn't ready to tell Kimberly the truth, I, not even that reluctantly, nodded my head in agreement.

Even though I had to sometimes push down worries about what the future might hold once our Day of Denial ended, what followed was one of the best and happiest days of my life. It wasn't as if we did anything special, really, it was just a day spent sharing the simple pleasures with the man I loved.

We walked through the park, we had breakfast at a diner, we watched people skate at Rockefeller Center (although, honestly, the most fun part of that was watching the ones who fell), we had a light lunch before catching a Broadway musical matinee, we went shopping at Macy's. That was it. And it was bliss. Granted, since J.J. and I rarely had the chance to spend time alone together, especially in public, it also felt wonderfully exotic, but it was still the daily furniture of domestication, and it could not have been better. Obviously since J.J. had been watched his entire life, even with his ball cap pulled low to ensure as little recognition from people as possible, it wasn't as if we could hold hands, or show any signs of affection, but we kept our eyes out for paparazzi, and it all seemed to go exceptionally well. Or so we thought. But the downside of modern technology is that it can be so unobtrusive, even people who think they are paying attention can be lulled into a false sense of security.

I'm talking, of course, about what happened at Macy's that day. Although the reality of it was so different than how it got portrayed in the gossip pages.

Earlier, right after we'd decided to spend the day together in denial, J.J. and I separately sent texts to excuse our absences. He texted Kimberly saying that he had unexpectedly been asked to play tour guide to a family friend in town for the previous night's party, but that he would be over later to take her out to dinner. Meanwhile, I texted Iris that I was out with a friend, but that I would be home in time to prepare dinner for the family as usual. Within a few hours, when each woke up at her own leisure, we received okay messages in response. (Well, mine said, "ok," from Iris. I think J.J.'s response from Kimberly was longer, and no doubt guilt-inducing, because he kept it far from my eyes. This would have been one of those moments when I had to push away my doubts and just bluster along in my happiness.)

Anyway, so after the musical, J.J. said he should probably pick up a little gift for Kimberly for when he arrived at the house later, and, again choosing to ignore my lurking feelings of doubt and guilt, I agreed.

As we walked through the various departments of the large store, we joked, admired, disapproved—all the usual things while leisurely shopping with a friend—but since we were secretly more than just friends, and indulging in the fantasy of a day spent only focused on each other, and since any couple in love will tend to imagine what their future might be like together . . . well, we got a little whimsical. The idea, actually, did not come from us, though. It was that damned couple, her with an almost tyrannical need to control every single item that went on their gift registry, and him with his passive-aggressive desire to hold out for the one thing he was going to dig in and defend his right to veto. I'm talking, of course, about china patterns.

As we strolled through the housewares department, veering away from the bickering couple's combat zone, I said to J.J., "I wonder if that would be us."

He stopped, eyed the couple and then the display of china patterns, and said, "Well, there's one way to find out. Pick your favorite, don't tell me, and I'll do the same."

"Really?"

"Why not?"

I know it's stupid, but the idea of playing this game made me almost deliriously happy. As we went our separate ways, wending through the multitude of choices for every taste, I couldn't keep a ridiculous grin off my face, whether I was looking at Wedgwood or Lennox, or stealing a giddy glance at J.J.

After several minutes of careful consideration, he said, "Okay, I've picked mine."

"Me, too."

"We'll each point to our favorite at the same time?"

"Count of three?"

"Deal. Should we cover our eyes?"

We did so, although I was wishing my hand was over my ears instead as I heard the unhappily betrothed continue their debate. ("No, my mother hates that color." "Well, then your mother doesn't have to eat.")

"One . . . two . . .three," J.J. said.

When I lowered my hand to uncover my eyes, he and I were pointing at the same china set, one with a white face, navy blue lip, and a single ring of gold.

"That's not a bad sign," I said.

"That's a very good sign, I'd say."

In the next half-hour, we decorated our imaginary home, agreeing easily on the silver, the crystal, linens, wedding invitations, and a double-wide chair with an ottoman. The couch required some negotiating.

Here's where the downside of modern technology comes into play. While we were keeping our eyes out for paparazzi, we weren't really thinking about the fact that pretty much everyone with an iPhone or cell phone has a camera, so there are more Big Brothers watching than George Orwell ever could have imagined.

And while I'd thought lying in bed after J.J. and I had our first fight seemed about as bad as things in my life could get, there was evidently more for me to learn. Because you know how they say it's always darkest before the dawn? Well, that's bullshit. Sometimes it just keeps getting darker.

CHAPTER 17

YOKO ONO

"What did you do this time?" Buck asked Kimberly as he peeked between the drawn curtains, investigating the source of the not-so-hushed murmur outside our house.

Looking panicked, Kimberly shouted, "Nothing!" to Iris, who practically leapt out of her chair to see about what Buck was talking.

"Damn it, Kimberly!" Iris said. Then, after pushing Buck out of the way and looking out for only a split second, she spun around. "What did you do?!"

"Nothing!" Kimberly jumped up, waving her arms for everyone to get out of her way, then pushed her eye to the break in the curtains. And gasped. (See, I'm not the only one.) As she spun around to face us, I could see her reviewing the previous night's events in her head. "I swear. J.J. picked me up, we went to dinner, he gave me a bottle of perfume, I smiled, I nodded, I waved, I did nothing that anyone could take offense to. I swear, Mom!"

As the only member of the family who had not seen whatever it was outside the window that was creating all of this commotion, I slipped over to take a look.

Holy shit. It was by far the largest congregation of people that had ever been there, blocking the street (which explained the cabs honking—more than usual, I mean), and basically creating an absolute logjam outside and a sickening feeling of dread inside. Why, this of all days, had I slept in, and hearing the others stirring, rushed downstairs to make breakfast without first checking my phone for warning texts from Duane?

As I turned around, it was as if we all got the idea at the same time. Our eyes simultaneously went to where Buck's laptop lay under the coffee table. But before any of us could make a single move towards it, we were startled by a loud pounding on the front door. *KNOCK-KNOCK-KNOCK*!

Everyone froze.

And then everyone else's eyes moved to me. "You get it," Iris said, her tone filled with more pleading than authority. I nodded. I tried to take deep breaths to calm myself as I walked determinedly to the front door. Was it J.J.? A reporter who was ignoring the protocol of waiting for someone to exit? An assassin who would blessedly put me out of my misery?

No, it was Duane. "I sure as hell hope I'm designing the dress," he said as he pushed his way into the house, the mass of reporters surging up behind him. Just before slamming the door on them, he stuck out a hand with his middle finger raised, yelling, "Ya'll stepped on my clean shoes!"

Once safely inside with the door closed, he brushed off his clothes, more for dramatic effect than necessity, and raised an eyebrow as he looked at me with a dubious expression. "Well, aren't you quite the secret keeper?"

"What are you talking about?" I asked, my eyes darting towards the door to the living room, hopefully communicating to him that curious ears were not far away.

"Don't play dumb with me," Duane said. "It ain't cute." As he said it, he pulled out from his armpit a copy of the *New York Times*, unfolding it to show me the front page. "WHEN WILL HE PROPOSE?!" was the caption beneath a photo of J.J. and me underneath the Bridal Registry sign in Macy's.

Maybe it was just the shock making me thickheaded, but at that moment all I felt was panic that J.J. and I had been photographed together without our knowing it, and someone had figured out that we were a couple, and now the entire world knew, and—

"I think I'm going to throw up," I said, turning and running for the downstairs bathroom. Even in my rush for the toilet bowl, I had the presence of mind to lock the door behind me, I guess my subconscious will to live knowing that once Kimberly and Iris found out the truth, a locked door would lengthen, by at least a few more seconds, my life.

I leaned over the toilet, trying to catch my breath, waiting for the nausea in my stomach to do whatever it was going to do, even though I, luckily, had not had time to finish making, let alone eat breakfast before the buzz from outside drew our attention. My entire body burned flush and I broke out in a sweat as I finally fully realized exactly to what my actions had led. Every minute of loving J.J. had felt like a fantasy, and now reality had come to collect.

That's when I heard Kimberly and Iris begin to scream. Which is also when the burning I'd been feeling over my entire body instantly turned to ice. I can't quite explain it, but almost without thinking, I reached out and turned the doorknob, determined to face them on my own terms, not to have them find me cowering in the corner of a hallway bathroom. It was like ripping a Band-Aid off; I just wanted to get the unavoidable over with. Each step through the hallway felt like walking through quicksand, but somehow that made me try to make it happen faster, so before I'd even thought of a single thing to say by way of explanation, I was standing in the doorway to the living room, and Kimberly and Iris were looking up from the newspaper and directly at me.

"How could you not tell us?" they screamed in unison.

But here's the weird part. They were smiling.

Huh? Then I realized I hadn't said it out loud.

"Huh?"

"I can't believe this!" Kimberly said, jumping up and down, and then bouncing over to me and throwing her arms around me. "I'm so, so, so, so HAPPY!"

Suddenly Iris was feigning a swoon onto the couch, Buck getting out of her way just in time. "Oh my god, what a relief," Iris said.

"You tricky little bastard," Buck said.

All I could think was that this wasn't really happening.

But it really was.

Just not in the way I thought.

Because that's when Duane crossed his arms and said, "So when is he going to propose to her?"

"Who?" I asked, my mind obviously overwhelmed and not processing at top speed.

"Very funny," Duane said. "If they time it right, the wedding dress could be my final project next semester."

Kimberly let out another high-pitched scream as she looked down once more at the front-page photograph in her hands.

This time when a *KNOCK-KNOCK-KNOCK* came from the front door, I was the only one left in the living room, because everyone else ran out to see who it was.

Almost numb with shock and confusion, I sat heavily on the edge of the couch as I rubbed my temples. I heard a whispered argument between the others still at the front door, quickly followed by Iris, Buck, and Duane rushing on tip toe back into the living room, throwing themselves into seated positions, Iris in her chair, Buck on the couch, and Duane also on the couch between Buck and me. All three attempted attitudes of casual lethargy, as if they hadn't stood up in hours. For Duane, this included casually draping his hand over Buck's thigh. I reached over and slapped it away.

"Bitch," Duane said.

Then we all listened. The door opened. The roar of noise from outside swelled, then quickly mellowed as the door shut. "Hi, J.J." Kimberly said.

"Good morning," J.J. responded. "Sorry about all that," he added, meaning, we all knew, the circus in front of the house.

"It's okay," Kimberly said.

"Where is everybody?"

"In there." And then they both appeared in the doorway. J.J. looked almost as nonplussed as I felt (and no doubt looked).

His eyes momentarily went to me before he smiled at Iris. "Good morning."

"So lovely to see you, J.J." she said. "How's your mother?"

"She's . . . fine. She sends her regards."

"Have you seen the paper?" Buck said, thrusting it at J.J. with his usual aplomb.

"Buck!" Kimberly and Iris said.

"Jeez, you two, like he hasn't seen it," Buck said. "I say let no elephant in the room be ignored."

J.J. gestured for Buck to keep the paper. "Yes, in fact, I did see it." He turned to Kimberly, "I'd asked Chris to help me pick out that gift I gave you last night, and evidently we walked by the Bridal Registry sign. It's crazy what the media will make up, isn't it?"

Her cheek twitched slightly as she struggled to hide her disappointment.

Iris, however, was not as successful. A low sort of moan briefly escaped her throat, before she covered it by pretending to be racked by a coughing fit.

"I'll run get some water," I said, jumping from my place on the couch and heading for the door. Even before I'd left the room, Kimberly slumped into the place on the sofa I'd just evacuated.

I looked behind me several times as I headed down the hallway to the kitchen, hoping that somehow J.J. would make some excuse to follow me, as he had done in the past, but to no avail. Even taking as much time in the kitchen as I could reasonably manage didn't help. Reentering the living room, I could see that everyone was pretending to feel differently than they did. As J.J. pretended his spring term classes were all he wanted to talk about, and Iris, Kimberly, and Duane pretended they were interested and not extremely disappointed that there did not appear to be a wedding on the horizon, and Buck pretended he wasn't wondering what was playing on ESPN at the moment, I pretended that I wasn't the textbook definition of miserable.

As confused as I was by everything that was transpiring, one thing was becoming very clear: I couldn't take much more of this. Something was going to have to change.

It was over a week before I could talk to J.J. alone. Part of me felt like he was purposefully making sure that there was always someone around specifically so that we couldn't talk, but it's possible that I was being paranoid. I was in a rather emotional state after all.

And there seemed to be no escaping it. Whereas the atmosphere at home had been so much better ever since Kimberly had met J.J. at the Autumnal Ball, ever since the gossip had started about a possible proposal, now that it was out there, there was the smell of possible failure thick in the air.

Things weren't much better at school. Some of that was simply my own distraction and worry, but my classmates weren't much help if school was where I was hoping to forget what was going on in the rest of my world. Besides the constant looks and inquiries about my sister and J.J., even Vibol wouldn't let me escape. The first thing he'd said to me upon our return from winter break was, "If what the papers said was true, I want a Kennerly letter of recommendation for medical school."

"You haven't even received your acceptance letters for undergrad."

"But those applications are finished. I'm just thinking ahead. You always say I'm the most prepared person you know."

"I think obsessive is the word I used."

He shrugged. "I'd do it for you."

There he had me, because for all of the competition between us, Vibol always wanted an even playing field.

"Honestly, I don't know anything more than you do. But should it happen, I'll see what I can do."

He held up a fist for a bump, which I hesitantly gave him.

The worst of it, of course, was my inability to turn on a TV or go onto the internet without seeing constant speculation as to when J.J. would propose. That one silly, inaccurate picture had taken on a life of its own, and one evening I stared unbelievingly at the surrealistic argument on a news program—a NEWS program, not even an entertainment or gossip one—where one talking head spouted statistics on divorces for people who married too young, the next one applauded J.J. and Kimberly's clear endorsement of traditional family values by avoiding temptation out of wedlock (how that person knew they hadn't already had sex, I'd definitely like to know), and a third one criticized J.J. for clearly pandering to the radical right in an attempt to begin building a centrist reputation for his future political campaigns.

To say that I wasn't sleeping well during all of this would be putting it mildly. Most nights I'd fall asleep at a decent hour, exhausted by the thick tension in my head, but by four or four thirty in the morning I'd wake up from a dead sleep on the verge of a panic attack. It was like that feeling when you realize you almost got knocked off the platform and into an oncoming train. Or like the feeling when you see a picture of you and your sister's boyfriend on the cover of the *New York Times*, and you think the world has discovered that you're lovers. But at four in the morning. And waking from a dead sleep.

While I could definitely say tiredness may have affected my mood when I finally managed to get some time alone with J.J., I can't really blame lack of sleep for how our conversation ended. The weight of our secret had been building up. For a while, the absolute joy of having met a guy who made me realize that I wasn't a freak, a deviant, an abomination, that I was as worthy of love as any other human being on the planet, had been enough to make me ignore my doubts and the inexcusableness of how we were misleading Kimberly and everyone else. The first time I kissed J.J., the first time we held each other, the first time we made love, each time was a confirmation that reverberated like a gong echoing through a never-ending cave that, for me, this was the only thing that was natural. Anything else would be a lie, an obscenity, a sin, despite what anyone of a different orientation tried to make me, or anyone else, believe. They were wrong. For me and millions of people like me, this was *right*.

Standing in front of the man who had made me feel okay about who I was, possibly for the first time in my life, certainly since beginning to realize that I was gay, and having to explain to him how being happy with him was making me miserable was easily the hardest thing I'd ever had to do in my life.

"But what does that mean?" J.J. asked.

Surrounded by the canned and dry goods in the kitchen pantry, where we'd hidden ourselves in our best attempt to make sure we weren't overheard, I shrugged. "It means that I can't keep doing this to Kimberly. I can't take the worrying about being caught by her or by some stupid person with a camera phone."

"That asshole."

"J.J., when I first saw that newspaper and thought that we had been discovered, I felt more fear and self-hate than I ever thought possible."

"Self-hate?"

"Because we've been lying to her, of course, but also . . . I don't know. There's something about hiding the way we feel that almost lets them win."

"Win? Who?"

"The people who would say we're wrong."

"But they're the people I probably wouldn't be able to influence if . . . I told the truth about myself. About us."

"That pisses me off, trust me, but it also pisses me off that I'm at least somewhat out, at least to my family, and yet I can't even let them know I'm in love."

J.J. smoothed down the loose label on a can of sweet peas. "I warned you about this from the start."

"I know, I know, you think you can do more for the cause of gay rights if they think you're straight. But, J.J., you're not. And I don't know how long you think you can keep that from tearing you up inside."

He looked at me with such pain that it was almost as if he were considering me the source of it. "You don't think this tears me up?"

"But then—"

"I don't know if someone who wasn't raised the way I was can understand this, but I was brought up to believe that with privilege comes responsibility, and sometimes that means sacrificing yourself in order to make other people's lives better."

"Yeah, I think it's called being a martyr."

"That's not fair."

I looked down at my hands. "Sorry. You're right. But how can you hope to do any good in the world if you're not at least a little bit happy?"

He leaned his back against the shelf, tilting his head up towards the light overhead, and I saw the bright glint of tears begin to sparkle in his eyes. "Do you really think most people in the world are happy? Do you think people who spend their lives trying to hurt other people, trying to tell other people they are bad, or evil, bound to go to hell, do you think those people are happy? No one who is happy makes it their life's work to make other people miserable."

"And you think the way to fight that is with your own misery?"

He sighed, long and deep, but almost silently. "What do you want me to do, Chris? You know that I love you. You have to know that. But you can't ask me to give up everything I've ever wanted my life to be just because of it. I realize this takes balls to say after how selfishly I've acted with your sister, but I just feel that putting myself before the good I know I can do would be more selfish than I can live with."

"But you can live with this?"

"Is it that awful?"

I nodded. "For me, it has gotten that bad."

He looked at me long and hard before swallowing, and in a voice, barely above a whisper said, "Worse than being apart?"

Up until that point, I thought I'd done a pretty good job of controlling my emotions. And even though some part of me had known that one of the possible outcomes of my ultimatum was what he had just said, hearing the words come from the lips which I so loved kissing was a shock, and suddenly tears began to course down my cheeks. "Aren't all miseries basically the same?" I asked.

"Why do we have to decide this now?" J.J. asked. "Maybe with a little more time Kimberly will realize I'm not everything she hoped I would be, and she'll want to break things off."

If I hadn't been feeling so miserably, I think I might have laughed at that idea. I wasn't sure if it showed more of his cluelessness on the state of my family's finances or what effect he had on people, especially single women, but either way, I could only shake my head in dismissal of the idea.

"Besides," he said, slight hope being renewed by a new tactic, "do you realize what your life would be like if we did come out to the world?"

"Yeah, I'd be more hated than . . ." I grasped for the right example.

"Yoko Ono."

"Who?"

"Yoko Ono. The woman people blamed for breaking up the Beatles. But it really wasn't her fault. She's actually very nice."

"You know her?"

He shrugged. "She's friends with my parents."

"Well, I was going to say more hated than Hitler."

"Oh, much better," J.J. said, almost sounding lighter. "But do you see why maybe we should just let things rest for a little while longer?"

"But it's never going to change, J.J. And I can't keep living like this."

What little levity we'd managed to distract ourselves with disappeared. Fresh tears springing into his eyes, J.J. gently pulled me forward until our foreheads touched. Our eyes held fast, neither of us blinking, as if we each thought he could prove his misery was the greater in a contest no one could win.

"Chris, I can't do it. I can't let my entire life be controlled by this one small facet of who I am. There's too much good I can do."

"And I can't keep living a lie," I told him, my own tears falling anew.

"So what do we do?" he asked.

"I guess we say I love you," I said.

"I love you," he said before I could finish.

"And goodbye."

The look on J.J.'s face combined surprise, horror, pain, and probably many uglier emotions than I was able to comprehend as I found myself running out of the room and racing upstairs to throw myself onto my bed, where I would spend the rest of the night crying, contemplating everything awful in the world, and wondering how I would make it through to the next breath, let alone the next day.

Chapter 18

French Fries Dipped in Chili Cheese

I don't know exactly what I'd expected to happen after that, perhaps because I'd mostly succeeded in avoiding the thought that I wouldn't convince J.J. that I was right, but what I—stupidly—did *not* expect was for him to keep showing up almost daily for dates with Kimberly. Each time I saw him it felt like I'd just eaten an entire vat of E. coli, but we both, of course, had to act as if everything in our lives was just fine. I excused myself with the old standby of having homework to do, but my concentration was practically nonexistent. So much so that one of my favorite teachers actually pulled me aside after a class to ask if anything was wrong. I lied, and said that I was fine, but she'd known too many teenagers to fall for it. "Mm-hm," she murmured through pursed lips. Then, putting a hand on my back to shove me out the door, said, "If that changes, I hope you know you can talk to me."

I was late to my next class, because even the hint of sympathy had sent me rushing into the bathroom to hide my tears behind a gray metal stall door. I wasn't eating, I wasn't sleeping, I don't even know if I'd call what I was doing living, but somehow a week turned into a second, and almost without my realizing, the gray cloud of a foggy January turned into February. And we all know what February means . . . Valentine's Day.

On the morning of February 1st, the brightly colored, Xeroxed "Send your Valentine a candy-gram!" postings showed up plastered all over school, and almost as if the great media minds of the world were still in high school, by that afternoon all anyone on TV, the internet, or the blog/Twitter-sphere seemed to care about was whether or not J.J. Kennerly was going to propose to Kimberly Fontaine on Valentine's Day. And as if it had all been choreographed by the powers that be, the American Heart Association was having the Love Your Heart Ball that night. It was as if the entire world was determined to rub my face in it. Everyone in the world gets to be in love, Christopher Bellows, EXCEPT YOU!

Now, if you're wondering why I didn't run to Kimberly and tell her the truth, I will say that only a few times while I was curled up in a sobbing ball on my bed did I briefly consider it. But never seriously. Just in that oh-god-I'm-going-to-steal-all-of-Iris's-Xanax-and-never-have-to-wake-up-to-this-horrible-world-again way. You know, a flight of imaginary fancy just to cheer myself up a bit. Even in the depths of my misery, I knew that it would only be my own selfishness, not a sense of justice or doing what's right, that would motivate me. And I simply could never disrespect J.J. in that way. Besides, who would believe me? Even if I tried to prove it by telling Kimberly intimate details about

J.J., she wouldn't have her own knowledge to either confirm or deny them, so what good would it do? I would just end up looking crazed and pathetic. And while I might be both, more than anything, I still felt the sorriest for J.J. What must it be like to go through every day of your life feeling the burden of that much responsibility on your shoulders? He was trying to do what he thought was right, and it wasn't his fault that the world was a needlessly messed up, hate- and ignorance-filled place that seemed to resent nothing so much as people being happy.

Yeah, so that's the kind of thing the words "Valentine's" and "Day" made me think of.

Having noticed my less-than-spirited state, Duane had suggested (i.e. insisted) that the two of us have a night out, and no matter how much I protested, on the first Saturday in February, there he was goading me to make myself pretty, or he'd drag me out in my stained t-shirt and sweat pants, and I'd just have to deal with everyone thinking I was a homeless person. With friends like this . . .

But he was right. Once I took a shower and got dressed, just knowing that something other than the same depressing thoughts would be filling my head for the next few hours made me perk up a bit. I even found myself feeling a little bit hungry for the first time in weeks. As I started thinking about pizza, I heard Duane talking to Buck in the living room.

"And then how many reps do you do of that?"

"Depends on the day. Some guys do the same number every day, but it's really better to vary your numbers so that the muscles can't get too comfortable. Muscles are like a brain; they get bored if things get too predictable."

"Well, I do like a man with brains," Duane said. "Can I touch it?"

Clearing my throat as loudly as possible as I entered the living room, I found Buck flexing his bicep, and Duane gingerly prodding it with his index finger.

"Don't let me interrupt anything," I said.

Buck rolled his eyes at Duane. "Chris thinks I'm teasing you."

"Chris should mind his own fucking business." Duane turned and smiled broadly. "Look at how big your brother's muscles are getting."

"They've always been big," I said.

"No, really," Buck said, "they're getting bigger. I found out almost all of the body builders at my gym are gay, and ever since I let them know I have a gay brother and I'm cool with that, they've been letting me work out with them, and I'm gaining mass like crazy."

"What else have they been teaching you?" Duane asked, not quite able to disguise the hope in his voice.

"Sorry, brah, I'm still all about the vag."

If you had told me, when I was fourteen and beginning to realize that I might be gay, that my muscle-bound, meathead of a jock stepbrother would turn out to be one of the most nonjudgmental people I would ever meet, I would never have believed you. And yet, it was the kind of surprise from the people you least expected that can give you hope that other people might also surprise you. But hope is a careless emotion. If you don't believe me, Duane's weary sigh would have proved my point.

"Let's go," he said to me, shrugging his shoulders.

"Tomorrow we're doing legs," Buck said.

"I'll be back," Duane said.

Once I'd gotten a little hungry, my appetite seemed to come raging back, and since I knew it probably wouldn't last, I indulged in every craving that entered my mind. Which was why there was pizza, french fries, a chocolate milkshake, and a chili cheese dog in front of me.

"That one's cute," Duane said, watching a preppy Latino guy walk past the window of the diner.

"Mm-hm," I said without really noticing, returning my gaze to the basket of fries I was working my way through.

"Or maybe you prefer Gaysians?" he said, gesturing at a group of Asian guys across the street.

"I don't have any preferences based on race." I dipped a couple of french fries into the chili cheese remains from my hot dog. "Why are you suddenly pointing out every guy who walks by?"

He casually reached over to take a few of the fries. "Because when you fall off a horse, you have to get back on quickly, or else you'll get too scared."

"What are you talking about?"

Duane cocked his head to the side, giving me an impatient look. "Chris, I know what a broken heart looks like. I know what it looks like, and I know what it feels like, and I also know the only way to get over it is to distract yourself with the plethora of possibilities walking the streets out there." He held up a hand before I could object. "I know it feels like you'll never love anyone else again, but Aphra Behn once told me that during the shock after the 9/11 attacks, she knew that the world would continue when she realized the only thing that made her feel better while watching the news was all of the hot NYPD and firemen in the background. I realize we were just little kids then, but the point is that it's human nature to find hope in the tiniest thing." Then with a Mae West delivery, he added, "Not that a lot of those boys are so tiny."

The food in my mouth suddenly seemed about as easy to swallow as a boulder of granite.

Sympathy returning to his eyes, Duane leaned forward. "She told me that story a couple of years ago when I had my heart broken for the first time. You'll get through it. Somehow we all do."

"How . . . what . . .," I said.

"I don't know how you've managed it, with all that's been going on in your house, or especially how you've kept it a secret—"

The chocolate shake I'd picked up to try to wash the fries down slipped out of my hand with a bang.

"It's that Vibol guy from school, isn't it?" Duane said. "I'm right, aren't it?"

I began to choke, a combination of the immediate relief from his way off-base guess and a laugh. Shaking my head, I eventually said, "No."

"No?" He looked disappointed.

Finally, having swallowed the food, I told him, "I'm not sure Vibol even plans on dating until after he gets his medical degree."

"I don't know. You ever look at videos online? Some of those Gaysians are damn freaky." Then he clarified, "I say that with admiration and respect, of course."

"Of course."

Duane looked at me expectantly.

"What?" I asked.

"Well, aren't you going to spill the beans now that you know I know?"

I returned his gaze, and found the temptation to finally be able to tell someone everything almost overwhelming. But years of holding back had taught me more restraint than was perhaps good for me. Cautiously, I asked him, "What exactly do you know?"

"Well," Duane said, reaching over to pick off a piece of pepperoni and tear it into little pieces that he ate as he spoke, "I don't know exactly when it started, maybe before we even met, which was only a few months ago, after all. But I know you had sex for the first time around your birthday, were so damn happy in love through all of the holidays, and then something went sketchy around New Years. And the last couple weeks you've been in heartbreak hell."

And here I'd thought I was so good at hiding things.

"How do you know all of that?"

"Duh, woman's intuition. Are you sure it's not Vibol? You don't know that many other people." I could see the wheels turning in his head as he considered other possibilities.

I shook my head. "It's not Vibol. I promise."

Suddenly, he gasped, his eyes popped open, and he grabbed a knife off of the table and pointed it at me. "If you tell me it's Buck, I will kill you. As hot as the idea of step-brother incest might be in a porn, if that man ever turns to dick, he is mine. Do you understand?"

I laughed.

"Don't laugh. I am one hundred percent serious."

I laughed harder.

To prove his seriousness, Duane reached over the table with the knife and began poking my hand. As it was a butter knife, the threat made me laugh even more.

"He *my* man," he said in a voice that I was pretty sure was an impersonation of someone. I gave him a look to let him know I didn't get the reference, and he said, "Hello, Rae Dawn Chung in *The Color Purple*."

"I've never seen it," I said, finally starting to recover from my laughter.

"Shut up! Oh, damn, girl, if you think you cried over having your heart broken, wait until you see this movie."

Reaching across the table in an overly dramatic way that let me know he was acting out something else from the film, he said, "Nothing but death will part us!" He frowned. "Or maybe it's nothing but death will keep me from writing? I forget. All I know is those bitches could have used a better texting plan."

I shrugged, apologetic. "Can't help you. Haven't read the book either."

For the rest of the night, even after we left the diner and wandered the streets of Chelsea, Duane acted out scenes from, first, *The Color Purple*, then he moved onto *Do the Right Thing*, *In The Heat of The Night*, and *Boyz In The Hood*, and then finally really confused me with his rendition of some ghost from *Beloved*.

By the time we got back to my place it was getting late, and although I invited him in, he said he had to get back to work. Ever since the New Year's Eve party, he had been crazy busy meeting with and making sketches for the society women who had loved his designs, and now with the new semester underway, he was finding himself overwhelmed. I told him I really appreciated his taking the time for me since he was so busy, but he responded that he'd needed the break. Besides, the other drag queens were mad at him because he'd been too busy to rehearse, so who else was he going to hang out with? All I knew was that, once again, my fairy godmother had come to my rescue. I was so exhausted from laughing that I was almost positive that I was finally going to get a good night's sleep.

As I dragged myself up the stairs and reached the second-floor landing, I heard a noise from down the dark hallway. Craning my neck and squinting to see who it was, nothing could have prepared me less for what I saw: J.J., with his hand on the doorknob, exiting Kimberly's bedroom.

After a long moment with us both standing motionless, J.J. put a finger to his lips as he crept softly towards me. The caution wasn't necessary because I doubt I could have formed words even if I'd wanted. As he stepped into the light of the stairwell, I looked into the dark brown eyes I had so purposefully avoided for the last few weeks. What I saw there had the odd effect of making me feel both better and worse. I felt better because I could immediately see that J.J. had been every bit as miserable as I had, and I felt worse because he was the last person in the world I wanted to be unhappy. Even more so than myself. I guess that's what love is. And somehow I could tell from the way he was looking at me that he was thinking and feeling the same thing.

"Do you want to talk?" he said.

I nodded.

"Where?" he asked.

I gestured with my head for him to follow me, then led the way up the stairs to my room on the third floor. Once we got inside, with the door closed, seemingly without thinking, we both sank down to sit on the bed facing each other. There couldn't have been more than a foot between us, and it took every ounce of self-control to keep myself from throwing my arms around him. Instead, I focused on the way his hands worried the cuff of his slacks.

"You were in Kimberly's room," I said, trying to keep the question out of my tone.

He nodded. "Yeah, it's . . . ." He sighed, then sat up a little straighter, trying to push his resolve. "I figured if I'm going to do this thing, I can't put it off forever."

Unable to contain my disbelief, I said "You mean—"

"No!" He met my eyes briefly before looking back down at his hands. "I mean, not yet."

"But you know that's what she's going to want. I mean, you went to her *bedroom*."

"Girls seem to *really* like to cuddle."

"So that's what you were doing in there?"

"Well, mostly. Some kiss——"

"You know what," I said, "I don't want to know."

He nodded.

Although I'd seen him come over to take her out night after night, I'd assumed it was still all for show, but now he was suggesting . . . well, what exactly had he meant by, "if I'm going to do this thing?"

So I asked. "What exactly do you mean, if you're 'going to do this thing?'"

"It's what she wants, Chris. It's what they all want. It's what the world wants. I'm going to . . . try. I can do it. It's not so bad."

"I don't think I understand," I said, fighting the panic that started to build as I feared that maybe I was understanding exactly.

He finally looked up at my face as he matter-of-factly said, "I'm going be straight."

"But you're not straight."

"Maybe not. But what does that matter?" A bitter resolve began to cloud his eyes.

I stood up from the bed, running my fingers through my hair, not believing what I was hearing. "But . . . but . . . but that's not fair to Kimberly."

"I'm sure I don't know everything about her either."

"But being gay is too big not to tell a woman you're in a relationship with."

"I'm not going to be gay."

"You will *always* be gay."

"Not if I don't act upon it."

"You will still *be* gay. Someone can die a virgin, but if they're straight, they're straight, and if they're gay, they're gay."

"Chris, none of that matters. I'm going to be in a relationship with Kimberly, and I'm not going to cheat, and I'm not going to do anything to hurt her. You and I had what we had, but from now on, I am going to at least *live* the life of a straight man. It's the only way."

I don't know if what I did next was a desperate attempt to remind J.J. of his true nature, or if I was selfishly trying to satisfy myself in what appeared to be my last chance, but I ripped my shirt off over my head as I threw myself at him, grabbing him to me, and covering his mouth with mine.

He began to respond passionately, but all too soon J.J. struggled to push me away, turning his face away from mine and into the bedspread.

Rejected and despondent, I fell off of him, burying my head into my pillow, already sensing the sobs that it was soon to stifle. With my face averted, I listened as he got off the bed and took the few steps towards the door.

After a lengthy silence, he almost successfully made his voice sound calm as he said, "I don't know how you'll get out if it, but maybe you shouldn't come to the ball next week."

"What ball?" I said into the pillow, reeling too much to understand anything but my own pain.

"The one everyone's talking about."

Finally, it struck me that what he meant was the Valentine's Ball at which everyone was speculating he and Kimberly were going to announce their engagement. Too stunned by this impossibility to feel anything, I bolted up to inspect his face to see if he was being serious. "What's going to happen there?" I asked, my voice suddenly rough from tightness and fear.

J.J. shook his head. "I don't know."

Then he let himself out, closing the door quietly behind him.

CHAPTER 19

LOVE YOUR HEART

If I'd thought I'd been sleeping badly before, now that my heartbreak was coupled with an almost unbearable anxiety about what might or might not take place at the Love Your Heart Ball, keeping my eyes open proved to be my biggest challenge. It was as if my heart and mind were so inundated with misery that they'd shut off in self-preservation. It was like when you sink to the bottom of a swimming pool and look above, the distorted sights and sounds ripple and surround you while your lungs burn with their need for oxygen. But it was every minute of every day, at school, in the kitchen making dinner, trying to help Duane as he altered the deep scarlet brocade of the dress he was creating for Kimberly. Only sleep felt real, and something in me craved it beyond all other things.

Because I was in such a fog, it wasn't until the night before the ball, when Iris told me she wanted everyone ready to go by seven the next night, that I realized that I'd done nothing about taking J.J.'s advice to avoid going. Oddly, the first thing that made me feel something clearly was the fear of even more pain if I had to watch him announce to the world that he was engaged to Kimberly. But Iris wasn't having it. Even after I said I thought I'd contracted a communicable disease, and spreading a new plague to everyone in the social registry not going to do her reputation any good. (I thought I saw her waver on that one, but then Buck had to open his mouth and say what a good impression a token gay in the family made on liberals like the Kennerlys. I pointed out that they'd already met me, and he countered that it would look like I was trying to make a statement. Which, in a way, I guess I was.)

Anyway, as it was a Friday, I'd barely gotten home from school when I opened the front door to find Coco Chanel Jones in full drag queen regalia. High-fashion, tasteful drag queen, but drag queen nonetheless. The dress was silver lamé, after all.

"What happened to the tux?" I asked.

"I've been making all of these fabulous dresses for every rich bitch in New York City, and I realized *this* bitch hasn't shown her fabulosity in months."

"Do you think that's a good idea for business?"

"If they can't take the competition, fuck 'em."

After he passed by, I stuck my head out to see what the paparazzi situation was, and Coco told me there were only a couple guys staked out across the street. "I guess the rest are waiting at the Met," I said.

Before he answered, Iris called from upstairs. "Is that Duane?"

"Sort of," I said.

"What does that mean?" she said, clearly irritated, but then poking her head from the top of the stairs, saw what I meant. "Oh. Right."

"Relax, Mama, *you* can handle the competition," Coco said, kicking off her stilettos and starting up the stairs, leaving the shoes in the entryway. As soon as they'd disappeared into Iris's room, I began to pace the front hallway, desperately trying to think of a last-minute way out of attending the ball. The irony that only a few months before I'd been trying to figure out a way to get *into* a ball, and this time I was scheming to get *out* of one, did not escape me. So much had changed since then.

"Chris, I need you!" Kimberly called from upstairs. Well, some things hadn't changed all that much.

Reluctantly, with feet that felt soaked in cement, I climbed the stairs, dreading being alone with Kimberly. I'd worked very hard to avoid her as much as possible the last few weeks, and because she'd been spending so much time with J.J., I was pretty sure she hadn't even noticed. But with just the two of us in her bathroom together, avoiding her was likely to be a little more difficult.

As I entered, she was trying to zip up the back of the red dress Duane had created for her, strapless with a sweetheart neckline, and a playful mini-bustle from which a chiffon train extended. She looked beautiful. "Can you help me zip this, please?"

Without answering, I approached her, zipped up the dress, which fitted perfectly, and as I looked the effect over, acknowledged, "Duane really knows what he's doing."

Kimberly beamed. "He's amazing," and then surprised me with a peck on the cheek.

"What was that for?" I asked.

"For introducing me to him."

"Oh." Then thinking back on how I'd first met him as I sat dejectedly on our front steps and he happened to walk by dressed up as Diana Ross, I shook my head with bemusement. "It's strange how the most important people can seem to fall into your life."

Kimberly nodded in agreement. "Yeah, like J.J."

Annoyance flashed across my face, but I tried to cover it, even as I said, "Well, actually, you and Iris basically hunted him down."

With a guilty yet impish grimace, she said, "Oh, yeah." Then barely waiting a beat, she asked, "Do you love him?"

I took two involuntary steps back away from her, stunned by her blunt casualness as much as by the fact that she'd figured everything out and had waited until now to question me about it.

"J.J.?" I asked.

Rolling her eyes, she said, "No, silly. Duane. Do you love him?"

Almost melting with relief as my heart began to beat again, I swallowed with difficulty, then moved over to the vanity to busy myself with straightening it up. "Duane isn't my boyfriend. We're just friends."

She frowned. "Oh." She joined me at the vanity, picking up a makeup brush and making slight alterations on her cheekbones. "I think it would be nice if you met someone."

I stopped what I was doing as I chewed my lip, wanting so badly to ask her all of the things that I'd been avoiding her for the last few weeks so that I *wouldn't* ask. Then, suddenly, before I could stop the words from coming out of my mouth, I heard myself say, "So, are you and J.J. announcing anything tonight at the ball?"

She scoffed. "If you mean all of that craziness the gossip people have been speculating about, let's just say it would be news to me. It's ridiculous what they get away with saying."

"So you two aren't . . . engaged, or whatever?"

"Do you really think we wouldn't tell you first?"

I nodded, relieved, but now that I'd broached the subject, I wanted to know more. "Have you ever discussed it?" I kept my eyes lowered, busying myself more intently than ever with the pencils, and creams, and powders scattered around.

Kimberly let out a soft sigh, lowering the makeup brush. "J.J. is amazing and smart and perfect and all of that . . . but he's not exactly the easiest person to get to know."

"What do you mean?"

"Look, I know he's been the center of everyone's attention since he was born, and everyone wants to be near him, and all of that stuff, so he has to have built up walls, but . . . ."

I looked up to find her watching me with uncertainty.

"What?" I asked.

She shook her head. "It's nothing."

"Kimberly," I said, "you can tell me anything."

"Do you ever feel like he's putting on a show for you?"

"How do you mean?" I asked.

"I mean, he never says or does anything wrong. He never gets mad, he never gets emotional, he never *doesn't* have the right answer. Everything about him is so perfect, and . . . well, I'm not. I mean, I want to be, especially when I'm around him. I'm not saying he's not a great influence, but I just keep wondering what he's doing with me. Duane says that's what everybody feels when they're in love, that everyone has self-doubts, but I don't know. I guess I thought being in love was supposed to make you feel better about yourself, not worse."

I don't know which I was less prepared for, that Kimberly had expressed such intimate thoughts to me, or to realize that she was as insecure as anyone else. But I also couldn't help but wonder if she would be feeling those things if the man she was in love with wasn't trying so hard to appear different than he really was.

"Have you ever said any of these things to J.J.?"

She sighed again, this time a little exasperated, picking up a lipstick. "He just shakes his head and tells me I'm crazy."

I probably should have let it rest, but having learned so much in the last minute or two, I had to make sure of one more thing. I stepped over to the door, closing it, so that no one passing by could inadvertently overhear. This action caught Kimberly's attention, and she watched me in the mirror with curiosity.

"What?" she asked.

"So if J.J. asked you to marry him, you wouldn't accept, right?"

"Are you kidding?!" she said. "Of course I would!"

"Wait, what? But you just said . . . ."

"But if he wanted to marry me, then I'd know I was just being stupid. Besides, who cares, I could afford all of the therapy in the world. Retail therapy, aromatherapy, psycho-therapy, you name it. And I'd be married to J.J.-freakin'-Kennerly! Can I get an amen?"

Of all the white girls in the world, Kimberly was among the least likely to pull that one off. "You've been spending too much time with Duane," I said.

She shrugged, then a devious smile rose on her lips. "Although it would be kind of fun to make Mom think I might say no. Just to watch her squirm."

"But you wouldn't say no?" I asked.

"Hell to the no."

"You've really got to stop trying to act black, Kimberly. Seriously." If I couldn't stop her from marrying a gay guy, this advice was the least I could offer.

The walk up the stairs to the Met was my first red carpet. Not what I'd expected. Not glamorous. Yes, there were lights, and cameras, and flashes going off, but the noise was off-putting. Everyone yelled to get Kimberly and J.J.'s attention first, then Jonas and Jennifer's, then Buck's (who it turned out now had a meme website dedicated to him, started by some girl who'd given up on her dream of marrying J.J.), and with Iris and Coco more than happy to take up what attention remained. I hung back as much as I was able and watched the forced cheerfulness from everyone—people on one side of the camera smiling to look as happy as the fantasy tells us some lives are, and those on the other side of the camera fawning with barely veiled desperation, afraid that they might not get the right picture to pay their next month's rent. Or maybe I was just in a bad mood. But it had definitely been more fun sneaking into the Autumnal Ball through the back door than arriving for this one "in style."

Once we'd checked our coats and Coco's large handbag, which she'd asked me to hold while walking the red carpet, she told me to keep the claim tag accessible because she would probably need to get to it several times over the course of the evening. Since her dress didn't have pockets, I didn't have much choice but to help out. Honestly, if I'd known what she had in mind (and in that bag), I probably wouldn't have had the nerve to carry it.

"What is in that thing anyway?" I asked. "It weighs a ton."

"Just the usual stuff. Makeup, hair spray, a tailoring kit just in case anything goes wrong with this or any of the other dressing I created for clients."

"Those things shouldn't weigh that much."

"Fine, a copy of *War and Peace* and two solid gold bars stolen from Fort Knox. Does that make you feel better? Maybe you should start working out with Buck if you think that was so heavy. Women are supposed to be so weak and frail, but we carry that stuff around with us all the time. If men only knew the effort and preparation it takes women to look the way we do." She huffed, crossing her arms at her waist, then realized she looked a little bustier if she squeezed.

"Dude," I said, "What is wrong with you?"

She pouted with comedic drama. "I'm just very tense. I have seven dresses coming here tonight."

"Well, Iris and Kimberly both look amazing."

She perked right up, beginning to smile warmly, but I quickly realized it wasn't because of what I'd said. A very handsome Latino waiter was walking towards us with a silver tray of champagne glasses and an appreciative stare focused directly on Coco.

"Champagne?" he asked in a way that somehow actually said, *I want to find an empty broom closet and and slip inside with you.*

Coco batted her thick, false eyelashes demurely. *"Papi,* I'm not old enough to drink."

"What are you old enough for?" he asked, clearly checking to make sure he didn't have to worry about being accused of statutory rape.

"Anything else," Coco said, her lips quivering in a way that under different circumstances would have gotten her diagnosed with Parkinson's.

"I shall find you again and again this evening. It will be easy. I must only look for the most beautiful woman in the room." As he turned and offered drinks to another group of guests, Coco began making a noise that was somewhere between a purr and a growl.

"The most beautiful woman in the room?" I said. "At what point are you going to fill him in on a few pertinent details?"

Coco, her mouth puckered tightly, turned slowly towards me, meeting my eyes with her eyebrow disdainfully raised. "Oh, he knows."

"Christopher!" I turned around to find Kiki Cacciatore, all in black, of course, smiling at me in a way that let me know she had more in mind than a simple greeting. She leaned in to air kiss both of my cheeks, while also evaluating Coco as she did.

"Kiki, this is Coco," I said, almost wanting to laugh as soon as both of their names came out of my mouth in the same sentence. I wasn't quite sure what Kiki's take would be from a media consultant's point of view, so I was guarded, but as she offered her hand to shake, the look on Coco's face was even more so.

Until Kiki spoke. "We need to get you a reality show," she told Coco.

"Finally someone in this crazy world is talking sense," Coco responded, taking a hand and clasping Kiki's forearm. "Make me rich, bitch."

"Make me richer, bitcher," Kiki said, staring Coco dead in the eyes. It was like the asexual version of the meeting between Anna Karenina and Count Vronksy, although hopefully with happier results. "Call me." Then Kiki turned her attention back to me. "I need you in about twenty minutes."

"For what?" I asked

She looked surprised that I didn't know. "For J.J.'s announcement."

Trying to keep down the panic that started racing up my body, I asked, "His announcement of what?"

"His opening remarks."

"So why do I need to be there?"

"You're all going to be there—Kimberly, Buck, Mrs. Fontaine, plus Jennifer and Jonas. You know, one big happy family."

"But—I—nobody told me—"

"I'm telling you. Twenty minutes. No, now you're making me nervous, make it fifteen." She looked at Coco. "If you don't have him at the Temple of Dendur in fifteen minutes, it could mean the end of your television career."

"He'll be there," Coco said. "I can't guarantee he'll be alive, but he'll be there."

"I love you already," Kiki said as she spun on her heel and left.

They had set up a podium on the large concrete platform that held the Temple of Dendur, so that whoever was speaking would be nicely framed by the stone gate overlooking the reflecting pool. A makeshift holding area had been created with some tenting to the side of the temple behind the gate, and this was where Coco led-slash-dragged me. We were two minutes early, or seven if you didn't take Kiki's precautionary buffer into account, and while people and press abounded in the gallery, none of my family or the Kennerlys appeared to have arrived.

"Maybe everyone's in the tent?" Coco said.

"Why don't you go in and check?"

"And leave you alone to scurry off like the cowardly little cockroach you are and ruin my television career? I think not." Getting behind me and pushing me towards the white canvas structure, Coco reached around and stuck her hand into my jacket pocket, pulling out the coat check numbered tag. "As soon as I hand you off to Kiki, I need to run get something."

"Any chance you carry cyanide capsules in that bag?"

"Don't get your hopes up, but I'll check," she responded dryly.

My intestines were as knotted as last year's Christmas lights, but when we stepped into the dimly lit tent and found it empty except for one attendant in a suit facing the back wall, I sighed, briefly relaxing a small amount. Until the attendant turned around and revealed himself to be J.J. Although not quite as loud as at some noted points in the past, my damned gasp returned.

An awkward silence followed, as J.J. and I looked squarely at each other, really for the first time since my rebuffed attempt at reminding him with a kiss how much we meant to one another.

Finally, J.J. cleared his throat and nodded at Coco. "Good to see you back in all your glory."

Coco curtsied demurely, but followed it with her usual brazenness. "Baby, if you ever saw me in all my glory, your life would never be the same."

I winced before I could stop myself, which she noticed, and smacked my shoulder roughly. Then looking back at J.J., she said, "Will you make sure this one doesn't run off anywhere? Kiki made me responsible, but I need to get something from my bag, so now he's your problem, ya hear?" Without waiting for a response, she disappeared out of the flaps of the entrance, leaving J.J. and me torturously, and at the same time blissfully, alone.

As badly as I wanted to spin around and flee, there was something about J.J. that drew me in, and almost against my own will, I found myself taking steps towards him. Our eyes were unblinkingly locked, and as I got closer, I realized that there was something odd about his skin. It looked different. *He* looked different. Then I realized what it was.

"Are you wearing makeup?" I asked.

J.J. let out a woeful sigh, dropping his chin to his chest and letting his head hang. "Kiki insisted. It's just base. Or concealer? Or maybe both. I don't know."

"Why?"

"To hide the dark circles under my eyes." He lifted his face, and I was surprised by the accusing look in his eyes. "I haven't been sleeping."

I tried for what I hoped was an equally accusing look when I said, "I was like that for a while. But now sleep is *all* I can seem to manage." That's when my attempt at a brave and resentful front betrayed me, and my eyes began to tear up.

Blinking repeatedly, J.J. looked down at his hands clasped in front of him. "I never wanted to hurt you, Chris. You have to know that."

Trying to avoid a discussion that could quickly turn me into sobs, I attempted to change the subject. "So what is it we're all here for? What's this big announcement?" Then, as soon as the words were out of my mouth, I realized that the thing I'd been so desperately wanting to know for weeks, might be a knowledge I'd gladly put off for every last possible second. But it was too late; I'd asked.

J.J. shrugged. "I don't know. I'm supposed to talk about having a healthy and happy heart or some other lie, I guess." He tried to force a laugh, but it was so soaked with bitterness and regret that it came out sounding somewhere between haunted and just short of crazy.

As awful as the last few weeks had been, hearing the same pain and misery in J.J.'s voice made me feel even worse, because I felt utterly helpless to heal it. I tried my best and offered what I could by reaching out and placing my hand flat upon his chest. "I just want you to be happy," I said. "Seriously. It's all I've ever wanted."

J.J. met my eyes, holding my gaze, finally saying, "Funny how everyone who says they love you, says that. But do they really mean it?"

"Isn't that what love is? Someone else's happiness being more important than your own?"

J.J. put his hand over the one I held to his chest, and as he took in a shuddering breath, his eyes, too, began to fill with tears. "Why can't what makes one person happy ever be the same thing that makes everyone else happy?"

"For a while I thought it was," I said.

No sooner were the words out of my mouth, than the clack-clack of high-heeled shoes warned us that our solitude was about to be invaded, and we stepped away from each other.

Kiki led the way in, followed closely by Kimberly, Jennifer, Jonas, Iris, and Buck. "So it'll be just a few minutes, and Lizette from AHA will come lead us to the podium. She's awesome, so everything should go off without a hitch." Then, winking towards J.J. added, "Unless, of course, you want to surprise everyone with some good news. I mean, it is Valentine's Day, after all."

J.J. smiled mechanically, or maybe it only looked mechanical to me, because I was closest to him, so the uneven light was not able to hide from me the perspiration that began to form on his brow.

"I'm still trying to put together my thoughts," he said. "Just ignore me for now." With that he turned away from them, walking to a corner at the back of the improvised room. Almost immediately, everyone went back to whatever they'd been talking about. Except for me, who had been talking to him, and Jennifer, his mother, who watched him with a curious, then slightly troubled, expression.

She bit the inside of her cheek, before softly walking up behind him. I couldn't hear what they said in their hushed tones, but I could see the genuine concern on her face as she spoke, and then listened, to him. They were still deep in conversation when the PR woman from the American Heart Association popped her head into the tent and said everything was ready.

CHAPTER 20

IMPERFECT

So, obviously, I'm almost up to the point about which most of you already know.

If you haven't believed a word I've written so far because it didn't fit into your own agenda, well, there's nothing I can do about that, but I will say that the conspiracy theory that outing me in such a public forum was to garner votes is absolutely ridiculous. For starters, even if J.J. had planned the whole thing all along—which makes no sense at all, but conspiracy theorists seem to have their own form of logic—fine. But there's no way the rest of us knew anything. Certainly no one in the Fontaine-Bellows camp, of that I would swear on a stack of Jane Austen's original manuscripts.

As we gathered behind J. J, he approached the podium with a bouquet of television and radio microphones waiting to record his every word. At this point I was so distracted with replaying in my head what he and I had just been talking about that I wasn't even aware enough of all the people watching us to be nervous, at least not about them. But I still managed to hear my name being hissed from the side, and when I looked over, Coco was waving a hand at me, while struggling to get past one of the PR assistants. Trying to not be too obvious, I signaled to the assistant that it was okay to let her join us, and reluctantly, he let her proceed. She blew him a kiss with one hand—more of triumph than gratitude—as she passed, burying her other hand in the flowing folds of her gown. I didn't think much of it at the time, which I'm glad about now, because who knows what I might have done if I'd known what she was planning.

"Happy Valentine's Day, everyone," J.J. said, leaning into the microphones, his voice carrying clearly throughout the broad space of the gallery.

"Will you be my Valentine, J.J.?!" a woman's voice called from somewhere in the crowd. She got a big laugh from the rest of the room. Even Kimberly laughed. (Iris, not so much.)

Smiling graciously, and probably blushing though it was hard to tell under the makeup Kiki had made him wear, J.J. continued. "In support of the great work that the American Heart Association does, they have asked me to say a few words to remind everyone of the little steps they can take to help make sure that we all do our best to take care of our own hearts. Which got me thinking. Always a dangerous proposition, right?" He winked, and the audience laughed.

As he warmed to his audience, and they warmed to him, I saw him transform from the suffering soul in the tent into the charismatic leader that he had been born to become. Some people blossom under the expectant gaze of an audience; they're not intimidated by it, not weighed down by it, but instead they're lifted up by it. I was not born to be that person, but J.J. was. And it was at this moment that something released inside me. It wasn't so much that the pain of losing

J.J.'s love went away, but I finally realized what a selfish thing I was guilty of in wanting him to ask less of his future by being with me. I finally understood the amazing things he might be capable of changing by making his personal sacrifice. People need leaders, and only a very few are drawn naturally to the calling. For J.J. it wasn't about his own ego, or accomplishments, or playing the adult version of King of the Mountain. It was about the prospect of being able to do good and to better other people's lives. And at that moment, I made a certain peace with the fact that if my own dreams were to be stifled by that sacrifice, that was something with which I could be okay. After all, hadn't I just told him that loving someone was about wanting them to be happy, even if it didn't make you happy? Even if that meant an entire country. I know that probably doesn't make sense to a lot of people, but hopefully, at least the honor in it is clear.

Caught up in my own epiphany, I hadn't really been listening to the content of what he was saying, but as he looked over his shoulder at Kimberly with the words, "in sickness and in health," drawing a hardy round of applause from the audience, my stomach dropped. Maybe I wasn't as okay with all of this as I'd just thought.

As those of you who have seen the footage of what happened know, it all went very quickly. But it didn't feel that way up on the stage. Granted, I was very much caught up in my own head, and, honestly, while you see my head turn towards Buck and Coco, I wasn't aware of what was going on with them.

Of course, you may not have even noticed that, because this was also the moment where J.J. seemed to freeze in front of the microphone, looking out at the audience with that inscrutable stare. For a while some political analysts tried to argue that he'd had a mini-stroke at that moment to explain what he was soon to do, but how a nineteen-year-old man having a stroke in front of cameras would be considered preferable to what actually happened, makes me think I had been stupid to think such a country deserved his or anyone else's sacrifice.

J.J. later told me that he thinks he maybe had a little bit of a nervous breakdown right then. He said as he looked out over all of these people looking up at him with all of their expectations, he was suddenly filled with a violent loathing. He hated every single one of them with every fiber of his being. It was like an explosion of hatred inside himself.

Now whether you were watching J.J., or Buck and Coco, during J.J.'s awkward pause, this is the part where Buck lobs the Ferragamo shoe that lands smack dab in the middle of the podium with a thud. And J.J. just stares at it for a long moment, but not half as long as it seemed at the time, to any of us up there. And this was when J.J. told me he had his own epiphany. He realized that those people watching him weren't the ones he hated—*he* was. He hated himself for not being what they wanted him to be. And that's when he understood that he had a choice to make. A choice between hate and love.

While he was mid-epiphany, most of the rest of the people on the stage scrambled about. Iris yelled at Buck, who pointed at Coco, saying she'd told him J.J. was in on it (which he wasn't, but how else was Coco going to get Buck to use all of that football throwing precision to give the shoe the best chance of hitting its mark?), Jennifer and Jonas tried to get everyone to save their squabbling for less public scrutiny, and Kimberly and I looked at each other, frozen, with plastic smiles on our faces—in a sense proving our possible mettle as future political spouses, I guess it could be argued.

Kiki and Lizette darted in from opposite sides to remove the shoe, but J.J. stopped them by holding out his arms to either side, sending them both away, then picked it up. Which was when I finally got a decent look at it and realized it was one with which I was very familiar. It was the Ferragamo I'd accidentally kicked at J.J.'s face the first time we met.

For some reason, this was the thing that shook me up the most. Having been so careful to keep J.J.'s secret, the idea that anyone knew made me feel like I had failed him completely. And that felt awful. I turned my head slightly to Coco, who was back beside me, and whispered, "How long have you known?"

She said, "Not long. I thought I'd finally put it all together a few days ago when Kimberly was saying J.J. sometimes felt like a stranger, but it wasn't until I saw you and J.J. together in the tent that I finally knew for sure. Only two people in love can look at each other with that much pain."

"You couldn't have waited to say something in private?"

She shrugged. "Maybe I'm more political than we thought."

By now J.J. was holding up the shoe for everyone to see with an intensely amused expression, which freed itself into a chuckle, then built into a laugh. And the crowd was more than happy to join in, eventually breaking into full-out applause. See how cool their future leader was in a crisis?

After the laughter and applause had quieted down, J.J. leaned forward to speak again. "We live in strange times. We say we want progress, but we also want to hold on to the good old ways that feel familiar and secure. We say we love freedom, but too much of it can seem scary. We say that individualism is the hallmark of what it means to be an American, but then many of us find that differences make us uncomfortable. I'm not a politician yet, but it has always been something I expected to be in my future. But there's one big thing I struggle with more than anything else when I consider that future, and I'm going to take this Valentine's event to get it off my chest. That should be good for my heart, right?"

He took a pause and looked carefully at the people who stood before him, waiting expectantly for whatever he was going to say next.

"That politicians lie is considered as much of a truth in our society as the notion that the sun comes up in the morning and goes down at night. I don't want to be that kind of politician."

Applause broke out, interrupting him, but he held out his hands to suppress it.

"The problem is, people want their leaders to conform to one idea of what is perfect. Something that no living human being has yet managed in the history of the world. It's almost as if we're knowingly choosing which lie we'd rather believe, even though we know both options are lies. And that's not okay with me. Because I'm not perfect. And I want each and every one of you to know it."

Again applause started, and although he'd tried to quell it almost immediately, his audience ignored his wishes and cheered his humble admissions. He waited with uncomfortable patience until they'd had their say before continuing.

"Not too long ago someone described pride to me as accepting who you were born to be and not trying to hide or deny it, so today I am here to tell you that I am proud to be who I am, even if that isn't everyone's idea of perfect. And on this Valentine's Day, I am proud to love someone else who might not be your idea of perfect."

My eyes slid over to Kimberly, who looked confused and not entirely pleased, until she thought of an answer she could live with and muttered, "Oh, the fat lady comment," to me. "Not my best moment." Then she beamed a smile at J.J. when he looked over in our direction. And for the briefest moment, as he began to walk across the expanse between the podium and us, just because it seemed like the least dramatic of the options I could think of, I almost hoped that he would take her in his arms.

Almost. Because although part of me crumbled inside when he put a hand on her forearm and softly said, "I am so sorry, and I hope someday you will be able to forgive me," the rest of me rode a wave of glorious hope that the imperfect person for whom he had just proclaimed his love was me.

Then in front of everyone in the room, and the world reachable via the cameras that recorded his every move, J.J. Kennerly took me in his arms, kissed me full on the mouth, and provoked the gasp heard around the world.

In the hysteria that immediately followed as Kiki rushed us like a linebacker, heading us off the platform and eventually through a series of hallways until we were spit out of the back entrance of The Met, yelling at us to grab a cab and get the hell away into hiding, while it's mostly a blur, I do remember the following moments:

★ Kimberly screaming, *This is all your fault!*" But she wasn't yelling at me. She was yelling at Iris.

★ Buck giving me a stunned high five, and then as Iris looked at me with horror and loathing, he yelled into her ear, "Relax, Mom, J.J. can still marry into the family." And then Iris body-chucking her way to the podium and shouting into the microphones, "*I supported marriage equality before it was trendy!*"

I thanked Coco as she struggled to keep up with our pace in her stiletto heels as we raced through the hallways. "You were our very own *deus ex machina!*" I said.

"What's that?" she asked.

"It's like the Greek version of a fairy godmother," I said, explaining as best I could under duress.

"The Greeks knew about their man-on-man love, so I'm down with that," she said, just as the heel on one of her shoes broke, and she stumbled. J.J. and I both threw out our arms to keep her from falling, but she told us to leave her alone—there was a cute security guard close by that she'd rather have help her. Then she slumped lavishly to the ground.

Getting into the first cab we could stop and being asked where we wanted to go, J.J. and I looked at each other, realizing that whatever answer we gave was the beginning of our public story as a real couple.

"Where should we go?" he asked.

"I don't know," I said. "I don't care, as long as I'm with you." J.J. smiled, took my face in his hands, and kissed me.

From the front of the cab, the driver's bored but good-humored voice said, "Yeah, yeah, yeah, you're here, you're queer, I'm used to it. The meter's running, so where do you two lovebirds want to go?"

ACKNOWLEDGEMENTS

Since a proper list of all the people who deserve thanks might run longer than the book itself, I'm going to break the first rule of writing by not being specific. I thank my family and friends; my teachers and students; the writers and artists who have made me laugh and cry; my Loyola Marymount University and USC colleagues; Evan Corday, Claire Abramowitz, and everyone at The Cartel; Kylie Brien, who was the book's first champion at Sky Pony and a fantastic editor to work with, Bethany Buck, Joshua Barnaby, Kat Enright, Cheryl Lew, Julie Matysik, and the entire Sky Pony team. To all those who have shared the journey of this book, and this life, I thank you.